Praise for the
Southern Sewing Circle Mysteries

"Sweet and charming . . . the bewitching women of the Southern Sewing Circle will win your heart."
—*USA Today* bestselling author Monica Ferris

"Filled with fun, folksy characters and southern charm."
—*New York Times* bestselling author Maggie Sefton

"[Mixes] a suspenseful story with a dash of down-home flavor. . . . Visiting with the charmingly eccentric folks of Sweet Briar is like taking a trip back home." —Fresh Fiction

"I love the setting and the coziness of the town. I've loved getting to know each and every one of [the] characters . . . and I've loved the murderous predicaments they've all found themselves in. But the camaraderie between the ladies is what makes the story so much fun!" —Marie's Cozy Corner

"Tori is fun, sassy, smart, and crafty in more ways than one. . . . I like feeling the connection to the characters, like they are old friends coming into my home for the night to sew and solve mysteries together." —TwoLips Reviews

"This series has its own brand of charm, intrigue, and unique characters." —Once Upon a Romance

"An excellent read for crafters and mystery lovers alike. Elizabeth [Lynn] Casey has a knack for threading together great story lines, likable characters, and surprises in every page." —The Romance Readers Connection

Berkley Prime Crime titles by Elizabeth Lynn Casey

SEW DEADLY
DEATH THREADS
PINNED FOR MURDER
DEADLY NOTIONS
DANGEROUS ALTERATIONS
REAP WHAT YOU SEW
LET IT SEW
REMNANTS OF MURDER
TAKEN IN
WEDDING DURESS
NEEDLE AND DREAD
PATTERNED AFTER DEATH

Patterned
After
Death

Elizabeth Lynn Casey

BERKLEY PRIME CRIME
New York

BERKLEY PRIME CRIME
Published by Berkley
An imprint of Penguin Random House LLC
375 Hudson Street, New York, New York 10014

Copyright © 2017 by Penguin Random House LLC
Penguin Random House supports copyright. Copyright fuels creativity, encourages
diverse voices, promotes free speech, and creates a vibrant culture. Thank you for buying
an authorized edition of this book and for complying with copyright laws by not
reproducing, scanning, or distributing any part of it in any form without permission.
You are supporting writers and allowing Penguin Random House to continue to
publish books for every reader.

BERKLEY is a registered trademark and BERKLEY PRIME CRIME and the B colophon
are trademarks of Penguin Random House LLC.

ISBN: 9780425282571

First Edition: June 2017

Printed in the United States of America
1 3 5 7 9 10 8 6 4 2

Cover illustration by Mary Ann Lasher
Cover design by Judith Lagerman
Book design by Laura K. Corless

For my readers who have loved reading about the Sweet Briar crew every bit as much as I've enjoyed writing them.

Thank you.
This one is for you!

Acknowledgments

It's hard to believe this book marks the twelfth title in the Southern Sewing Circle Mysteries. It seems like just yesterday *Sew Deadly* (book #1) came out. I'll never forget the thrill it was to see that book on store shelves all across the country. And I'll never forget the equal thrill that came when I started getting letters from readers just like you—readers who'd taken a chance on me and my book and fell in love with Tori, Margaret Louise, Rose, Leona, and the whole Sweet Briar crew.

Writing has been my dream since I was a little girl about Lulu's age. So whether you found me through these books, or the many series I write under my real name, Laura Bradford (www.laurabradford.com), the fact that you're here—with one of my books in your hand—is an honor.

Thank you!

Chapter 1

Tucking her tote bag beside her feet, Tori Sinclair Wentworth glanced over at the sixtysomething woman beaming at her from behind the sun-faded steering wheel.

"I really appreciate the ride, Margaret Louise." Tori reached up, grabbed hold of the seat belt, and fastened it across her lap and shoulder. "Saves Milo the hassle of having to drop everything just to pick me up."

Peeking into the rearview mirror, Margaret Louise Davis yanked the station wagon to the left and pressed down on the gas. Hard. If she noticed the way the back of Tori's head smacked against the headrest, she didn't let on. Instead, she turned left out of the parking lot, her smile widening with each additional number gained on the speedometer. "I don't think there's *anything* that sweet husband of yours wouldn't drop for you, Victoria."

"And knowing Milo, you're probably right. But he's

already doing me a huge favor. On his Saturday, no less."
Tori tried not to grimace as they sped around the corner.
"I just hope whatever is wrong with my car isn't anything
too expensive. I kind of went a little crazy on our trip to
Heavenly, Pennsylvania, last month, you know?"

At the end of Main Street, Margaret Louise turned
right and then left at the next four-way stop. "Bring it to
Jake. There ain't nothin' he can't fix."

"But he has a business to run and I don't want to take
advantage." And she didn't. Just because Jake was Margaret Louise's son didn't mean he should have to drop
everything to work on her car.

Margaret Louise waved Tori's protest aside as if it were
a pesky gnat. "I love you. Melissa loves you. And all eight
of my grandbabies love you. That right there is why Jake
would move your car to the front of the heap. Well, that
and the fact he's just the sweetest, most wonderful son a
mama can ask for. Been that way since the day he was
born. No fussin' and no troublemakin'. Ever."

"Spoken like a proud mama."

"There ain't no prouder, Victoria." At the next stop
sign, Margaret Louise stayed on the brake. "Victoria?
Would you mind if we stop out at the garage before I bring
you home? All this talk about my boy is makin' me want
to give him a hug."

She felt the smile as it raced across her face. "Hugs
are good."

"Woo-ee." Margaret Louise looked both ways and then
found the gas pedal with a heavy foot. "Wait 'til you see
his place, Victoria. Jake calls it state-of-the-art. I call it
fancy—*real* fancy."

There was no denying the way Margaret Louise's

natural enthusiasm for life bubbled over the moment the subject of her son, his wife, or their eight children came up. Even if the woman didn't utter a word, the love she had for them was as tangible as the polyester warm-up suit covering her plump form.

Tori swung her attention off the road in front of them and back onto her friend. "So the renovations are done?"

"Yes siree, Victoria. And it sure looks mighty purty out there now."

"And the partnership with Noah is working out okay?" Tori asked.

It was quick. And it was fleeting. But there was no missing the way Margaret Louise's smile faltered in response.

"Margaret Louise?"

Again, Margaret Louise waved at the air with her hand, only this time it was a tad bit less emphatic. "Don't mind me, Victoria. I'm just a mama bear with a memory that won't quit. But I'm workin' on it. For Jake's sake."

"I know I wasn't living in Sweet Briar when Jake was in high school, but I also know that was a long time ago. Surely an old football rivalry is long dead and buried." Though, even as the words left her lips, Tori knew she was speaking from a place of ignorance. Sweet Briar was a small town. A small southern town, for that matter. Ninety-five percent of the residents had been born there, as had their fathers and mothers before them. It was a dynamic she found both endearing and, at times, a little disconcerting, too.

Sure enough, Margaret Louise stiffened in her seat, her gaze firmly fixed on the road. "You might think that, Victoria. But defeat don't always go down easy. Especially when it was suffered in front of friends and family the way Noah's and Noah's mama's and daddy's was. Memories like that don't just fade away."

"Eighteen years isn't exactly fading away, Margaret Louise. Life goes on, you know? They're grown men, with jobs. And, in Jake's case, a family." Tori reached across the seat and squeezed her friend's shoulder. "And, from what I can see, Noah has done pretty well for himself since high school. Because here's the thing: The clubs you belonged to and the awards you won in high school might have mattered at that time, but in the real world no one really"—she stopped, mentally called back the word she was seconds from uttering, and opted to get the point across with a slightly softer touch—"thinks too much about it, you know?"

Margaret Louise said nothing as she turned right at the end of the block. There, in front of them, loomed the new sign for Jake's Garage—bright and eye-catching. "I guess, if nothin' else, Jake's business will increase now that Team Noah won't be drivin' clear into another town just to have their cars fixed."

"Team Noah?" Tori echoed.

"The folks who favored Noah as quarterback that last year were called Team Noah. The folks with workin' eyes were Team Jake." The car slowed as they approached the building but resumed its normal speed as a quick perusal yielded a CLOSED sign on the door and no sign of Jake's car in the lot. "Well, I'll be darned. Looks like that hug is gonna wait 'til I drop you off after all, Victoria."

She was pretty sure she nodded in response, but really, her thoughts had yet to fully leave the previous conversation. "So these teams were essentially made up of family, I take it?"

"Family, friends, people in town. Everyone picked a team. Though it ain't any coincidence the nicer folks are Team Jake."

"Are?" she repeated, only to pause as Margaret Louise made a U-turn in the middle of the road and headed toward Tori's side of town. "You say that like these teams still exist."

"Because they do." Margaret Louise swerved to avoid a squirrel, her eyes darting between the road and Tori. "And they're just as loyal and adversarial now as they were then."

"You can't be serious."

"Ask Leona sometime. Bein' a business owner in this town gives her a front-row seat to the inner workin's of Team Noah. Why, she can tell you a story or two 'bout Team Noah that'd curl your toes."

Tori winced as they narrowly missed yet another squirrel, and then looked back at the driver. "What's your sister and her business got to do with this?"

"Noah's money is all over this town these days. And as for Leona, she's Team Jake by default on account of bein' kin."

"Okay, slow down. You lost me on the money part . . ."

Margaret Louise opened her mouth to speak but closed it as Tori's phone began to ring. Reaching down, Tori fished it out of the center compartment and glanced down at the screen.

"It's Charles. Do you mind if I take this? He was on tap for checking on Rose this morning, and I want to see how it went."

"Put him on that speaker thingy so I can hear, too. Saves him another call that way." At Tori's raised eyebrow, Margaret Louise shrugged. "I'm worried 'bout her, too, Victoria."

Nodding, Tori hit the green button and the speaker button in quick succession. "Hey, Charles. I'm in the car with Margaret Louise. She's giving me a lift home from the library."

"Puh-lease tell me you are wearing your seat buckle, sugar lips. You know how that woman drives . . ."

"I am, I do, and . . . you're on speaker."

Silence filled the station wagon as she exchanged glances with a clearly amused Margaret Louise.

"Why, Victoria, it's gotten mighty quiet on Charles's end, wouldn't you say?" Margaret Louise teased. "Maybe our resident Yankee has gone and found some crow-flavored Pixy Stix?"

Charles cleared his throat, coughed, and then repeated the sequence once again. When he was ready, he spoke, his voice a poor disguise for the embarrassment he was still working to overcome. "I, uh . . ."

"How was Rose this morning?" Tori asked.

If relief wasn't an audible emotion before, it was now. The only thing missing was the visual of Charles's shoulders as they sagged against the wall he was undoubtedly leaning on in the back room of his new shop, Snap. To. It. Books & Café. His rush to take advantage of the shift in conversation, though, sufficed. "Honestly, Victoria, I'm worried."

Tori felt her body stiffen. "Worried? Why? What happened? Is Rose okay?"

"Nothing happened, per se. She just seemed to have a

harder time moving around her place than she had even at last week's sewing circle meeting."

"And she wasn't movin' 'round good then, neither."

Tori nodded along with Margaret Louise's words even as her gaze skipped to the dashboard clock. "I'm going to be bringing a dinner plate over to Rose later this evening, so that'll give me a chance to see if there's any improvement." The words tasted bitter on her mouth as the reality she'd been trying to ignore the past few weeks loomed large.

Rose Winters's health was failing, plain and simple. Yes, Tori could continue to chalk it up to the cooler than normal spring temperatures, but Leona had been really good about keeping their shop, SewTastic, at a comfortable temperature. And Tori could continue to explain away Rose's hit-or-miss attendance at the sewing circle's weekly meetings as a few repeated bouts of fatigue, but even that made no sense. When Rose wasn't doing anything but staying home, there really was no reason for her to be so tired.

She could feel Margaret Louise looking at her, but she refused to make eye contact. If she did, she knew the tears she was trying so valiantly to keep from her voice and her cheeks would finally win.

"You'll give me a ring after you see her, won't you, sugar lips?"

"I will."

"Well, I better get back out on the floor before closing time." Charles sighed, then hesitated, and then sighed again. "Margaret Louise?"

"Yes, Charles?"

"I adore you. You know that, don't you?"

"I do. That's why I reckon I'll swing by and pick *you*

up just as soon as I deliver Tori back to that sweet husband of hers." Margaret Louise winked at Tori just before she slammed on the brakes at the next four-way stop. "Why, maybe we can drive clear out to Breeze Point and see us a movie . . ."

"I—I have plans with your sister tonight."

"Oh?" Margaret Louise taunted.

"I . . . yeah . . . we're . . . um . . ."

Tori savored the emotional reprieve offered by Charles's hemming and hawing and grinned back at Margaret Louise.

Margaret Louise winked and turned up the pressure a notch. "Because my car *can* fit three people, you know . . ."

"Uh . . . we're . . ."

Tori hit mute just long enough to give in to the laugh she could no longer keep at bay. "You can almost *hear* him sweating, can't you?" she whispered.

"Wait! We're . . . um . . . having a photo shoot with Paris," Charles said as Tori un-muted the call. "Yeah, that's what we're doing. And it . . . um . . . has to be . . . um . . . in her own environment!"

"You sure? 'Cause I got me a full tank of gas and I'm revvin' to go somewhere."

"No. No. I'm good. I—I'll have to take a rain check on that revvin'."

"How 'bout tomorrow, then?"

Charles's silence hung heavy in the air before it was broken by something that sounded suspiciously like a clap. "I'm sorry, ladies . . . a . . . a customer just came in. So as much as I hate to cut this short . . . I have to go."

And then he was gone, Margaret Louise's answering chuckle the only sound that remained.

"So you know?" Tori asked.

The car slowed as they turned onto Tori's street. "You mean 'bout the paper bags he breathes into every time he's sittin' in my backseat?"

Tori swallowed, unable to speak.

"What do you think I am, Victoria? Three pickles shy of a quart? Course I know." Margaret Louise sideswiped the curb in front of Tori's house and slid the car into park. "It don't make no sense, if you ask me. I don't drive any faster than anyone else."

Tori resisted the urge to snicker and, instead, offered a noncommittal shrug. "Well, thanks for the ride. It was a huge help."

"Anytime, Victoria. You know that." Margaret Louise released her hold on the steering wheel long enough to capture Tori's chin between her fingers. "I know you're worryin' somethin' fierce 'bout Rose. We all are. But the only thing we can do is exactly what we're doin'. Keepin' a close eye on her."

"But what if something happens when none of us are there to help?"

"She has her phone in her sweater pocket at all times, Victoria. She'll call for help."

But what if she falls and knocks herself out?

What if she's too weak to dial?

What if . . .

Tori shook the troubling thoughts from her head and took a long, deep breath. She'd taken enough of Margaret Louise's time already.

Plucking her bag off the floor, she opened the passenger-side door and stepped onto the sidewalk. "Thanks again."

"You get *that* out to Jake this evenin', you hear?"

Tori followed the path forged by Margaret Louise's finger and sighed when she saw her car in exactly the same spot it had been in when it started making weird noises that morning. "It's Saturday night, Margaret Louise. He's already gone home for the day, remember? Besides, he's probably got a long list of customers ahead of me."

"Knowin' my Jake, he'll be back at the garage after dinner tyin' up one loose end or the other. Been doin' that for years." Margaret Louise returned her hand to the gearshift and her foot to the gas pedal, but stopped short of actually engaging either as she smiled out at Tori. "And you ain't just a customer, Victoria. You're as good as family. Jake knows that."

Chapter 2

She felt the warmth of his breath on the top of her head a split second before his hand snaked around her waist and shut off the kitchen faucet.

"I admire your thoroughness, but you're going to scrub a hole right through the middle if you don't stop."

Tori looked from the gleaming plate in her hand to the handsome man standing just over her shoulder and shrugged, then smiled. "Oh. Sorry. I guess I was zoning out a little bit."

"A little bit?" Milo's rich, deep laugh tickled her ears as he liberated the plate from her hand and the dish towel from the counter and began to dry. "You've been zoning out off and on since we sat down to dinner. Did everything go okay at work today?"

"Everything was fine. In fact, I'd go so far as to say that for a Saturday, the library was mighty quiet."

He finished the plate and stacked it atop his own. "I'm sure it was just the weather, baby. With the cooler than normal temps we've had these past few months, a day like this probably had most of your regulars wanting to be outside—catching some rays. Which, coincidentally, was the one saving grace about your car being on the fritz. It had me outside. All. Day. Long." He thrust out his arm, pushed his short sleeve up to his shoulder, and grinned. "See? I even got a little bit of color."

She turned so she could have a full view of his face and then leaned back against the counter. "I'm sorry about the car, Milo. I know it's coming at a bad time."

"Bad time?" He tossed the towel onto the opposite counter and stepped closer. "You mean moneywise?"

"I know we kind of went all out on our trip to Heavenly, Pennsylvania, last month and—"

Reaching out, he silenced the rest of her words with a gentle finger to her lips. "I'd do it all over again tomorrow if we could pull off another long weekend. That trip was amazing, Tori. You know that."

"Oh, I know it was great. The bed-and-breakfast, the tours, the people, the quiet time for you and me . . . I loved every minute, too. But it still cost money."

"Money well spent." He pulled her close for a kiss and then stepped back so he could see her once again. "I don't want you stressing over money. An elementary school teacher and a librarian are never going to be rolling in it, but I don't need that to be happy. I just need you."

"But my car—"

Again, he silenced her worries. "Look, I'll admit, I'm at a loss for why it's making that noise. But somehow, someway, I'll figure it out."

"Margaret Louise says we should drop it off at Jake's tonight. That he'll be able to figure out what's wrong and make it right."

"Would that make you less stressed?" he asked.

She looked up at him, his brown eyes clouded with worry. "I'm not stressed, Milo."

"You barely touched your chicken parm tonight, and it was really good."

"I don't know—I guess I wasn't hungry. But I'm glad *you* liked it." Pushing off the counter, she wandered over to the table and lowered herself onto her chair, her thoughts rewinding ten, fifteen minutes. "I'm sorry if I was lousy company during dinner. It wasn't you. I promise."

He joined her at the table and reached for her hand across the top. "What's on your mind, Tori? Is it really just worry about the car and the money? Because we're fine. Really."

"I'm worried about Rose." There, she said it.

Tightening his hold on her hand, he leaned forward. "What happened?"

"Charles said she was moving slower than normal this morning."

Relief relaxed his grip. Understanding had him scooting close enough to guide her eyes onto his with his index finger. "She's going to have mornings like that, Tori. It's part of the aging process."

"But it's happening so fast now. Six months ago, she was helping me get ready for our wedding . . . and, up until a month ago, she was spending nearly every day at SewTastic, running the register and helping customers from the moment the store opened until the moment it closed."

"And she will again."

She heard the words, knew they reflected Milo's hope, but she also knew they were lacking any sort of conviction. A glance at her husband's face only served as confirmation of the latter.

"You see it, too, don't you?" Tori whispered. "Rose is failing. In mind and spirit."

Leaning back in his chair, Milo raked his fingers through his burnished brown hair. "I don't know, Tori. It seems like maybe . . . yeah. But I don't know. Maybe it's just carryover from a longer than normal winter-like season."

Oh, how she wished he could allay her fears, arguing her every worry with examples to the contrary. But he couldn't. Because to do so would be an exercise in futility.

For a moment she said nothing, her emotions a jumbled mess. Eventually, though, she got herself together enough to stand. "Rose likes my chicken parm. Maybe it'll give her a much-needed boost."

"Mind if I come?" Milo asked.

"I'd actually love that. And so will Rose." Nibbling at the answering tremble in her lips, Tori crossed to the refrigerator and the plate she'd carefully wrapped for her elderly friend. It was more food than she knew Rose would eat, but maybe, just maybe, she'd eat some of it. "I need her, Milo. I—I don't want anything to happen to her."

In a flash, Milo was off his chair and pulling her close. "I wouldn't write Rose off just yet, baby. Rose is a fighter."

"I know. And I thought SewTastic was the thing that would keep her fighting."

"So let's give her something else to fight for."

Slowly, she pulled back and gazed up at her husband,

his very nearness making it easier to think. "Something else to fight for? Hmmm . . . I like that."

He tapped the tip of her nose with his index finger, took Rose's covered plate from her hands, and then guided her toward the back door. "I'll drive your car and you drive mine. After we drop yours off at Jake's, we can make our way over to Rose's together in mine."

Tori met Milo in the parking lot and pointed through the open bay door to the pair of boots sticking out from beneath a sporty-looking silver car. "Looks like Margaret Louise was right. Jake's back at it again."

"That's because he always finds his way back to the garage after dinner. Even if it's just for a little while. The guy is a workhorse."

"Said the pot to the kettle."

"I grade papers. He fixes cars."

"You teach children, Milo." She rose up on the toes of her shoes and planted a kiss on his cheek. "Never, ever underestimate that."

Then, lowering herself back down, she gestured toward the boots. "Let's check and make sure he's okay with us dropping off my car before we head over to Rose's. For all we know, he might be way too swamped to take on another car."

"I don't imagine that'll be the case, but I'd rather hand him the keys than put them in a drop box, anyway." Milo guided her toward the boots with a gentle hand to her back, a low whistle escaping his lips as he did. "Wow. What a difference an influx of cash can make, huh?"

She followed his gaze to the newly sided building that

now boasted five bays rather than just the original two. To the left, where the cramped waiting room had once been, was a much larger area with big floor-to-ceiling windows and what appeared to be a flat-screen television and an assortment of cozy seats. Before she could point out those changes to Milo, though, a quick rolling sound from the middle bay brought her attention back to what was now legs and a torso and . . .

"Hey, Jake!" Milo waved at the grease-smeared face of Margaret Louise's only child and then gestured toward their surroundings without breaking stride. "I hardly recognize this place."

The surprise that had been evident on Jake's face as he appeared from beneath the car was quickly replaced by first recognition and then—

Irritation?

Tori glanced at her watch, noted the time, and felt her pace slow in response. "Milo," she whispered, "maybe we should wait until Monday and—"

"Looks like your new partnership is really working out. This place looks amazing, my friend."

Jake tucked the crowbar he'd been holding behind the back tire, ran the back of his grease-smeared hand across his brow, and then sat up, his smile wary at best. "Milo. Victoria. What brings you by this evening?"

"Tori's car is making a racket. Started this morning when she tried to leave for work. So I dropped her off in my car and then went back and tried to smoke out the source of the noise."

"And?" Jake prodded.

"I came up with nothing."

Jake stood, retrieved a cloth from a box beneath the window, and wiped his hands. "Did you bring it by?"

"We did." Milo hooked his thumb over his shoulder. "It's in the parking lot."

"If you're too busy, we could just bring it back home and wait until you have an opening."

Jake's dark brown eyes shifted in Tori's direction. "You do realize my mother would have my head if I told you anything other than I'll move it to the top of the list. So I'll move it to the top of the list."

She ignored Milo's answering laugh. "Your mom's not here, Jake. And Milo and I are very aware of the fact you have a business to run. The last thing we want you to do is risk irritating one of your customers by delaying work on their car to look at mine. We can wait."

"Oh, hey, it looks like you cut yourself."

Tori followed Milo's finger to the cloth in Jake's left hand. Sure enough, a big red streak of blood was visible amid the grease.

Jake glanced down, inspected his hand closely, and then wiped it with the cloth once again. "Par for the course around here." When he was done, he shoved the cloth into his back pocket. "Leave the car. I'll give it a look either before I head home tonight or after church tomorrow. If it's something big, I'll give you a call. If it's not, I'll just take care of it and let you know when it's done."

"Sounds great, Jake. Thanks." Milo again gestured to their surroundings. "So, the partnership is working out okay, I take it?"

"It's"—Jake stopped, floundered his head from side to side, and then exhaled loudly—"*working.*"

Tori felt her internal radar beginning to ping, but it was Milo who voiced the feeling aloud, with a simple but no less effective "Uh-oh."

Jake hesitated a moment, then motioned for them to follow him across the empty bays to their left. "Look, don't mind me. I'm pretty jazzed by the things this new partnership has allowed me to do—I really am. I just didn't look past the possibilities to see the probabilities."

"I take it Noah is being difficult?" Milo asked.

Again, Jake seemed to weigh his words before answering. "Not anything I can't handle."

They followed in step behind him as he pointed to the new lifts, the new tools, the new everything. But no matter how many *ooh*s Milo offered, or how many times Tori echoed them with an *ahhh*, nothing seemed to unearth the face-splitting smile Jake shared with his mother. In fact, if anything, Tori got the sense the tour was being given out of some sort of obligation rather than a genuine desire to show them around his newly renovated shop.

When they reached the waiting area, Tori stopped and sent what she hoped was a nonverbal plea to her husband. When he didn't respond, she tapped the face of her wristwatch. "Milo, it's getting late. We still need to stop in and check on Rose, and I would imagine Jake would like to finish up on that car he's working on so he can get home and spend a little time with the kids before they go to bed for the night."

A glance at Jake's face showed her words were met with relief. The quiet sigh he released a second later simply served as confirmation she hadn't really needed.

"Oh, man, I'm sorry, Jake. I guess I got so caught up in this place I forgot how late it is. I hope we didn't eat up too much of your time."

She knew Jake was anxious for them to leave. That much was obvious. But still, she was surprised when he didn't offer even a perfunctory argument to Milo's apology.

Swallowing quickly, she turned on her heel and led the way back across the garage to their starting point. As they approached the silver car Jake was working on, Milo's laughter echoed around the cavernous room.

"I probably shouldn't say this," he said, "but there's something a little bit comforting in knowing that the expensive cars aren't completely immune to issues. Though, even with that, they still manage to look good, don't they?"

She supposed Jake answered but she couldn't be sure. Her attention had followed Milo's to the sports car, where it parted long enough to travel down the passenger side and stall on the partially opened trunk door. With nary a second thought, she crossed to the back rear tire and pressed down on the trunk. When her effort failed, she circled around to the back of the car for a second try. But just as she readied her hands for a stronger push, she noticed a scrap of navy blue fabric peeking out near the center of the trunk. Lifting the door a smidge with her left hand, Tori grabbed hold of the fabric with her right and shoved it back inside, her fingers recoiling as they grazed something that felt an awful lot like—

Swaying backward, Tori thrust out her hands to keep from falling and, instead, grabbed the cold, stiff arm of Jake's new business partner, Noah Madden.

And, just like that, everything went black.

Chapter 3

Milo turned off the engine and reached for her hand across the center console, the concern in his eyes serving as proof the past two hours had, in fact, been real. The dull throbbing in the back of her head from where she'd hit the ground simply sealed the deal.

"Are you sure you don't want to just go home, baby? You've had quite a shock."

Looking down at their intertwined fingers, Tori waited for the warmth of his touch to chase the persistent chill from her body. "Rose needs to eat. It's the only way we can keep her strength up."

"But it's nine o'clock, Tori. She's probably in bed."

"My guess is she's asleep in her chair in front of the television." Tori gave up on the warmth that simply wasn't hers to have and, instead, studied the windows she could see from the passenger side. Sure enough, Rose's bedroom window was dark, while the living room window in front was ablaze with light. "See? She's watching TV."

"That doesn't mean she's going to want to eat right now."

"Maybe, maybe not. Either way, I want to check on her. Especially after what Charles said earlier." She swallowed hard against a wave of nausea, then winced as the back of her head hit the headrest.

Milo, of course, noticed and traded her hand for the side of her face. "Hey . . . Hey. Are you okay?"

"I'm fine. I just forgot about my head for a minute."

"And the way you touched your stomach before that? What was that about?"

"I felt a little queasy, that's all. But it's gone now."

Milo straightened in his seat. "Tori, you heard what the EMT said. Any nausea could mean a concussion. I really think I should either take you home or, better yet, to the actual hospital for a more thorough once-over."

"No. Please." She, too, sat up straight and did her best to project the strength she needed to have at that moment. "My head is just a little sore. That's all. And the queasiness came from thinking about Noah and the way his arm felt when I reached inside the trunk."

"Tori . . ."

It was her turn to reach for him, to squeeze his hand with as much reassurance as she could muster despite the parade of images that kept firing away in her head—Noah's terror-filled eyes, wide and staring . . . the grimace of pain plastered across Noah's face . . . his bloodied head . . . the feel of Noah's cold, stiff arm beneath her fingertips . . .

Blinking away the troubling images, she found the smile Milo needed to see and did her best to make the tone of her voice match the effort. "I'm fine, Milo, really.

I promise. If that changes, you'll be the first to know. But in the meantime, I really want to check on Rose. If she's not hungry, I won't push. It *is* late, and eating a full meal at this time of night might not be the best thing."

"You're sure you're okay? Because I—"

She quieted his concern with a kiss. Then, pulling back, she met his worried gaze head-on. "What just happened—it was a lot, Milo. Part of me is still shaking, and part of me is still convinced it was all just a bad nightmare. But all of me really needs a dose of Rose right now." And it was true. All through her childhood, her great-grandmother had been her go-to during stressful times. Now that her go-to was gone, Rose had unknowingly stepped into that role.

"Tori, I—"

"Milo, please. I need to do this. We'll keep the visit short if that'll make you feel better. But I have to see her."

He searched her face—for what, she didn't know, but eventually he lifted his hands in surrender. "Okay, let's do this. Just know that I'm going to hold you to the whole keep-it-short thing."

"Noted." Tori reached down, lifted the tote bag with the wrapped plate off the floor of the car, and joined Milo out on the sidewalk.

Together, they walked up the single porch step and crossed to the front door. After a few soft knocks, Tori knocked a little louder.

Soon, the single curtain panel covering the door's sidelight was shoved to the side and Rose peeked out. Tori and Milo waved in unison.

"Hi, Rose," she called through the still-closed door. "We brought you dinner."

Rose pointed at her ear, indicating she couldn't hear, and then swung the door open. "Good heavens, Victoria, don't you young people sleep anymore?"

Milo's laugh just over her shoulder brought a much-needed smile to her face, too. "We wanted to stop by and bring you this." Tori reached into the tote bag, retrieved the covered plate from inside, and held it up for Rose to see. "It's chicken parm. I thought you might enjoy some."

Rose looked from Tori, to the plate, and back again. "Two hours ago, I might have. But it's nine thirty. At night."

"Our intention was to be here by seven. But . . ." Her words trailed off as her mind's eye returned to the open trunk and Noah Madden's lifeless body. She shuddered.

Stepping back slowly, Rose waved them inside, plucked the plate from Tori's hand, and shoved it into Milo's as they passed. "Put this in the refrigerator, will you?"

"Of course." Milo kissed the elderly woman's forehead, winked at Tori, and then disappeared down the hall.

"You got yourself a real keeper with that one," Rose said as she turned and headed toward the living room and the canned laughter coming from the television. Halfway to her favorite chair, she turned back to Tori. "C'mon now, Victoria, you didn't come all that way just to hand me a plate and leave. So take a seat on the sofa and I'll give you the answers you're looking for."

"Answers?" Tori crossed to the couch and sat down. "I'm not sure I know what you—"

"Yes, a little. Not much. A little winded. And I'm still here, aren't I?"

She heard the refrigerator door close, knew the follow-up clinking noises were Milo pouring water for them, but other than that, she was at a loss. "Rose, you lost me."

"Yes, I ate dinner . . . a little, anyway. I didn't do much today. I didn't fall and break anything, but I *am* a little winded. And, last but not least, I'm still here, so you should all just quit your worrying." Rose pulled her cotton sweater more closely against her body and pinned Tori with a tired stare. "I did get them all, didn't I?"

Milo entered the room with a glass of water for Rose and a glass of water for Tori and then disappeared into the kitchen long enough to retrieve his own. When he returned, he claimed the empty couch cushion next to Tori. "So, what did I miss?"

"I answered all of the questions Tori has been sent—or, more likely, sent herself—to ask. So there's no need to linger." Rose's stance softened a smidge as she leaned forward for a closer look at Tori. "Maybe *I* should be asking how *you* are, Victoria. You look about as bad as I feel."

"So you *don't* feel well," Tori surmised across the rim of her water glass.

Rose threw her body against the back of her chair, muttered something beneath her breath, and then glowered. "You're all the same, you know that? Just a bunch of vultures waiting for me to slip up and give you even more of a reason to keep checking up on me."

Tori swallowed, sans water. "Rose, we're just worried is all. You haven't been yourself these last few weeks."

"And that's going to happen more and more, Victoria. I'm not getting any younger." Rose took a sip of water and then, with trembling hands, set the glass on the table beside her chair and turned back to Tori. "Now it's *your* turn. Did *you* eat dinner? What did *you* do with your day? Are *you* feeling okay? Are *you* sure? Are *you* really sure? Are you *really, really* sure?"

At a loss for how to respond, Tori looked down at Milo's hand now resting atop her own and tried to steady her breath.

"No one means any harm, Rose," Milo said. "In fact, it's quite the contrary."

A flash of guilt forced Rose's gaze to the ground momentarily. "I know. And, believe it or not, I'm grateful. I just don't want to be a burden or a have-to."

Tori snapped up her head. "You're a want-to, Rose. Please know that. In fact, by the time the cops got done with us at the garage, I knew it was probably too late for you to be eating dinner. But *I* wanted to stop—*needed* to stop. *For me.*"

"The police?" Rose asked.

Tori looked at Milo and, at his nod, took a deep breath and released it slowly. "Noah Madden is dead."

Rose's gasp sent a renewed chill down Tori's spine. "Noah Madden? But he's too young . . . What happened?"

"Tori found his body in the trunk of a car Jake Davis was working on at the garage," Milo said.

"In the trunk of a car?" Rose repeated. "What on earth was it doing there?"

"That's what the police are going to be trying to figure out. But it appears someone hit him over the head hard enough to kill him."

Rose shifted her focus off Milo and back onto Tori. "Are you okay, Victoria?"

"Just a little shaken up, I guess." She pulled her hand out from under Milo's and swiped it down the side of her slacks. "I—I noticed the trunk wasn't shut completely. I tried to close it, and when it wouldn't, I figured it was because of the scrap of blue fabric that was sticking out. When I tried to tuck it back inside, I touched No-ah's arm."

Milo slipped his arm behind her shoulders, nodding as he did. "I was standing toward the front of the car with Jake when Tori let out a half shriek, half gurgle. By the time I got my wits about me, she was already down on the ground."

Rose sat forward, her bifocal-enlarged eyes ricochet-ing between Milo and Tori. "She fell?"

"Hit her head pretty hard on the cement floor, too. She came to pretty quick, but I'm worried about a concussion."

Seeing the concern on Rose's face, Tori held off the rest of the blow-by-blow with a subtle elbow to Milo's side. "The EMTs checked me out thoroughly, and other than a little soreness where my head hit the ground, I feel okay."

"But just now, in the car, you said you felt queasy," Milo reminded.

She felt Rose studying her in the wake of Milo's words and did her best to smile away the woman's unspoken concern. "I think anyone who reached inside a trunk and found a body would be a little queasy. But really, that's gone now."

"Whose car was he in?" Rose finally asked.

"His own." Grateful to be out from under the glare of the spotlight, Tori rushed to fill in as many details as she could. "You know he went into a partnership with Jake at the garage, right?"

Rose rolled her eyes. "I might be slowing down, Vic-toria, but I haven't gone completely senile yet." Then, "Of course I know that. Thought it was a bad idea the moment Margaret Louise first told us at that sewing circle meeting back around Thanksgiving time. But I kept my mouth shut when she told us the deal was signed earlier that day."

"Why did you think it was a bad idea?" Tori asked.

"They don't get along," Milo said.

She looked at Milo. "Wait. You knew this?"

"Sure," he said, nodding. "They're both members of my men's club. When one shows, the other doesn't."

Rose pitched forward with a heavy cough and then threw her shoulders back against the chair. "Those two boys haven't gotten along since high school, Victoria. And bad blood like that doesn't just go away with the snap of a finger."

"But they were high school kids, Rose. Their quarterback days are long gone . . . for both of them."

"You ever notice the way Margaret Louise's smile faded every time someone so much as mentioned either Noah or his family? Happened every time. Like clockwork."

"No, I guess I never did."

"That's because you didn't know the history. Because the mere mention of Noah's name meant nothing to you. But for anyone who's lived in Sweet Briar for the past two decades, that name lowered the temperature in any Team Jake room by a good ten degrees. Maybe more."

"Wait." She made a T in the air with her hands and then dropped them back to her lap. "So you're telling me this Team Jake thing was real?"

"As real as real gets, Victoria."

"Margaret Louise mentioned it earlier today, but I assumed she was exaggerating."

"She wasn't exaggerating." Rose removed her glasses, used the bottom of her sweater to clean each lens, and then returned them to the bridge of her nose. "You've seen the way everyone flocks to the high school to see football games. It's an event around here. It's been that way since early on in my teaching career. Leona, of course, would say it's because there's nothing else to do in Sweet Briar on a Friday night. And maybe she's right. But whatever the reason, watching high school football is a staple in just about every home in this town come fall."

"Rose is right." Milo pulled his arm from around Tori and used it, instead, to pillow the part of his head that wasn't supported by the couch. "Even my third-graders can recite stats on players. And a few of them even understand what those stats mean."

"Okay . . ." Tori said, her curiosity at an all-time high.

"It was highly unusual for one class to produce two stellar quarterbacks. But Jake's year did." Rose shook her head at the memory. "Some thought Jake was better, some thought Noah was better. And each camp, as they came to be known, would thumb their nose at the other when their boy did something really good. On nights Jake played, Jake's camp whooped and hollered. On nights Noah played, Noah's camp whooped and hollered. And, for a while, it was just that—bragging rights. But as the season went on, and they were in position to go all the way, that's when the nasty stuff started."

"What kind of nasty stuff?" Tori asked.

"Cars were keyed in the parking lot, Noah's parents' trees were covered with toilet paper, eggs were thrown at Margaret Louise's home a few times, and—"

"Eggs?" Tori echoed. "Seriously?"

"Whoever was playing on any given night ended up being the target."

"Because the other camp was irritated their quarterback didn't play?"

Rose nodded. "That's right."

"And that went on for the whole season?"

"It did."

"But what difference did it make who was playing when they won? Weren't the fans just happy for the win?"

"You would think so, of course." Rose lolled her head back against her chair and sighed. "Most people would. But it didn't work that way. Everyone had a favorite and it became a competition. An unhealthy competition."

Tori drew back. "I can't see Margaret Louise being part of something like that."

"You know how she is about that boy, Victoria."

"But to TP someone's house because Jake didn't play one week?"

"I didn't say Margaret Louise did that. I said people in Jake's camp did—people who preferred Margaret Louise and her husband over Noah's family. But even if she did nothing wrong, you have to know she got swept up in the enthusiasm for her boy. Most mothers would, I imagine. Especially someone who loved being a mother as much as Margaret Louise did."

"Wow. Just wow. I had no idea."

"Those two boys used to be thick as thieves when they were in my kindergarten class. Why, the two of them would spend their recesses tossing a ball or searching for bugs or climbing on the monkey bars together. Stayed that way all through elementary school and into high school. But once they started competing to play, it changed. And I blame the adults in this town for that. They're the ones who made those boys see each other as competitors instead of teammates."

"I get that," Tori finally said. "I do. But that was almost twenty years ago, Rose. Why would people who were once part of Team Noah be so entrenched in the past that they'd take their cars to another town to be serviced rather than give their business to Jake?"

"Was that seriously happening?" Milo asked.

Tori nodded. "According to Margaret Louise, yes."

"Man, I knew there was something up there, but I didn't really pay it much mind. Some personalities just don't mesh in life. We all know that."

"The last straw was the state championship game." Rose scooted forward on her chair. "Jake was picked to play and he played his best game ever. Even got some big award with a bunch of letters."

"MVP," Milo said.

"Yes, that's it!"

Tori looked from Rose to Milo and back again. "Shouldn't everyone have just been happy the school won?"

Rose's frail body lurched upward with a shrug. "It sure seems as if they should have been, doesn't it, Victoria?"

"Wow." Tori looked up at Milo. "Crazy, isn't it?"

"You're not going to get any argument from me. I mean, I knew football was a big deal when I interviewed for my teaching job, but I didn't realize it was as big as it is until I actually got here."

"It's best just to stay out of that stuff completely, if you ask me." Rose slowly pushed her way off her chair and onto her feet. The movement, while simple enough, was accompanied by heavy breathing and more winces than normal.

Tori jumped up, only to root herself to the ground as the room spun ever so slightly.

"Tori?" Milo, too, stood, and gazed down at her. "Are you okay?"

She forced herself to take slow, deep breaths. When the unexpected motion stopped, she laughed. "Note to self: When you come across a dead body, stay upright." Then, before the inevitable questions began, she turned the focus back on her elderly friend. "How long have you been breathing like that, Rose?"

"Since I got old!"

A glance at Milo revealed the same concern she'd seen in his face since she came to on the garage floor, but now his concern for Rose was every bit as prevalent. At the caution in his eyes, she made an effort to soften her tone. "Do you think it's time for another treatment at the hospital?"

"Why? Because standing up hurts?" Rose groused. "No, Victoria, if I went in for a treatment every time my arthritis was acting up, I'd be a permanent resident."

There was no denying the quiver in Rose's voice or the fact that it came with the final part of her sentence. Somehow the thought of living in a facility had moved from never-going-to-happen into a real possibility for Rose.

Tori's heart ached for her friend and, for a moment, she wasn't sure what to say. But before she could settle on something, Rose began shooing them toward the door.

"If I'm breathing heavy, it's because I should have been in bed thirty minutes ago."

Tori opened her mouth to protest but closed it as Milo's hand settled against her back. "Rose is right, Tori. It's past everyone's bedtime."

Defeated, she let Milo guide her across the living room with Rose leading the way. When they reached the front door, Rose tried to open it, but lacked the strength to do so.

Tori looked over her shoulder at Milo and then back at Rose. "Rose? Are you sure you're okay?"

When Rose's only answer was a glare, Milo reached around Tori and opened the door. "You have a good night, Rose. You know how to reach us if you need anything."

"I do, Milo. Thank you." Rose accepted his kiss on her cheek as he passed and then shook her finger at Tori as she, too, stepped onto the porch. "Let him look after you. You've had quite a shock."

"Leona will be by in the morning to . . ." She let the rest of the sentence go unspoken as she realized her mistake.

Uh-oh.

Rose's eyes narrowed behind her glasses. "How do you know what Leona will be doing tomorrow morning?"

She looked to Milo for help, but, in the end, she knew she had to come clean. Rose would see through anything else. "We all love you, Rose. Everyone just wants to make sure you're okay. Including—"

With little more than a glance at her feet, Rose pushed the door shut.

Chapter 4

The sliver of sunlight peeking around the edges of the window blinds preceded the telltale creak of the bedroom door by a yawn. Maybe two. Rising up on her elbow, Tori did her best to shake the sleepy haze from her head.

"Why are you awake so early?" she asked around another yawn.

"It's eleven thirty."

"In the morning?" At Milo's grin, she tossed back the covers and flung her feet over the edge of the bed. "Milo, I'm supposed to be at the library in thirty minutes. Why didn't you wake me?"

"Because I called Nina and asked if she could cover your shift today."

She slipped her feet into her slippers, grabbed her robe from its resting spot at the foot of the bed, and stood. "Why did you do that, Milo? This is her weekend—Whoa!"

In a flash, Milo was at her side, taking hold of her arms until the room stopped spinning. "*That's* why."

"Wow." Reaching behind her head, she was able to find the point of impact quickly thanks to a protrusion that hadn't been there when she went to sleep. "Ouch."

"Take it from a former little boy, head injuries always seem to be worse the next day." With his hands still holding her arms, he stepped back to give her a more thorough once-over. "You okay now?"

"I am. But wow—I didn't expect this"—she pointed at the spot—"or that wave of dizziness." She dropped her hand back to her side and took a long, deep inhale. "Thanks for the catch, by the way."

"Always."

"I'm going to hold you to that."

He shadowed her across the bedroom, down the hallway, and into the kitchen. "So what would you like for breakfast? I could make you some bacon and eggs or some pancakes . . ."

"Did you eat?" she asked.

"I did. But that doesn't mean I can't make something for you now."

"I'll figure something out."

"It's settled. I'll make you some bacon and eggs," he said.

"You're incorrigible, you know that?"

"I do." When she was settled in her spot at the table, he headed toward the cabinet where the frying pans resided. "Scrambled or over easy?"

Her stomach roiled at the notion. "Actually, can we skip the eggs and just go with the bacon?"

He pulled two frying pans out, only to put one back. "You can't just eat bacon, Tori."

"Hmmm . . . Never thought I'd hear you utter those words in my lifetime."

The plunk of the pan against the stove top was no match for his laugh as he turned and made a face. "Wise guy."

"Sorry, I couldn't resist." She leaned forward, pushed the salt and pepper shakers closer to one another, and then dropped her hands back into her lap. "Let's just start with the bacon. I'll probably make some toast to go with it."

"*I'll* make the toast."

"Milo, I'm not an invalid. I fell and bumped my head, that's all."

He sprayed the frying pan, turned on the burner, and then crossed to the refrigerator for the bacon. "And I want to take care of you. Is that so wrong?"

"No."

"Then let me."

She said nothing as he placed what appeared to be seven or eight pieces into the pan and waited for the tantalizing aroma to follow. But even as it did, her thoughts, her senses, returned to Jake's garage and the moment she'd touched Noah's—

"It's Charles. I think he smelled the bacon."

Confused, she shook the troubling memory from her thoughts and looked up to find her vibrating phone in Milo's outstretched hand. Sure enough, a peek at the screen yielded Charles's name. "Good morning, Charles."

"Morning?" he repeated in her ear. "It's almost noon, sugar lips. You on the floor?"

"Nope."

"Your office?"

"Nope."

"Ooohhh, wait. I love twenty questions. I'm a certi-fia-ble master."

She didn't need the benefit of sight to know he'd just snapped a triangle to emphasize his credentials. She also didn't need the benefit of sight to tease him a little, either. "Certifiable has five syllables, not three."

When she was pretty confident the tongue he'd stuck out was back in his mouth, she filled in the blanks. "I actually didn't go into work today. Nina took my shift."

"*You* didn't go into work?" he repeated. "But when does that happen?"

"When my husband goes into my phone, finds Nina in my contacts, and asks her to cover my shift because he remembers what it was like to be a little boy."

"You lost me, sugar lips."

"I fell—or, rather, fainted—yesterday. Bumped my head pretty good."

"Always worse the next day," Charles said by way of agreement.

"Little boy days?"

"I was four and trying to learn how to pirouette."

There was no mistaking Milo's smile at the sound of her laugh. And there was no mistaking the way her head throbbed in the wake of that laugh. She closed her eyes and waited for the pain to stop.

"Anyway, the reason I'm calling, sugar lips, is to let you know Rose was feisty to the core this morning."

"You saw Rose? Where? When?"

"At her house. About two hours ago. I brought her

some of Debbie's famous chocolate-dipped donuts, like we discussed."

When the throbbing subsided, she opened her eyes to find Milo and a plate of bacon headed in her direction. "Like we discussed with *Leona*, you mean?"

She reached for a piece of bacon, smiled at her husband, and waited for her friend to respond. But there was only silence.

"Charles?"

"You were supposed to ask me about the feisty thing with Rose . . ."

"And I will. After you get to the part explaining why you're the one who brought Rose her Sunday breakfast instead of Leona."

Silence, part two.

"I'm waiting . . ."

"I plead the Fifth."

She nibbled her way through the first piece of bacon and reached for a second. "You can't."

"Are you eating?"

"Uh-huh."

She crunched down on the second piece and followed it up with an air kiss at the man now standing by the toaster.

"You're eating bacon, aren't you?" Charles asked, mid-gasp.

"I"—Tori set her half-eaten piece of bacon on the plate Milo had slyly placed at her spot and readied her fingers to snap—"plead. The. Fifth."

Milo laughed.

Charles didn't.

"Okay. Okay. You win. I had a message on my phone when I got out of the shower this morning. It was Leona."

A plate of buttered toast appeared next to the one with the half-eaten slice of bacon. "Thank you."

"You're welcome," Charles replied.

"I was talking to Milo."

"Was that for the bacon you think I'm too clueless to know you're eating?"

"No. That was for the toast he made *in addition* to the bacon." She allowed herself a moment to savor her ensuing chuckle and then moved on. "I take it Leona asked you to bring the donuts to Rose?"

"She did."

Tori rolled her eyes and reached for the toast. "And what was her excuse for shirking that job off on you?"

"She didn't say."

"Unbelievable," she mumbled, dropping the toast back onto the plate, untouched. "She *said* she'd take this morning."

"It's no big deal, Victoria. Really. It's not like I wasn't going to stop at Debbie's on the way to the bookstore, anyway."

"That's beside the point. Leona said she was going to do it. She *volunteered*, remember?"

She shivered at the memory, the unexpected truce between the longtime nemeses as hard to fathom now as it was when they first decided to go into business together in the fall. Rose and Leona . . . Who knew?

"I don't think it was deliberate, Victoria."

The shiver turned into a laugh. Only it wasn't a happy laugh as much as a sarcastic one. "Of course it was deliberate, Charles. Leona took this morning's shift in front of everyone in that group chat we set up after last week's sewing circle meeting. And she did it then because she wanted the public *atta-girls* for being a team player." Tori pushed the plate of toast into the center of the table and dropped her head into her left palm. "I just can't believe it took me this long to figure it out."

"Look, I realize I'm still a relative newcomer to this group. And while Leona and I have traded some pretty juicy secrets over the past eleven months or so, I wouldn't pretend to know her better than you do." Charles inhaled sharply and then released his breath in a veritable windstorm against her ear. "But, Victoria, you didn't hear her voice on that message this morning."

"Meaning?"

"Leona didn't call to cancel out on Rose. That happened during the message."

Tori sat up tall. "Come again?"

"From what I could tell, she called to see how I liked the shampoo she gave me yesterday." Charles's voice picked up in both pitch and speed. "Which, by the way, was fabulous. Simply *fabulous*."

"Keep going . . ."

"She sounded like she was drinking her age-defying tea because I heard her take a sip."

Age-defying tea?

Certain the question, if repeated aloud, would send Charles off on a sidebar of epic proportions, she opted to keep it to herself. Instead, she did her best to keep him focused. "What happened next?"

"I heard her set her cup down—it makes the same dainty sound every morning when we talk—and pull the rubber band off the morning paper." Charles stopped, cleared his throat, and dropped his voice to a near whisper. "And that's when everything changed, Victoria."

Before she could fully process his words, he continued. "I heard her mutter something about Sweet Briar and the fact that its Sunday edition is such a waste of paper and, the next thing I knew, she gasped."

"She gasped." Tori saw Milo point at her toast in an *eat-that* sort of way. She shrugged, made herself take a bite, and then returned to the conversation in her ear. "That's it?"

"At first, yeah. Then I heard a string of *oh-no*s. They were loud at first, but then they grew kind of hoarse, like this." He demonstrated.

"Did she say what she was *oh-no*-ing about?" she asked.

"No. But the last *oh-no*? She eked that out like she was trying not to cry."

Tori sat up tall. "Cry?"

"I know, right? Listening to this message was like watching an episode of *Hair Today, Gone Tomorrow*. I was on the edge of my seat. Which is why, by the way, my hair looks awful today."

"I don't understand."

"If I don't dry my hair imme-diate-ly"—he snapped— "I'm done for the day."

She considered pointing out his inability to count syllables once again, but let it go. Instead, she waited for more on Leona. Charles, of course, didn't disappoint. "So there I was, with my hair drip-drying, listening to Leona sniffling, when it all changed."

"What changed?"

"Leona got mad. Really, really mad. And that's when she told me she had to go and she hung up."

"I don't—"

"The next message was her calling back. Asking me to take her shift with Rose so she could be with Margaret Louise."

A chill moved down her spine and radiated out to her limbs. "Margaret Louise?"

"That's what she said."

"Charles, I've gotta go." Without waiting for a response, she pulled the phone from her ear and made a beeline for the front door and the Sunday paper.

Chapter 5

She was six blocks from Margaret Louise's home when her phone rang from inside the cup holder between the seats. She considered letting it go to voice mail but picked it up when she saw the name on the screen.

"Hey, Debbie."

"I just got back from church with Colby and the kids and saw the morning paper. What on earth happened last night?" The bakery owner stopped, took an audible breath, and then rushed on, the pitch of her voice a good indicator of the worry that had prompted the call in the first place. "And, more importantly, are you okay?"

"Physically? Yes, save for a bump on the back of my head and the on-again, off-again nausea it seems to be causing."

"I saw the picture. You looked dazed."

Ah, yes. The picture the *Sweet Briar Times* reporter

had managed to snap while Tori was being looked at by one of the local EMTs. Saying she looked dazed was one of many examples of Debbie Calhoun's generosity. Tori said as much aloud.

"So is it true?" Debbie asked. "Is Noah Madden really dead?"

"Considering I saw and touched his body, yes, I can verify that he is, indeed, dead." She shook away the memory that accompanied her verbal flashback and focused, instead, on the four-way stop she was approaching.

Two more blocks . . .

"What was he doing in the trunk of his own car?"

"That's a good question. And one Chief Dallas and the crew will be figuring out in the days to come, I imagine."

"I couldn't believe it when I saw the paper. Noah Madden is *my* age. People my age don't just show up in trunks." A voice in the background of the call quieted Debbie, but only for a moment. "Okay, Colby is right. Age isn't likely a factor in the location in which a body is found."

Nodding, Tori turned onto Margaret Louise's road and headed toward the third house on the left. In spite of the reason for her visit that morning, there was something about the grandmother of eight's home that always made Tori smile. Part of it, she supposed, was the cheerful yellow flowers that lined the walkway up to the front door, as if calling to passersby to stop by and stay awhile. Part of it, too, was the chalk-drawn pictures that covered every inch of the woman's driveway. In between the cats and smiley faces, the words "I Love You Mee Maw" invariably showed up in the handwriting appropriate for whichever grandchild had a few hours with grandma that particular day. Even Molly Sue, who wasn't in school yet, found a way to proclaim her love with backwards letters and almost no vowels.

"Victoria?"

"I'm still here." Not wanting to drive across the colorful images, she bypassed the driveway and parked alongside the curb.

"Do you know how he died? The paper didn't say."

Again, she flashed back to Jake's garage, Noah's eyes staring up at her with frozen fear, his head and face covered in blood. She swallowed back the bile rising up her throat and willed herself to breathe. To think. To remember. But other than Noah's eyes and the feel of his arm, there was nothing.

Nothing except blackness.

"From the moment my brain registered what I was seeing, I don't think I was upright for more than a second. But I know there was blood, and I knew he was dead."

"Oh, Victoria. I hate that you had to be there."

"So do I. But Milo was with me and he made sure the EMTs looked me over from head to toe." And it was true. Milo made everything better somehow. Even finding dead bodies. "Once we got home, he sent me straight to bed and arranged for Nina to cover my shift at the library today."

"You found yourself a good one with that guy, that's for sure."

"You'll get no argument from me."

Colby's deep voice in the background was followed by another question from Debbie. "How's Jake?"

"I don't really know. I know he was talking to the police, but honestly, as much as I hate to admit it, what you saw of me in the paper this morning was pretty much my state of mind right up until we got to Rose's with her dinner plate."

"You still went to Rose's after all that?"

"Trust me, she was a much-needed tonic."

"I'm glad." Debbie grew quiet for a moment, a sure sign she was thinking. When she finally spoke again, it was not without hesitation. "I . . . take it you saw the article? On the front page of this morning's paper?"

Tori looked up at Margaret Louise's front door and heard the answering roar of dread in her ears. "I did."

"That headline was over-the-top," Debbie said.

All Tori could do was nod and swallow.

"Sadly, though, there are an awful lot of folks in this town who would have gotten there without that headline."

"That stuff was *twenty years* ago, Debbie. They were *kids*! On a *high school football team*!"

Debbie's sigh was laden with dread. "*You* know that . . . and *I* know that. But that doesn't change reality, Victoria."

"And what reality is that, exactly?" she asked, even as she braced herself for the answer she knew would come— an answer that had prompted her to drive across town in pajama pants and slippers.

"The police need to figure out what happened to Noah—stat. Before Team Noah unleashes its wrath on everyone and everything connected to Jake Davis."

Leona answered the door, her brown eyes surveying her sister's front yard and the street it bordered before coming to rest on Tori.

"I came as soon as I saw the paper," Tori said in greeting.

"That's why you sleep in silk, dear. So if you have to run out without dressing, you still look"—Leona paused, took a slow, pointed glance at Tori's fuzzy pink slippers, and then rolled her eyes in utter disgust—*"attractive."*

"I'll remember that for next time." Tori gestured past Leona into the house. "Is she here?"

Leona made one more visual pass of the grounds behind Tori and then waved her inside. "It's only a matter of time before the vultures start circling."

"Vultures?"

"The press, dear."

"You really think they'll—" She stopped her personal naiveté-powered train in its tracks and cocked her ear toward Margaret Louise's most heavily utilized room. But instead of pans being extracted from cabinets and mixing bowls being set atop counters, there was only silence. Save, of course, for an occasional hiccup/sniffle combination.

Swinging her focus back to Leona, she noted the uncharacteristic lines around the Botox-assisted (*thank you, truth-serum brownies*) face. A closer inspection yielded—gasp!—a hint of darkness beneath the sixtysomething's lower lashes.

Tori inhaled sharply. "Tell me."

"Robert called about thirty minutes ago."

"Robert?"

"Good heavens, Victoria, must I hold your hand through everything, dear?" Without waiting for a reply, Leona barreled on without so much as a glance at her nails or a touch-up of her lipstick. "Robert Dallas, of course."

Tori swallowed against dread's encore. "And?"

"I should be furious at him for jumping to conclusions, but at least he had the decency to call so she didn't have to hear it across the back fence."

Tori tried to read between the lines, but she was at a loss. The roar in her ears was making it difficult to think, let alone decipher. "Leona, please . . . English."

"I knew it was bad when I saw that headline, but I never, in a million years, thought anyone with half a brain would take it seriously. Then again, we are talking about Sweet Briar Police Chief Robert Dallas."

Tori made a T in the air with her hands. "English, remember?"

Leona craned her head in the direction of the kitchen and then stepped closer to Tori. "They've arrested Jake, dear."

Her gasp echoed in the paneled hallway as she fell back against the wall. "Wait, what? You—you can't be serious!"

"It's true, Victoria. They've arrested my Jake!"

Spinning around, Tori's gaze fell on the kitchen doorway and the puffy-eyed woman staring back at her with such gut-wrenching sadness it took everything in her power not to look away. "Margaret Louise!"

With several long strides, she closed the gap between them and pulled the heavyset woman in for a hug. "Margaret Louise, I'm so sorry. They're making a huge mistake. There's no way Jake could have been involved."

"Just the very fact he was working on the car Noah's body was found in makes him involved, Victoria," Leona said.

Slowly, she stepped away from Margaret Louise, the

anguish she'd felt just moments earlier catapulting into anger—anger at Leona.

"And *I'm* the one who *found him*, Leona," she hissed through clenched teeth. "Which means if there is any basis to your logic, I must be involved in Jake's murder, as well."

Leona raised Tori's clenched teeth with a death glare. "It's not *my* logic, dear. It's the logic that had half the police force summoning Jake to be questioned in the first place."

"They didn't summon *me*," she protested.

"Nor have you been in a lifelong rivalry with the victim." Leona stepped around Tori and, with a gentleness rarely seen with anything other than Leona's beloved pet rabbit, Paris, took her sister's arm and guided her back into the kitchen and over to the spot at the table that was littered with crumpled tissues. "We really should get word to Melissa."

Tori stopped in her tracks. "Melissa doesn't know?"

Margaret Louise flopped into her chair, plucked another tissue from the box atop the table, and blew her nose like a trumpet. When she was done, she hiccupped twice. "She knows he went to the station to talk 'bout what happened last night, but she doesn't know he was arrested."

"When are you going to tell her?" she asked.

"When I can quit my cryin' and take care of my grandbabies so she can go see Jake." Margaret Louise stared at the tissue in her hand as if it were some sort of foreign object, her words taking her somewhere far beyond the confines of her normally bustling kitchen. "I just can't bear thinkin' 'bout them youngins growin' up without their daddy!"

Leona clapped her hands. "If you keep thinking like that, Margaret Louise, you'll never quit crying. And if we don't move this along, Melissa is going to find out Jake has been arrested from someone other than you!"

Seconds stretched into minutes as Margaret Louise wiped her eyes, blew her nose, and, eventually, squared her shoulders with a resoluteness that propelled her up and out of her chair. "Jake needs me right now. He needs me to be strong for Melissa . . . strong for those youngins . . . and strong for him, too. I owe my boy that."

"Wait right there." Leona disappeared into the living room only to return less than a minute later with her makeup bag in hand. "By the time you get to Melissa's, the puffiness should be gone. But this"—Leona whipped out her favorite concealer—"should help with the redness. *If* you don't start crying again."

When the redness was muted enough to fool the casual observer, Margaret Louise took an audible breath and did her best to smile at Tori. But the effort, while commendable, didn't fool any of them.

"Let me take you," Tori said, hooking her thumb in the direction of the front door. "I have Milo's car, so that's not an issue. Plus, if I'm there, I can keep the kids busy while you break the news to Melissa."

Margaret Louise's eyes filled with tears all over again. "You'd really do that for me, Victoria?"

"Are you kidding me?" Tori gathered Margaret Louise's hands inside her own and squeezed. "I'd do anything for you. Anyone would."

"Then help me find 'im."

"Find who?" Tori asked.

"The person who *really* killed Noah Madden."

Chapter 6

It was nearly five o'clock before Tori had her first minute alone with Margaret Louise. The car ride to Melissa's hadn't counted, as her main focus had been keeping Margaret Louise from crying. After that, it had been all about keeping the kids busy while Margaret Louise told her daughter-in-law about Jake's arrest, and then continuing to keep them busy in the aftermath of that conversation so they didn't question why their mother was running out of the house or why news trucks were beginning to assemble on the street outside their home.

Fortunately, Margaret Louise's cooking skills and affinity for knowing what her grandchildren liked for dinner had bought them a little time to regroup.

Stealing a peek through the sliding glass door that led to Melissa and Jake's patio, Tori silently counted seven heads around the table, all eagerly munching on the hot dogs and macaroni and cheese their Mee Maw had made and then shooed them outside to eat. Which left just one more set of ears—the baby's.

"So, how'd it go with Melissa?" Tori turned back to the kitchen and the woman staring, unseeingly, in the direction of the baby swing and the sleeping child nestled inside. "Was she completely devastated?"

When there was no answer, she came around the center island and lowered herself onto the stool next to her friend. "Margaret Louise? Are you okay?"

"My Jake is in jail," Margaret Louise said, her tone void of anything resembling its normal exuberance. "For murder. How can anything ever be okay again?"

"He didn't do it. *That's* how everything is going to be okay." She hated to see defeat on anyone's face, but to see it on someone who normally crackled with joy was painful. "Why, he's probably on his way back here with Melissa right now, laughing at the ludicrousness of this whole thing."

Margaret Louise's wide shoulders rose and fell with obvious effort before the eyes that had been staring off into space swung around to meet Tori's. "There won't be any laughin' anytime soon, Victoria."

Unsure of the best response, Tori simply reached out, encased her friend's pudgy hand with her own, and waited.

"I ain't tryin' to take nothin' away from the acclimatin' you've done since you've been in Sweet Briar, Victoria. You've brought somethin' mighty special to this town. The folks who've gotten to know you rave 'bout you, and rightfully so. But there's a lot you don't see workin' in the library, eatin' at Debbie's, or even walkin' in the park with Milo."

"Then tell me what I'm missing so I can understand."

Margaret Louise pulled a hot dog off the platter she'd tucked to the side, considered it for a moment, and then returned it to its original starting place. "I can't remember the last time I went hours without eatin'."

"You should, you know. Melissa and Jake don't need you getting sick right now."

"If you listen to my twin, I could stand to miss a few meals."

"And if I listened to Leona, I'd spend most of my day fussing over the way I look. But if I did that, I'd miss out on the stuff that really matters." Tori slid off her stool, crossed to the cabinet for two plates, and then topped each one with a hot dog and a helping of leftover maca-roni and cheese. "So I smile politely when she tells me what I need to do, and then do what I want, anyway. Which is what you're going to do with this food."

Margaret Louise stared down at the plate Tori placed in front of her and then pushed it off to the side. "Leona ain't why I'm not eatin'. What my Jake is goin' through is why I ain't eatin'."

"What Jake is going through is exactly why you need to eat." Tori pushed the discarded plate back in front of her friend. "*He* needs you to be strong. And I need you to get me up to speed on this ugly side of Sweet Briar I don't know."

After a quick glance at first the patio and then the baby swing, Margaret Louise picked up the hot dog and added a thick line of ketchup. "Maybe it's better I don't tell you 'bout them other parts of Sweet Briar," Margaret Louise said between bites. "'Cause if I do, you just might up and move back to Chicago."

"Look, as long as you, Leona, Rose, and the rest of the gang are here, Milo and I aren't going anywhere." Realizing she'd forgotten drinks, she returned to the cabinet for glasses and then stopped at the refrigerator for cold water. "That said, if I'm going to be able to do what you asked, I need to know the history."

Swiping the back of her hand across her mouth, Margaret Louise dislodged a few hot dog bun crumbs from her lips and then swiveled to the left to accept the water Tori held in her direction. "What did I ask?"

She stared at her friend. "For me to find Noah's real killer."

Hope skittered across the woman's face. "You're really goin' to do that?"

"Of course." Tori wandered back to her stool and the hot dog she'd yet to touch. For some reason, her stomach didn't seem as enthralled with the sight as her eyes did. "I love Jake and Melissa, too, you know."

The tears were back, bringing with them a mental visual of Leona's concealer-related warning. "No . . . no . . . don't cry. Please." Tori yanked her chin in the direction of the patio. "Those grandbabies of yours are going to be coming through that door any minute looking for dessert and you don't want them seeing you cry."

"I didn't tell them there was dessert."

"You don't have to. You're their Mee Maw."

Margaret Louise's answering smile disappeared behind her napkin as she dabbed at the tears. "I swear, Victoria, you've been a blessin' to me since the day Mayor Georgina brought you to your first sewin' circle meetin'. Why, when I left that night, I told Leona you were goin' to be a special one, and I was right."

"Trust me, Margaret Louise, you've been every bit as much of a blessing to me these past few years. Probably even more so."

A hint of crimson crept into the woman's cheeks. "You really think so?"

"I really *know* so." She straightened up on her stool, did another mental count of the occupants at the picnic table, and then gathered up her plate and her napkin and carried them to the trash can in the corner. "So tell me more about this so-called rivalry between Jake and Noah. How it started, how bad it got, when it ended, that sort of thing."

"There ain't no so-called 'bout it."

"Okay . . ."

"As far as how it started and how bad it got, I can tell you all about that. But that last part? The one 'bout when it ended? It hasn't."

Movement from the swing waylaid her intended return to the counter and, instead, had her making a detour toward the newest addition to Jake and Melissa's large brood. The smile she earned in return brought a laugh from the vicinity of the island.

"Well, would you look at that, Victoria? He just lit up when he saw you."

With a flick of the switch, the baby swing slowed to a stop and two little arms extended in Tori's direction. "Oh, sweetie, aren't you precious." She lifted the baby into her arms and pressed her lips to his forehead, the sweet smell of his skin akin to a lighthouse in the crazy storm that had been her past twenty-four hours. "Hmmm, he smells so good."

"Give 'im time. It won't be long before he'll be diggin'

'round the dirt just like his big brothers." Margaret Louise chuckled. "And just like his daddy was always doin'. Why, Jake could've found mud in a desert when he was a youngin. Especially if he was wearin' one of them fancy schmancy outfits his Aunt Leona sent him when she was livin' in the Big Apple."

Tori laughed at the image, but it was short-lived thanks to the way the same memory shifted Margaret Louise's aura back to sad. "There's a lot I don't get about this whole rivalry thing between Jake and Noah that I want to know, but the part that makes absolutely no sense to me at all is the fact that you think it's still going on. I mean, how can you say that when Jake took Noah on as a business partner at the garage? Surely he wouldn't have done that if this rivalry was still an ongoing thing, right?"

Margaret Louise's gaze moved past Tori and Baby Matthew to fix on something clearly beyond the confines of her son's and daughter-in-law's home. "Jake's daddy loved him with all his heart. He was a wonderful husband to me and a wonderful father to Jake. He worked hard, worshipped our Lord, and lived a life of honor. But he wasn't no wealthy man. Not in the way money makes a person wealthy, anyway. But it didn't matter none. We had each other and we had Jake. That was more'n enough."

Tori carried the baby closer to the island and bounced him gently on her hip. "I've never really heard you talk much about your husband. He sounds exactly how I'd picture someone lucky enough to be married to you."

"I was the lucky one, Victoria. Jake Thomas Davis was my one true love. Then he gave me my next true love in the form of another Jake Thomas Davis." Margaret Louise took a sip of her water and then wiggled a finger at her youngest grandchild. The baby, in return, squealed in delight. "Anyway, all my yakkin' is to give you a little understandin' 'bout things. It's not that I didn't *want* to help Jake fix up his garage. Why, I'd do anything for my boy—you know that. But money is somethin' I just don't have."

Finally, the reason behind her friend's lengthy lead-up clicked into place. That, along with her limited knowledge of Sweet Briar and its residents, got her to a workable starting place. "Surely he could have gotten a loan from the bank, though, right?"

"He wasn't willin' to put this house up as collateral. Not when he had Melissa and them youngins out there countin' on him the way they do."

"Okay, I get that. But why Noah? Especially if the blood between them was as bad as you say? Why not ask Leona? I'm sure she would have helped."

Margaret Louise started shaking her head before Tori was even done. "Leona was talkin' 'bout openin' Sew-Tastic. Jake didn't want to change her plans. Especially when we realized she was wantin' to include Rose in them plans."

"So how did he make the leap from Leona to Noah? That's the part I don't get."

"Seems Noah heard rumblin' 'round town—probably from Arden at the bank—that Jake was wantin' to fancy the garage up. So he reached out to my Jake and made him an offer he couldn't refuse."

"Jake gave Milo and me a quick tour yesterday when we dropped off my car after dinner. The place is amazing."

When Margaret Louise said nothing, Tori continued, her thoughts jumping from the baby in her arms to the man who had seemed less than thrilled to see her and

Milo the previous evening. "Okay, so in this deal between Jake and Noah, Jake got the spruced-up, state-of-the-art garage he wanted. What did Noah get?"

"Half of all the profits for twenty years or until Noah's death, whichever came first."

"Until Noah's *death*?" she repeated as a chill skittered down her spine. "And *then* what?"

"I'm not sure what you're askin', Victoria."

She tried again. "What happens after Noah's death if it's before the twenty years?"

"You mean in terms of his share of the profits?"

Tori nodded, unable to speak.

"Why, they go right back where they belong—in my Jake's pocket."

Chapter 7

Tossing the car keys onto the hall table, Tori did her best to resist the overwhelming urge to scream. How life could go from relatively calm to all-out crazy in a matter of a single weekend was mind-boggling at best. Still, if it weren't for the fact that Milo was likely grading a mountain of second-grade papers at that exact moment, the scream could at least count as doing something.

"Hey, babe. I'm back here."

She smiled to herself as the smell of her husband's favorite coffee beckoned her down the hall and across the living room to the tiny den that served as his paper-grading station on Sunday evenings and her sewing room a few evenings a week. At the doorway, she swept her hand toward the stacks of marked papers on his left, and the slightly smaller-sized single stack of unmarked papers to his right. "Looks like you're making really good progress . . ."

"Only because you haven't been here." He underlined a sentence near the bottom of the page and then stopped, his amber-flecked eyes widening. "Wait. I so did not mean that the way that it sounded. I just meant—"

"I know what you meant. And I'm sorry. I had no idea things were going to go the way they did when I ran out of here earlier today." She picked her way across the mounds of graded papers, bent down, and kissed the top of his forehead, the warmth of his skin beneath her lips a welcoming albeit brief tonic for the chill that had been hers since Margaret Louise shared details of Jake and Noah's business arrangement.

With a gentleness that made her heart full, he book-ended her face with his hands and lowered her lips to his. Then, after a moment or two, he pulled back, grinning. "I have to say, the pajama-pants-and-fuzzy-slippers look works well on you."

"It's a good thing Leona isn't here right now. I think she'd stone you for saying that." Tori straightened and wandered over to the single window and its view of the driveway and the magnolia trees that grew, canopy style, along its western side. It was a view she realized she'd come to take for granted, like everything else about the home she shared with Milo. "It's kind of scary how fast things can change, isn't it?"

"Meaning . . ."

She took one last look out the window and then turned back to Milo, the red pen in his hand and the stack of papers at his side eliciting a sigh she was powerless to stop. "I'm sorry, I shouldn't be in here, distracting you. You have work to do. We can talk later. When you're done."

"Oh no you don't." He scooped up the stacks of graded

papers, deposited them into his work bag, and then stood. "C'mon, let's sit in the other room."

"But you still have all of those to do," she said, pointing at the untouched pile still on the floor.

"And they'll get done. *After* I spend a little time with my wife." He waited for her to take his hand, then led her into the living room and over to the couch. "I'm assuming Margaret Louise fed you, but if you're still hungry I could throw in a bag of popcorn or something."

"No. I'm good."

Shrugging, he lowered himself onto the couch and then pulled her down beside him. But instead of heeding his invitation to snuggle into the crook of his arm, she grabbed the closest throw pillow and hugged it to her chest. "Oh, Milo, it's bad. Real bad."

"Please tell me Team Noah didn't show up?"

"I can't really say one way or the other. Margaret Louise and I were more focused on keeping the kids away from the front windows so they wouldn't keep asking about the news trucks."

"News trucks? Are you serious?" Milo raked a hand through the top of his hair and exhaled loudly. "I mean, I guess it stands to reason they might swarm the garage and all, but Jake's house?"

And then she knew.

Milo had no idea Jake had been arrested. She'd been too busy to call and tell him, of course. But she'd assumed he'd have heard it on the local five o'clock news. Then again, he had graded a good 75 percent of his students' papers . . .

Casting the pillow off to the side, she scooted forward just enough to afford direct eye contact with her husband.

"Jake was arrested this morning. Right before I got to Margaret Louise's, in fact."

"Arrested?" Milo repeated, his eyes wide.

"Chief Dallas was considerate enough to give Margaret Louise the heads-up before it got out to the public, but . . . yeah . . . they arrested him."

"Arrested *Jake*?"

"Yes."

"Please tell me you're joking."

"I wish I could." She watched him push off the couch and begin to pace—moving between the fireplace and the couch with steps that managed to seem both purposeful and aimless at the same time. "That's why I was gone so long. Margaret Louise was a mess when I got to her place. Leona and I had to get her calmed down so the kids wouldn't know something was wrong the minute she walked into their house to tell Melissa."

Milo froze. "Melissa didn't know?"

"Margaret Louise told Chief Dallas she wanted to be the one to tell her. So once she got her own emotions under control, I drove her to Melissa's myself. While she broke the news to Melissa, I played with the kids in the backyard. Then, after Melissa took off for the police station, I stayed to help Margaret Louise with the kids."

He cupped his hand over his mouth, only to let it slip back down to his side in a fist. "*Jake Davis?* They arrested *Jake Davis* for murder?"

Since it was clearly a rhetorical question designed to convince himself of what he'd just heard, Tori said nothing, the shock on her husband's face not out of line with what she, too, was still feeling. Only the reason for hers was very different.

Sure, she'd found the initial news of Jake's arrest for Noah's murder every bit as ludicrous as Milo did. But now, in light of what she'd unearthed about Jake's deal with Noah, her shock was partnered up with something that felt an awful lot like dread.

Milo turned and headed back toward the fireplace, only to stop midway and turn back. "Look, I get that these two were football rivals. I even get that high school football isn't just high school football around here. But c'mon . . . And, if they want to bark up that tree, why would *Noah* be the one dead in the trunk and not Jake? *Jake* is the one who got the coveted MVP award at State that year, not Noah."

It was, essentially, the same argument Margaret Louise had been making when the sliding glass door opened and seven dessert seekers ranging in age from fifteen down to two swarmed into the kitchen. Looking back, Tori had been as grateful for that distraction as she was for the one now knocking on her own front door.

"Are you expecting someone?" Milo asked.

"No. But with everything going on, I guess I'm not really—"

The telltale creak of the front door drifted into the room a half second before the no-nonsense tone of an all-too-familiar voice. "Victoria? Milo? Are you here?"

"Georgina?" she whispered to Milo before rising to her feet and turning toward the hallway. "We're here. In the living room."

Georgina Hayes, the town's mayor and an original member of the Sweet Briar Ladies Society Sewing Circle, breezed into the room with her trademark straw hat firmly in place atop her head. In her hands was a simple purse and a pair of car keys. "I just had to see you with my own two eyes!"

Looping around the back side of the sofa, Georgina nodded a greeting at Milo and then directed Tori to turn in a circle. When they were facing each other again, Georgina smiled. "You appear as if you're in one piece."

"I am."

"Andrew at the fire department said you took a nasty fall?"

"I hit the back of my head on the concrete floor when I passed out. But I'm okay now. Really."

Georgina looked to Milo for confirmation of Tori's words, but he was studying Tori. "No more queasiness? No more dizziness?"

"You were queasy?" Georgina snapped, not unkindly. "Andrew didn't mention that."

"That's because it didn't start until after we left the scene. But really, it's subsided quite a bit."

"I take it you've heard the news? About Jake Davis?"

"I did."

Milo moved in beside Tori, slipping his arm around her waist as he did. "With all due respect, Georgina, you've gotta know the chief is reaching with this one. Jake Davis is a good man, a good husband, a good father. Taking someone's life isn't who he is."

"Noah Madden's body was found in the trunk of a car Jake was working on, Milo. A crowbar, recovered at the scene, had Noah's blood and Jake's fingerprints on it."

Something jiggled in Tori's memory, but it remained at large as Milo splayed his hands in frustration. "Maybe he touched it, maybe he didn't notice the blood, maybe—"

Georgina silenced the rest of Milo's supposition with

her hand. "I agree that there might be a very logical explanation, Milo. But Team Noah would have our heads on a silver platter if we ignored the evidence."

"Team Noah?" Milo repeated. "Really?"

"Wait." Tori stepped away from Milo's arm and slowly backed up against the couch until her only option was to sit. "So you're saying the reason they arrested Jake is just because of this football thing?"

"We have what looks to be the murder weapon. We also have two men who have had issues with each other for a very long time. Arresting Jake is the best way to make sure the"—Georgina paused—*"little issues* that still rear their heads from time to time don't escalate to the level of old."

"What *kind* of little issues?" Tori asked.

Georgina pulled her hat off and tucked it beneath her elbow. "Do you remember that broken window in Leona's antique shop last summer?"

"How could I forget? The guy who came to replace the window was no more than twenty-two and he was positively smitten with Leona. She, of course, let him down gently when he asked for her number, but boy did she talk about that at the next sewing circle meeting."

"Make that the next *several* sewing circle meetings," Georgina corrected. "Now, do you remember the big crack in Margaret Louise's windshield later that same day?"

Tori grinned. "Sure. Margaret Louise calls stuff like that their twin moments. Charles and I prefer to call them their twin-pathy pangs. Get it? Twin-pathy?"

Any laughter was short-lived as Georgina proceeded ahead, her eyes never leaving Tori's. "And what about

Lulu's stolen bike during the first week of school in the fall?"

"Of course I remember that. Lulu loved that bike." Tori looked up at Milo to see if he was following along better than she was, but all she saw in his face was a noticeable tightening of his jaw. "I don't understand what any of this has to do with this Team Noah/Team Jake stuff."

Milo whistled softly. "Oh man. I had no idea."

"No idea about what?" Tori looked from Milo to Georgina and back again, her confusion growing with each pass. "What am I missing?"

"What's the common denominator in all of those incidents, Victoria?" Georgina asked.

"I don't know. Leona and Margaret Louise are twins . . . Lulu is Margaret Louise's granddaughter and Leona's great-niece . . . But Lulu's thing had nothing to do with a window."

"You're right—it didn't. But all three of them share something else in common, Victoria. Or, rather, some*one* in common."

She stared at Georgina, waiting for more, but it was Milo who finally delivered the answer Tori sought.

"They share *Jake*."

Chapter 8

She could feel Nina's eyes following her as she made her way down the mystery aisle, shelving the night depository's last few titles.

A Churn for the Worse by Laura Bradford . . .

A Story to Kill by Lynn Cahoon . . .

A Cry in the Night by Mary Higgins Clark . . .

Tori slid the last book into place and sighed. Granted, it was odd to wish for another stack of returned books, but then again, the task had served as a much-needed distraction. Without it, her mind was free to wander, stirring up the same guilt that had left her tossing and turning the entire night.

"That's it. That right there . . ."

She turned and looked a question at her assistant, Nina Morgan.

"Don't you look at me like you don't know what I'm talking about, because we both know you do." Nina did a quick scan of their surroundings, and when she was satisfied that no patrons had magically appeared in any of the library's nooks and crannies, she folded her arms across her chest and waited.

Tori released a second, louder sigh, and headed back to her starting point and the list of tasks she wished she hadn't already completed. "You really should've taken today off, you know?"

"Why?" Nina challenged. "The Brown Bag Mystery Lovers group is coming in at noon today."

"I know, but they're easy. They run their own meeting."

"I'm on the schedule." Nina's arms remained crossed.

Winding her way through the opening in the otherwise circular desk, Tori perched on the edge of the stool closest to the computer. "But you weren't on the schedule yesterday and you ended up coming in to cover me. Last minute, I might add."

"And if Milo hadn't called and asked me to cover you, you'd have been in here, putting your health in jeopardy."

"I bumped my head, Nina. That's all. Milo was being overly cautious. You know how he is."

"He loves you. And he was worried. Consider yourself one of the lucky ones." Nina released her arms, pulled the second stool alongside Tori's, and took a seat. "So how are you? Really?"

"I'm okay." More than anything, she wanted to reach across the keyboard and turn on the monitor, but to do so would be rude. Instead, she mentally picked her way through the minefield of possible answers before landing on the most innocuous of the bunch. "My head was still sore when I brushed my hair this morning."

"Passing out on concrete will do that, I imagine."

"Tell me about it." She brought her hand to the back of her head and winced as her fingers grazed the bump. "But it'll go away soon."

"Sleeping would probably help with that."

Tori withdrew her hand. "I slept until almost lunchtime yesterday."

"I'm talking about last night," Nina countered.

"What makes you think I didn't sleep last night?"

"Um, maybe the circles under your eyes that you better hope Miss Leona doesn't see?"

"We're not all blessed with her skin. Or her plastic surgeon."

Nina leaned forward, decreasing the already small gap between their stools. "There's also the way I had to say hello to you three times this morning before you even noticed I was sitting at my desk."

"I guess I was a little distracted, that's all."

"That much was obvious," Nina said.

Tori cast about for something to say that would explain her behavior, yet keep Nina off the true scent. "Milo told you what happened, yes?"

At Nina's slow nod, Tori continued. "Well, I guess I keep seeing Noah's body in that trunk. Not exactly a fun sight."

For a long moment, Nina said nothing, her dark eyes searching Tori's face like one might search for treasure. What, exactly, she was looking for was anyone's guess, so Tori used the opportunity to shrug and scoot her stool a hairbreadth closer to the still-darkened computer screen.

"I know we're not as close as you are to Miss Leona or Ms. Rose or Ms. Margaret Louise, but after two-plus years of working together here at the library, I know when something isn't right. And something isn't right with you."

Tori paused her hands atop the keyboard, took a long, slow breath, and then turned back around to face Nina. "Don't discount what you mean to me, because I certainly don't. And you're right—I didn't sleep very well last night. But honestly, it's just the fact that every time I close my eyes, I feel that arm . . . and see those eyes staring up at me as if pleading for me to help. But it was too late."

The fact that what she was saying wasn't a complete lie made it easier to justify in her head. After all, the sensation of Noah's skin beneath her fingers *had* surfaced a time or two over the past twenty-four hours. The fact that it wasn't the true reason for her sleepless night, though, was inconsequential. Besides, admitting her status as an awful human being to Nina wasn't exactly a productive or pleasant way to start their respective workdays.

Nina opened her mouth to protest but closed it as a sudden swath of sunlight across the top of the information desk redirected her attention to the front door and their first patron of the day. Tori sagged her back against the counter in relief—a relief that only magnified as the elderly man requested help with the public computers, a timely task that would no doubt enable Tori to busy herself with budgetary reports that would be too difficult to break away from when Nina returned.

Sneaky, yes. But Tori was desperate.

"Hey, sugar lips, how's that pretty head of yours doing today?"

Startled, Tori looked up to find Charles smiling down at her from the other side of the counter. "Where did you come from?"

"From the front door," Charles said, hooking his thumb over his shoulder. "But considering how preoccupied you obviously are, it's no wonder you didn't notice."

She straightened up on the stool and stole a glance at Nina before dropping her head into her hand. "What is it with you guys? Do I really have to be Polly Positive twenty-four/seven?"

"Personally, I see you more as Sally Sunshine than Polly Positive, but that might just be because I have a thing for yellow at the moment." Charles pointed at his now-yellow-tipped hair. "I thought it was time to retire the green for a little while and try something more spring-like. What do you think? Is it me?"

"Is it *you*?" she echoed, laughing. "Well, considering you've sported purple, red, green, and blue tips since we met, I'm not sure how to answer that question. But yes, you look . . . happy. Like the sun."

"Just call me Mr. Sunshine and I am"—he readied his fingers at the top of his triangular snap formation—"at. Your. Service."

"I'll remember that, thanks."

He dropped his elbows onto the counter and propped his chin atop his left palm. "Soooo. What's got you so glum, chum?"

"Look at you rhyming. I'm impressed." She leaned over, neatened a pile of scratch paper intended for patrons, and then moved on to the jar of miniature pencils to its left. "But really, I'm fine. Just a little tired is all. Finding a dead body has a way of messing with a person's sleep, you know?"

"So *lack of sleep* is what's behind this sudden urge to clean an already clean desk?" Charles rolled his eyes in a near-perfect imitation of Leona and followed it up with a soft *tsk*ing sound. "Do I look like I fell off one of those carrot trucks Margaret Louise is always talking about?"

"You mean a turnip truck . . ."

"Semantics." Elongating his neck to almost giraffe-like proportions, Charles took in the empty aisles and chairs he could see from his vantage point and then lowered his voice to a whisper nonetheless. "So what gives?"

"I'm a horrible friend." There, she said it.

Charles's answering gasp was so sudden and so loud, Nina left their only patron to hurry over to the desk. "What's wrong?"

"Nothing." She shot Charles a warning look and then gestured toward him for Nina's benefit. "I just told him about a sale on scarves at Thurman's that he didn't know about. And, well, you know how he is about his scarves . . ."

"That was about *scarves*?" Nina asked.

Charles nodded dutifully and then waited until Tori's assistant was out of earshot once again. "For the record, Thurman's doesn't carry scarves, sugar lips. But that was a valiant effort."

"Thank you."

He reached across the counter, took hold of Tori's hand, and led her out from behind the counter. Then, with a series of chin motions for Nina's benefit, he tugged her toward the back hallway. "C'mon. We can talk in your office."

She tried to stop, but he kept on pulling. "Charles, I can't leave Nina on the floor alone."

"Because she can't handle the one person who's here right now?"

"No. Of course she can. But someone else might come in."

"And if they do, she'll be fine."

It was no use arguing. Unless . . . "Hey, why aren't you at the bookstore right now?"

"It's Monday. I don't open until eleven o'clock."

Drat.

When they arrived at the office she shared with Nina, Charles reached around the corner, flicked on the overhead light, and then motioned her inside and over to her desk.

"Has anyone ever told you you're kind of pushy?" she asked as she dropped onto her chair. "Because you are, you know."

"They have and I know." Bypassing his usual stop at the coffeemaker on the table just inside the door, he ventured over to her desk and the folding chair to its side. "Okay, so let's revisit what you said out there, shall we?"

"I would, but you said Thurman's doesn't sell scarves," she quipped in a feeble attempt to keep some semblance of control over the conversation and, better yet, her emotions.

"I take it no one has ever clued you in to the fact that you stink at stall tactics."

She leaned heavily against the back of her chair. "Nope. You're the first."

"I'm honored. But really—you're a horrible friend?"

His artfully shaped left brow inched upward a half second before he pulled his phone from his back pocket. "I think it's time to call in the troops."

"The troops?"

He paused his finger on his phone's keypad and nodded at Tori. "It sounds to me like someone in this office needs a hug intervention."

A hug inter—

Flinging her body forward on her chair, she shoved her hand across the top of Charles's phone. "No. Please. Don't call anyone. I don't need a hug intervention."

"Are you going to talk?" he asked, pulling his phone out of her reach. "Because I will call them all—Rose, Dixie, Beatrice, Leona, Georgina, Margaret Louise . . ." His voice faded away, only to return with a quick head shake. "Actually, Margaret Louise is probably a little too busy with her son's ridiculous arrest, but I'm sure that'll be over soon."

"I'm not so sure about that," Tori whispered.

"No, really, even Debbie says it's a matter of time before Jake is back with Melissa and the kids." Charles drummed his perfectly manicured fingernails on the edge of Tori's desk, his excitement over being in the know palpable. "Seems Debbie talked to Georgina just before I got to the bakery this morning and Georgina said Jake's arrest is just about dotting *i*'s and crossing *t*'s and once that's done, Jake will be let go on account of there being no real motive."

Aware of the lump moving up her throat, Tori swiveled her chair around until she was looking out over the library grounds. Normally, the mere sight of the hundred-year-old moss-draped trees and the smattering of park benches most heavily utilized by readers calmed her to the core. But not today. Not even close.

Charles spun her focus back onto him. "What's going on in that gorgeous head of yours?"

The way she saw it, she had three options. She could admit her traitorous thoughts aloud. She could continue to let them fester until the breakfast she'd barely been able to eat made the encore it had been threatening since she left the house. Or she could simply distract him with talk of scarves until he had to make haste to open his shop.

She glanced at the clock on the wall above the door. *Ten o'clock.*

"Don't worry, sugar lips. I've got a good forty-five minutes—*fifty* if I gallop."

"Gallop?"

Charles picked at the nail on his right index finger and then gave up and pointed at Tori. "You need to talk. Now."

He was right. She did need to talk. "Okay." Tori stopped, took a fortifying breath, and then continued, her voice barely more than a whisper. "What happens if there *is* a motive?"

"You mean for Jake?"

She could only nod.

"Puh-lease, Victoria." Hiking his left foot across his right knee, Charles removed a piece of lint from his bright blue sneaker. "*Everyone* had issues with someone when they were in high school. Jake did, Leona did, *I* did . . . It's a given in much the same way waxing is superior to tweezing."

"Waxing?"

"It's true. Ask anyone." He let his foot bounce a few times before swapping it for the right.

"Leona has talked to you about her high school years?" she asked, before waving off the question. "Actually, that shouldn't surprise me. She tells you things—behind-the-scenes things she doesn't tell anyone else."

Charles took a few moments to preen and then returned to the subject at hand. "High school was horrid, simply horrid. I spent the majority of my freshman year having my face shoved into lockers, walls, turf, bleachers, you name it. Sophomore year, most of the brainless brutes who'd tortured me the year before were busy chasing the kind of girls who, for some unknown reason, find that type enchanting, so they more or less left me alone. It helped, of course, that I arrived as the first bell was ringing and timed my departure each day with that of a few of the teachers. Junior year was more or less a rinse-and-repeat, although I did start an after-school book club that netted me a friend or two."

He dropped his foot back down to the ground, pushed off the chair, and wandered in the direction of the coffeemaker. When he got there, his arms remained at his sides.

"And your senior year?" she prodded.

Reaching forward, he grabbed a stirrer from the holder beside the coffeemaker and slid it between the teeth on the left side of his mouth. "I met my first true adversary."

"I thought that distinction belonged to Rickie Meanypants Rogers—the kid who stole your meat loaf sandwich in second grade and your favorite eraser in third grade, and chipped your tooth in fifth grade."

He worked the stick around his mouth in very un-Charles-like fashion. "That was my first bully. I'm talking about my first real adversary."

"What do you call the jocks who made your freshman year a living hell?"

"Them?" Charles withdrew the stirrer from his mouth and gave it a little wave. "They didn't know what to make of me, that's all. I could've left my hair its natural color, and chosen clothes that weren't so . . . pastel-y. But I didn't. I think part of me felt as if I was playing the tortured victim in *Crime Spree*." His eyes widened at the memory. "That was such a gripping show, wasn't it? And Ted Walker? The lead detective? Completely and utterly adorable. Ask Leona."

She raised her hands in surrender. "No, I'm good. Anyway, get back to the part about your first true adversary . . ."

Charles shuddered once, twice, and then tossed the nibbled stirrer into the trash can and leaned against the wall alongside Nina's desk. "Robert Shannon—aka Shanny."

"Go on . . ."

"As we've already established, I wasn't Mr. Popular. So when I was one of two nominees for Best Smile in our graduating class, I was beside myself."

"I take it this Shanny person was the other nominee?"
Charles nodded.

"And he won?" she surmised.

"Only because he told everyone my smile had been altered." He turned around, hooked his index finger into the side of his mouth and pulled, drawing her attention to the slight imperfection in his top front tooth he'd shown her a few months earlier.

"But I knew you for months and never noticed it! And—and I only found out about it in the first place because you pried back your mouth the way you did just now and showed it to me!"

Charles turned back to the window. "Well, Shanny knew, and he made sure everyone in our class knew."

She stood, sidled up next to him, and rested the side of her head on his shoulder. "For what it's worth, I'd have voted for you."

"Thanks, sugar lips. That means a lot." Silence filled the office, only to be broken a few moments later by Charles. "I actually wrote an acceptance speech."

She popped up her head. "Acceptance speech?"

"For Best Smile."

"I'm sorry you didn't get to give it."

"Oh, I gave it. To my mom. And she clapped like there was no tomorrow."

It felt good to smile, good to lose herself in a moment of lightness. Even if she knew it couldn't last.

"I tell you, Victoria, it was months before I stopped plotting ways to get revenge on Shanny. But here's the thing—life got better after high school. I discovered my passion for bookstores, I found a fabulous hairdresser, and, eventually, I found true friends in you and Leona and Rose and the whole gang. And poof! I couldn't care less about Shanny." Charles pointed at a squirrel scurrying across the grounds with a scrap of sandwich bread in his mouth, and then, when he'd watched it as long as their vantage point would allow, he made his way back to the folding chair. "And that's with *Shanny* winning! This Noah Madden person didn't win. So why would Jake feel the need to kill him at all, let alone twenty years later?"

She knew he wasn't expecting an answer. A rhetorical question didn't need one. Then again, it wasn't really a rhetorical question if an answer was available . . .

"Because twenty years ago, Noah's life wasn't the only thing standing between Jake and his dream."

Chapter 9

It was all there—the ham sandwich, the bag of pretzels, the apple Milo would later pretend he accidentally put in her bag instead of his, and a chocolate chip cookie. Yet nothing appealed to her despite her later-than-normal lunch break.

Charles pointed at the apple and, at her nod, pulled it across the picnic table, studying it as if it were a crystal ball capable of solving life's mysteries.

"If you see something in there that fixes all of this, you'll tell me, right?"

He looked up, the worry in his eyes unmistakable. "I spent the whole time you were on the phone with the library director trying to pretend this wasn't happening. And then, when Nina called you up front to help with a few of your patrons, I even pinched myself a few times. You know, just in case I was having some sort of nightmare."

"Welcome to my life for the past"—she glanced down at her wristwatch—"nineteen-plus hours. That said, I'm still surprised you called in one of your part-timers to open the bookstore."

"I just . . . couldn't." Dropping his head onto the table, Charles unleashed a dramatic sigh.

Movement from midway up the tree canopying their chosen table stole Tori's attention from her unexpected lunch companion. But no matter how hard she tried to lose herself in the beauty of the young finch carefully watching them from its temporary perch, her thoughts yanked her right back to reality. "I know I had to have reacted when Margaret Louise was telling me about the death clause in Jake's agreement, but she didn't seem to notice."

"Jake could've been holding the murder weapon and Margaret Louise wouldn't notice. You know how she is about him." Slowly, Charles sat up. "Side note, do we even know how Noah was killed? Was he strangled? Poisoned? Shot?"

"He was hit in the head. With a crowbar."

"How do they know it was a crowbar?"

"Seems they found it at the scene. With Noah's blood on it."

Charles cringed. "That's a nasty way to kill someone."

"Is there a nice way?" she asked.

Shrugging, he took a bite of the apple and then swapped it for the bag of pretzels. "I don't know, maybe a pillow over the face would be a nicer way."

"Okay, this is turning a bit too macabre. Next topic, please."

He popped a pretzel into his mouth and began to chew. "What . . . are you . . . making . . . for tonight's meeting?"

Her stomach churned.

"I—I don't know, Charles. Maybe we should hold off on the sewing circle until next week."

"No sewing circle?" He stilled his pretzel-holding hand midway to his mouth and pouted his lips. "Why?"

"Isn't that obvious?"

His eyes narrowed as he shook the pretzel at her. "I thought the sewing circle was as much about spending time with each other as actually sewing."

"It is, but—"

"What Margaret Louise is going through right now is *exactly* why we need to have tonight's meeting."

Twenty-four hours earlier, she'd have made the same case. But now? Knowing what she did about Jake? Not so much.

"What's that face about, sugar lips?"

She shook off her woolgathering, only to wave off the final pretzel from what was once her bag. "There's no face."

Charles tossed the empty bag into Tori's paper lunch sack, then voided his face of all emotion. "*This* is no face, Victoria. And *this*"—he cast his eyes downward, crinkled his forehead, frowned, and drooped his shoulders—"*is* a face . . . which I'm looking at right now."

To argue or pretend otherwise would be futile. Charles was perceptive. And even if he weren't, she was a lousy poker player when it came to keeping her emotions hidden. "See? This is why we can't have a meeting. Or why I can't attend if there is one. Everyone will know something is wrong. Especially Margaret Louise."

It was Charles's turn to slump. "I hadn't thought of that."

"I haven't been able to think of anything else." She surveyed what was left of her lunch and then pushed it across the table to Charles. "I keep seeing it in my head. Jake will get released, Margaret Louise will be beside herself with relief, and there I am, thinking her son actually did it."

Charles gasped. "You really think he did?"

"I don't *want* to think it, Charles. Jake is my friend! I've been to dinner at his house; he's been to barbecues at mine. He was at my wedding; I was at the baby's christening. I adore his wife. I consider his mother one of my very best friends." It was becoming harder and harder to speak with each passing sentence. Finally, she lurched forward against the table, bookending her face with her palms. "Yet I'm privy to a piece of information that could destroy not only him but his entire family—a family I couldn't love any more if they were my own."

She closed her eyes against the ensuing silence and prayed that when she opened them again, she wouldn't see the same disgust on his face that she felt in her own heart.

"Maybe the police won't find out about the business arrangement." Charles broke a piece of bread off the still-uneaten sandwich and tossed it toward a bird hungrily pecking its way across the grass.

"But *we* know."

Charles snapped his attention back to Tori. "What are you saying?"

"I'm saying that we know about that agreement. That Jake has regained one hundred percent of his garage *because* Noah is dead."

The earlier silence returned, only this time she didn't close her eyes or send up any silent prayers. No, this time she just watched as confusion gave way to understanding before settling into the same despair she felt to the very core of her being.

"If we say nothing and Jake did this, we're essentially setting ourselves up as accessories after the fact, aren't we?"

"I don't know the legal terms, but"—she mustered a shrug—"yeah, I would imagine we could get in trouble. And even if we couldn't, a man is dead. It's not in my makeup or yours to stay silent about something like that."

Charles held up his hands, crossing-guard style. "While I appreciate your steadfast belief in my moral character, there are a few people who, under this same circumstance, I wouldn't rush to help."

"Such as?"

"Anyone who would hurt you, for starters." Charles scattered the rest of the sandwich bread around the grass and then stuffed the ham and cheese back into the sack. When everything was neat and tidy, he pointed at her cookie. "Are you going to eat that?"

"Be my guest." She watched him nibble his way around the outer edges of the cookie and then grabbed the paper sack and stood. "I've got about ten more minutes. Any interest in taking a quick loop around the library?"

He stood, stuffed the rest of the cookie into his mouth, and met her on the far end of the table. "I'll be the one if you want."

"Be what one?" she asked as they fell into step beside one another.

"The one that tells Robert."

She stopped mid-step and grabbed hold of his arm. "No. I dragged you into this mess. I never should have told you about any of this."

"You told me because I asked."

"I could have dodged your questions. That's what I did with Milo when we were getting ready for bed last night, and it's what I was actively doing with Nina just before you showed up this morning."

"Hence the reason I am here, sugar lips."

"Excuse me?"

"Oops." Charles covered his mouth.

"Charles . . ."

His hemming and hawing gave way to a guilt-ridden shrug. "Now, don't give him a hard time, love. He was just worried about you is all."

"He? As in Milo?"

"He called me as he was on his way to the school. Said you seemed preoccupied and asked if I would talk to you." He looped his hand through the crook of her arm and guided her down the library's outer path. "And then, when you weren't looking, Nina motioned for me to talk to you."

She wasn't surprised, really. Her move to Sweet Briar had netted her so much more than the librarian job she'd sought. It had filled her life with the kinds of people who made her smile from the inside out and made her a better person in the process.

"How do I do this, Charles? How do I deliver up information that could destroy Margaret Louise?"

It was Charles's turn to stop. "If Jake did this, Victoria, it will be on him, not you."

"But if I'm the one who— Wait. I'm getting a call." She reached into the front left pocket of her slacks, pulled out her phone, and glanced at the screen.

Uh-oh . . .

"Who is it?" Charles asked.

Swallowing hard, she held the phone out for Charles to see.

"You have to take it," Charles concluded. "She'll worry if you don't."

Once again, she closed her eyes. Only this time, in addition to the silent prayer, she found herself counting to ten. At nine, the vibrating stopped.

She slumped in relief. "I didn't answer fast—"

Again, her phone began to vibrate and, again, Margaret Louise's name and face-splitting smile filled the screen.

"She's going to hate me, Charles." She swung her gaze up at the sky and slowly brought the phone to her ear as Charles moved in to listen. "Hey there, Margaret Louise, how are you holding up—"

"Is Nina workin' today?" Margaret Louise asked in a rush.

"She is. She's inside at the moment, but I can get her if you'd like to talk—"

"I need you, Victoria!"

Tori pulled the phone closer to her ear. "Margaret Louise? What's wrong? Where are you? Did something happen to one of the kids?"

"I'm . . ." The woman's words gave way to such gut-wrenching sobs Tori thought her own heart was going to break.

"Shh . . . shh . . . It's okay. I'm here."

The sobs intensified.

Charles flapped his hands as raw panic raced across his face. "Make her stop! Make her stop! Make her stop!"

"Please, Margaret Louise," Tori pleaded. "I need you to stop crying so you can tell me where you are."

"I—I . . . I'm here . . . in town . . ."

Spinning around, she took in the whole of Main Street with one quick visual sweep. "I don't see your station wagon."

The cries quieted enough to allow a few sniffles through.

Tori tried again. "Where *are* you? I can't help you if you don't tell me where you are."

"I'm . . . I'm at the . . . police . . . station."

She felt Charles pull away from the phone, but she kept her focus on the woman now hiccupping in her ear. "Talk to me, Margaret Louise."

"They . . . they say they're . . . not . . ." Margaret Louise sucked in a breath and then let it out along with a second stab at her sentence. "They say they're not releasin' Jake!"

A knowing chill skittered down her spine.

After a moment, Margaret Louise sniffled again. "Did you hear what I said, Victoria? They say they're not releasin' Jake!"

A gentle elbow in her side broke through the roar in her ears enough to voice the response Charles was silently mouthing. "They're *not*?"

"No!" Margaret Louise wailed. "They say this business with Noah ain't 'bout football."

Unsure of what to say, Tori said nothing at all. But it didn't matter. The cries and the hiccups had stopped.

"They say it's 'bout the garage. They say he had motive."

She felt her knees begin to buckle and was grateful for Charles's answering hand on her back. "M-motive?" Tori stammered.

"I keep sayin' they're crazy, but they ain't listenin'. They say they have proof."

"Proof?"

"Some sort of papers."

"I—I don't know what to say, I—"

"Please, Victoria, I need you to come to the station. I need you to tell them Jake didn't do this."

"Margaret Louise, I don't know what I—"

"And if they won't listen, you'll just have to show 'em the truth. Just like you always do."

Chapter 10

Until that moment, Tori had never considered the click of a door as it closed. It had always been such a normal, almost inconsequential sound. But now, standing there in the same room as Jake, she heard something very different—a finality.

The guard, stationed just inside the doorway, nodded as if he understood, but really, his nod was likely nothing more than a standard run-of-the-mill greeting. Only for Tori, there was nothing run-of-the-mill about being in the cinder block room generally reserved for criminals and their attorneys.

She'd argued that point with Margaret Louise, but it hadn't worked. To Margaret Louise, Tori was Jake's way out of jail. Like somehow she could snap her fingers and make the damning contract between Jake and Noah cease to exist.

Margaret Louise, of course, was determined to find out who had anonymously sent a copy of the contract to Chief Dallas earlier that morning. But really, it didn't matter. What mattered was the fact that the contract not only existed but gave the woman's son a motive for murder. The fact that Noah's body was found in the trunk of his own car—a car Jake was working on, no less—just served as the proverbial cherry on top of the sundae that was his case.

Which meant one thing. Jake needed a lawyer, not a librarian.

She'd tried, of course, to tell that to Margaret Louise as the woman was shoving her toward the aforementioned door, but her efforts and her viewpoint had fallen on deaf ears. Charles had tried, too, even going so far as to volunteer to do what he could to find the best criminal attorney around. But that, too, had been waved away with the same diatribe now looping its way through Tori's thoughts.

"Jake don't need no lawyer, Victoria. He didn't do nothin' wrong. Which is why we need you and your sleuthin'. When you find the person who did this, my Jake will go free. And when he does, there best be a whole lot of pies showin' up at his door. A whole lot of pies."

If only it were that simple.

She stepped away from the door and into the middle of the room, her eyes coming to rest on a beaten-down version of Margaret Louise's son. His head hung low, his eyes hooded, Jake Davis exuded a potpourri of emotions—fatigue, anger, confusion, and even fear.

Slowly, he lifted his chin and motioned toward the chair on the opposite side of the square table. "Please, sit."

She did as he asked.

"Not exactly the usual venue for seeing one another, but it's the best I could do under the circumstances," he quipped, although his attempt at humor was perfunctory at best.

She swallowed. Hard. "I—I'm sorry this is happening to you."

"So am I. But, even more than that, I'm sorry it's happening to my mom, to my wife, and to my kids."

"The kids know?"

He tilted his chin up until his focus was on the drop ceiling. "Melissa kept them home from school today thinking I'd be released. But now, with"—he spread his hands to indicate their current setting—"*this*, they're going to find out. Melissa can't keep them locked in the house forever."

At a loss for what to say, she merely nodded and shifted in her seat.

After a few moments, he, too, shifted in his seat. Only instead of shifting from side to side, he threw his weight forward until his chest was one with the edge of the table. Then, stealing a glance in the direction of the bored guard, Jake modulated his voice down to a volume just loud enough for Victoria to hear. "We need your help, Victoria."

"You know I'll do whatever I can to help with the kids," she said. "And—and I know Milo will keep an eye on things at school to make sure no one is giving them a hard time."

Jake reached out and almost placed his hand atop hers, but he pulled back at the last minute. "And I'm grateful for that. I really am. But I was thinking more along the lines of the way you figure things out with stuff like this."

"Meaning?"

His inhale was audible, as was the beat of pure silence that followed. "I know how it looks, Victoria. I really do. But it's not right. I didn't do this. I didn't kill Noah."

More than anything, she wanted to nod, to offer the reassurance she knew he needed to hear, but she couldn't. Not yet. Instead, she mulled over her options and then matched his lean with her own. "I remembered something on the way over here, something I'd forgotten in the aftermath of finding Noah. You were holding a crowbar when Milo and I saw you . . . you had blood on your hands. Milo thought you'd cut yourself."

"And so did I."

"But you'd been using that crowbar . . ."

"You're right. I was. Because I was working on his car."

"Where did it come from?" she asked.

"You mean the crowbar? It was behind the tire when I got back to the garage—exactly where I left it when I went home for dinner."

"And you didn't notice it had blood on it?"

"No. I just wanted to finish his car and be done with it."

She studied his face for anything to indicate he was lying, but she saw nothing. Nothing besides despair and fear. "So I hear someone sent a copy of your contract with Noah to Chief Dallas."

"That's right."

"Any idea who might have done that?"

Again he looked toward the guard before he answered. "I don't know. But the section detailing the reversion of the garage back to my complete control in the event of Noah's death was highlighted."

"Highlighted?" she echoed.

"That's right."

"But why?"

"From where I'm sitting, only one thing makes sense."

"And that is . . ."

"Someone is trying to set me up."

All fidgeting stopped. "For Noah's murder?" At Jake's nod, she leaned forward again, her voice a dead giveaway for the shock his words had ignited. "Who on earth would want to set you up for murder?"

Jake palmed his face, only to let his hand slip back down to the top of the table. "The *real* killer."

No matter how hard Tori tried, she simply couldn't wrap her brain around the month's budget report. Every number she tried to plug into the spreadsheet gave way to the image of Jake's face as he'd looked when they parted ways. Every column she tried to close out bowed to yet another question . . .

Was he right? Was someone trying to set him up?

But who?

And why?

On one hand, she could point to a basic principle of Psychology 101. Jake's back was most definitely up against a wall and it was human nature he'd come out swinging.

But she also knew Jake. She knew him as Margaret Louise's son. She knew him as Melissa's husband. She knew him as Lulu's and the rest of the kids' dad. And she knew him as a person who'd done his best to keep her aging car on the road, who'd helped her set up countless library events over the past few years, who'd sat on her back deck for barbecues, and who'd celebrated the birth of his eighth child like it was his first. Did someone like that really just change on a dime? With not so much as a passing thought for his loved ones?

No.

Not if you're Jake Davis, anyway.

Tossing her pen onto the center of her desk, Tori sat up tall. Did she have answers? No. Did she know where and how to find them? No. But she knew Jake. And the Jake she knew would never jeopardize a life with his family. Not even for his garage.

Suddenly, the guilt that had marked the first half of her day parted like clouds after a storm, and she sank back against her chair with palpable relief. Now she could look Margaret Louise in the eye. Now she could stop avoiding Milo. Now she could look at herself in the mirror and not feel like the biggest heel on the face of the—

"Nina told me I'd find you back here." Leona strode into the room, set her purse atop the folding chair, and gave Tori a once-over. "She said you seemed troubled."

Tori stood, kissed her stylish friend on the cheek, and motioned toward the coffeemaker in the corner. "Can I get you a coffee? A glass of water?"

"A more comfortable chair would be my preference, dear. I don't do folding chairs unless it's absolutely necessary."

"Oh. Sure." She crossed to Nina's side of the office, liberated the unused chair from its spot at the desk, and wheeled it over to her own. "Here you go."

"You take that one, dear. I'll take yours." Leona sashayed over to Tori's chair and lowered herself onto it with the grace of a queen. "You don't look terribly troubled to me. In fact, I'd go so far as to say that when I walked in just now, you looked almost gleeful. Which, I must say, is entirely inappropriate considering my nephew's current circumstances." Leona crossed her ankles in her usual delicate way. "You are aware, of course, that he's still in jail, yes?"

"I am. I spent some time with him shortly after lunch."

"You did?"

Tori retrieved her pen from the desk and twirled it slowly between her fingers. "He says he's being set up."

"Well of course he is, dear," Leona droned. "That isn't exactly earth-shattering news."

For the briefest of moments, she considered admitting to Leona her initial skepticism, but on the advice of the little voice in her head vehemently protesting that thought, she opted for a shrug.

Followed by a flinch.

Uh-oh . . .

"Have you not heard what I've said about shrugging, Victoria? And the little lines that shoot across your forehead when you do?"

She said nothing.

Leona, in turn, gave no indication she even noticed. "I can only do so much, dear. Adherence is up to you."

"Adherence is up to me. Got it." Tori reached around to the front of her desk, yanked open the bottom drawer closest to her temporary seating, and plucked out the bag of pretzels tasked with getting her through some of the most grueling parts of her day. She removed the chip clip at the top and held the opened bag in Leona's direction. "Have one. Milo and I brought home like ten of these bags when we were in Heavenly, Pennsylvania, in February. They're incredible."

"Incredible, dear?"

"Yes." Ignoring Leona's answering eye roll, Tori helped herself to a handful of pretzels and then set the bag on the desk. "So, what brings you by the library at"—she glanced up at the clock above the door—"four thirty on a Monday?"

"I want in."

She stopped chewing and stared at her self-appointed life coach. "In?"

"That's what I said, dear."

"No, I . . . heard . . . you." She swallowed the rest of her pretzel and then popped another one into her mouth. "I . . . just . . . don't . . . know . . . what you're . . . referring to."

"You do realize you're chewing and talking at the same time, yes?"

"Uh-huh."

Leona pinned her with a stare.

She swallowed again and tried not to look too forlornly at what remained of the handful of pretzels piled in front of her on the desk. "Um, so, what do you want in on?"

"I want Margaret Louise's spot."

"Margaret Louise's spot? I don't understand."

"In your car, dear."

"We're not going anywhere, Leona."

Leona rolled her eyes again. Only this time, an exasperated sigh was added to the gesture. "I'm talking about when you do your snooping."

"My snooping?"

The sigh was back. "Victoria, dear, are you always this dense?"

"I'm not being dense, Leona." Slowly, and subtly, she walked the fingers of her right hand up the edge of the desk and over to the remaining pretzels. "You're just being cryptic."

Leona's hand came down over top of Tori's, bringing with it a crunching sound.

Tori's shoulders sank.

"I want to help clear my nephew's name."

Her eyes left the remains of her next pretzel and traveled back to Leona. "I don't understand."

"Surely you're going to heed Margaret Louise's request and track down the person responsible for this debacle."

Tori didn't move.

"*Victoria?*" Leona prompted.

Tori looked back at the carcass belonging to her last pretzel and waited for the protesting little internal voice to return. But it didn't. In fact, the only thing playing in her head at that moment was the same thing now making its way past her tongue . . .

"Okay, okay, you can help. But this business of getting Margaret Louise's spot? What happens if she wants it for herself?"

"She can't. She's promised Jake she'll focus on the children and Melissa."

No surprise there, but still . . . "If you take her spot, it's only temporary. Though, if I were you, I wouldn't count on Charles giving it up without a fight."

"Oh?" Leona stuck her hand into her purse, pulled out her phone, dialed a number, and placed the call on speaker. "We'll just see about that, won't we?"

Two rings later, Charles's voice filled the room. "Snap. To. It. Books & Café. This is Charles. How may I help you today?"

"I want Margaret Louise's spot in the car for Victoria's investigation into Noah's murder," Leona purred. "That's not a problem, is it, Charles?"

"Of course not."

Leona leaned forward, ended the call with a perfectly manicured finger, and then dropped the phone back into her purse. "Done."

Chapter 11

Tori shifted Milo's car into park and leaned forward, resting the side of her face on the edge of the steering wheel. There was no getting around the fact that she was utterly exhausted. The stress of seeing Margaret Louise so upset, her own worry about Melissa and the kids, and the subsequent lack of sleep leading into a full workday had officially caught up with her over a steaming spaghetti pot.

Milo, of course, had tried to convince her to skip the evening's sewing circle meeting in favor of sleep, but the sight of the brownies she'd made for the occasion had won out. She knew it was a silly reason to go, especially in light of the fact that a normal meeting netted enough dessert to feed a small army. Still, routine was routine, and time with friends was time with friends.

She allowed herself a pair of yawns and then made

herself sit up, remove the keys from the ignition, and gather up her meeting essentials—the brownies, her sewing box with its assorted threads, and the pair of shirts she was planning on mending for Milo. Surely her energy would resurface once she got inside Dixie's house. And if it didn't, she could always be the first to leave. Either way, she'd make it work . . .

Swinging her gaze toward her hostess's front window, Tori was able to make out a few of her fellow sewing sisters. Debbie was standing in front of Beatrice Tharrington's chair, swapping tales, no doubt, about the latest PTA meeting at Sweet Briar Elementary School. To their left, she spotted Mayor Georgina, hat on head, playing referee in what appeared, even from the road, to be a heated conversation between Dixie and Leona. Dixie, in her usual indignant way, had her hands on her hips and was holding her own against a clearly perturbed Leona.

When she saw no sign of Margaret Louise, Rose, or Charles, she peeked in her rearview mirror.

Nothing.

With one last glance at the house, Tori set the brownie plate on her lap and carefully peeled back a section of plastic wrap. When the opening was big enough for her hand, she reached in, extracted one small square, and popped it into her mouth.

Mmmm . . .

A sudden knock on her door made her jump.

The jump made her swallow sooner than planned.

The unexpected swallow kicked off the choking that yielded the driver-side door being flung open by Charles.

And Charles, in turn, barked at her to sit forward so he could smack her on the back.

Like an obedient puppy, she did as she was told and, sure enough, the coughing subsided enough that she was able to eke out something resembling a sentence. "You . . . really . . . shouldn't scare . . . a person like that!"

"Seems to me you got caught with your hand in the cookie jar, or should I say"—he readied his snapping fingers—"the. Brownie. Plate."

She considered denying the accusation, but to do so would be futile. Especially when the plastic wrap was still peeled back and a glance in the rearview mirror revealed a sizeable brownie crumb lodged in the corner of her mouth. Instead, she played the pity card and embellished it with a side order of ego stroking.

"With everything that's going on right now, I couldn't shake what you said to me earlier."

Batting his eyelashes, Charles placed his palm on his chest. "What I said?"

"You know, about tonight's sewing circle meeting being important." She pushed the brownie crumb into her mouth and then wiped any residual signs of her duplicity off with a dampened finger. "And you're right. Margaret Louise needs all of us surrounding her tonight—letting her know that we're on her side, no matter what."

"Margaret Louise isn't coming tonight."

She took in Dixie's front window one more time and, once again, the faces she could make out didn't include the grandmother of eight. "Did something else happen?"

"No. She's just helping Melissa with the kids."

It made sense. It really did. But still, the thought of a sewing circle without Margaret Louise wasn't exactly appealing. Sure, she loved all of her sewing sisters, but seeing Margaret Louise in any given setting instantly made everything more fun.

"Sugar lips?"

She shook herself back into the moment, fixed the plastic covering she'd breached, and stepped out onto the sidewalk next to Charles. "Yes?"

"Can we skip the buildup and just get to the part about the brownie?"

"I needed the sugar boost if I'm going to stand a prayer of staying awake through this meeting." There. She said it.

"Oh, I don't think you have anything to worry about on that front." He closed her car door, pointed at the lock button on her key fob, and then tucked his arm through hers for the walk across the street to Dixie's front step. "Unless you're deaf."

"Deaf?"

When they reached the sidewalk on Dixie's side of the street, Charles gestured toward the open living room window. And that's when she heard it.

Dixie and Leona weren't simply disagreeing.

They were out-and-out arguing. In full voice.

"What on earth?" She shoved the brownie plate on top of Charles's dessert offering and took off up the stairs and into Dixie's front hallway. Charles followed on her heels. "Hello! We're here! Where is every—"

"I've always known you have no fashion sense whatsoever," Leona shouted from the room at the end of the hall. "One only has to look at the tents you call clothing."

Tori's gaze dropped to her day's attire—gray dress slacks, lavender blouse, simple black heels . . .

"She's not talking to you, sugar lips," Charles hissed.

"I wouldn't be so sure if I were—"

"And I always knew you had it in you to be vengeful. We all had a bird's-eye view of that little fact the moment the library board handed your job to Victoria."

Uh-oh . . .

A glance at Charles revealed the same horror she felt as Leona's tirade continued at top volume. "But—but . . . *this*? You've stooped to a new low, Dixie Everdeen Dunn—a new low!"

"Wanting *justice* means I'm stooping to a new low?" Dixie bellowed back.

Leona's slender body leaned across the already minuscule gap between the women just as she stuck her finger within an inch of Dixie's face. "You think convicting my nephew of murder is *justice*?"

"If he did it—yes!"

Tori flung her sewing box and Milo's shirts onto the hall table and took off in a sprint down the hallway. When she reached the living room, she stepped between the warring women and placed a hand on Leona's shoulder.

Leona shook it off, her brown eyes filled with a rage trained solely on Dixie. "This so-called friend of my sister's believes Jake killed Noah!"

Tori heard the gasp from just over her left shoulder and knew Charles's shock echoed her own. "Dixie? Is that true?"

"I know that young man is dead. And I know that he's been a thorn in Jake's side since they were in high school," Dixie said, her voice thick with anger. "On the football field, off the football field, Margaret Louise's boy never missed an opportunity to show Noah up. The more public the better."

Leona spun around, plucked a nose-twitching Paris off Beatrice's lap, and turned back to Dixie. "I will not spend one more minute in the home of a traitor!"

Dixie spread her right arm toward the hallway from which Tori and Charles had just come. "Good. Because you're no longer welcome here."

"Wait! Wait!" Tori grabbed hold of Leona's upper arm. "Leona, please. Stay. We'll figure this out."

"There's nothing to figure out," Leona spat back. "This meeting—*this group* is over." Then, yanking her arm free, she spun around once again, snapping her fingers in the direction of the trio of pale-faced women staring back at them. "Let's go, ladies."

Debbie crossed to a rocking chair on the other side of the room, retrieved her sewing tote from its side table, and fell in line behind Leona.

"Wait . . . Debbie—"

Leona silenced Tori with a raised hand and then craned her head around Debbie. "Beatrice, get your things."

The British nanny looked from Leona to Debbie, to Georgina, to Dixie, and finally to Tori as uncertainty turned to fear. "I—I . . ."

Leona's jaw tightened. "Georgina?"

The mayor crossed her arms in front of her chest. "I'm staying right here."

Leona gasped. "You're *staying*?"

"That's what I said."

Leona fisted her non-Paris-holding hand at her side and then turned her attention back on the twentysome-thing now trembling from head to toe. "Beatrice?"

When Beatrice remained frozen in her seat, Leona pinned her with a flesh-melting stare and then headed toward the hallway with Debbie in tow. "Charles . . . Victoria . . . let's go."

Charles took his place behind Debbie but stopped when he realized Tori hadn't moved. "Sugar lips? Aren't you coming?"

The *tap tap* of Leona's stilettos against the hardwood floor in the hallway ceased. So, too, did the softer thump of Debbie's ballet flats. And, like clockwork, all three sets of eyes turned to meet Tori's.

Squaring her shoulders, she took a step toward the makeshift parade, only to step back just as quickly. "No, Charles. I'm going to stay here. With Dixie."

Chapter 12

Milo looked up from his latest thriller novel the second she walked into the bedroom and motioned toward the clock atop his nightstand. "So much for thinking you were too tired to go tonight."

"Actually, I should have heeded your advice and stayed home." Tori reached down, worked her shoes off her feet, and tossed them through the open closet door on her side of the bed. "If I had, I wouldn't have had to deal with all of that." She stopped, brought her fingers to her temples, and slowly kneaded. "Ugh . . . my head. It's spinning."

He slid his favorite student-made bookmark into his book, closed it, and set it beside the clock. "Why don't you get ready for bed and I'll go grab you something for the headache."

"It's not that kind of spinning." She dropped onto the edge of the bed and then slowly lowered herself down until her head was perpendicular with Milo's chest and she was looking up at the ceiling. "You should have seen it. It was a disaster from start to finish."

"What was?"

"Tonight's meeting. It was"—she stopped, squeezed her eyes closed against the image of Dixie throwing Leona's store-bought cake into the trash, and made herself breathe—"awful. Absolutely awful."

"What happened?" He rolled onto his side and gently smoothed her hair away from her face. "Did something happen with Rose?"

She tried to lose herself in his touch but it wasn't happening. "Okay, so maybe there was one good thing about tonight—two if you count Margaret Louise."

His hand stilled. "I'm trying to follow along, Tori, I really am, but I need a little help here."

"Rose passed on tonight's meeting. She apparently called Dixie and told her she was too tired." Pushing up on her left elbow, she turned her head just enough to make out the clock. Ten thirty. "It's too late to call her now, but I'll check in on her in the morning."

When she didn't return to her starting spot, he patted his chest. She waved off the offer. "And Margaret Louise, she was at Melissa's, helping get the older kids ready to return to school tomorrow.

"Funny thing is, it actually went through my head, as Charles and I were walking up to Dixie's door, that the meeting might have been a nice distraction for Margaret Louise." She shook her head, then stood. "Shows how much I know, doesn't it?"

"I take it there was an issue?"

She didn't mean to laugh. She really didn't. But it was

hard not to react to the understatement. "Uh, yeah, there was an issue. A *big* issue. Colossal, actually."

"Okay, c'mon, the suspense is killing me." Milo propped himself against the headboard and followed her around the room with his eyes. "What happened? Did Leona forget one of her travel magazines? Or—noooo . . . Did Charles step on Paris or something?"

At the window, she parted the curtain just enough to provide a view of the darkened street and then let it swish back into place of its own accord. "Did you know Dixie was—*is* Team Noah?"

"Oh no . . ."

"Oh yes." Inhaling sharply, she slowly turned until Milo was back in her sight line. "Seems Dixie would sometimes babysit Noah on the weekends if his parents had plans. Watched him"—she modulated her voice until it was a near-perfect mimic of the former librarian—"grow up right before her very eyes."

"Seriously?"

"Wait. There's more." Slowly, she made her way back to the bed, only this time, instead of wandering back around to her own side, she stopped beside his. "Dixie and her late husband, Ed, apparently went to every single one of Noah's games all through his high school years. They were—and I quote—*so very proud of that young man*. In fact—and I must quote her here, too—*he was like a surrogate son to us in so many ways*."

Milo palmed his face. "Tell me she doesn't think Jake killed him."

"Oh, Milo, I wish I could. But word of that contract clause that was anonymously highlighted and sent to Chief Dallas has gotten out. And it's not earning Jake any supporters, that's for sure." She reached around to the back of her neck and unhooked the clasp on her necklace. "You should have heard them, Milo. It was like they weren't friends. Like they hated each other."

"Who?"

"Dixie and Leona." Draping the necklace over her fingers, she crossed to the jewelry box that had belonged to her late great-grandmother. Then, with careful fingers, she opened a long door on the left side of the box and hung the delicate chain and its accompanying locket on one of four hooks. It was a nightly ritual that normally brought her peace. "Leona was so angry she walked out of the meeting before it ever really started. And she took Debbie and Charles with her."

"You mean because she drove them?"

"No. They left in a show of support for Jake." She captured the locket in her hand for a brief moment and then closed it inside the mahogany box. "Georgina and Beatrice stayed behind with Dixie. Leona, of course, was enraged."

Milo's whistle cut through the room. "I take it they're Team Noah, too?"

She moved on to the top drawer of the dresser and gazed down at the sleeping shorts and T-shirts she preferred over the silk counterparts Leona had insisted she purchase during a recent shopping trip. "Beatrice? No. I think Beatrice just wanted to pretend nothing was happening."

"And Georgina?"

"At first, I thought she was just being obstinate. You know how she stiffens anytime Leona utters anything that sounds the least bit like an order . . ." She grabbed a pair of baby-pink shorts and a white T-shirt and shut the drawer. "But once Leona and the others had left, and Dixie had stamped her feet a few dozen times, it started to become apparent that Georgina, if not Team Noah, isn't necessarily a card-carrying member of Team Jake, either."

A sudden intake of air from the vicinity of the bed made her turn around.

Sure enough, Milo was staring at her as if she'd grown two heads.

"Trust me, I was just as surprised as you are. I mean, we're talking about Jake Davis—*Margaret Louise's son*. Georgina and Dixie have always seemed as happy as any of the rest of us to see the latest pictures of his kids. But now? After tonight? I have to wonder."

The look on Milo's face didn't change.

"What's wrong?" she asked.

"I—I can't believe you stayed."

She carried her pajamas into the adjoining bathroom and set them on the edge of the counter. Then, one by one, she unbuttoned her way down her blouse, tossed it into the hamper behind the door, and turned back to the shorts and T-shirt that suddenly looked like heaven. "I'm telling you, hearing those two go at it like they did snapped me right out of that fatigue I had during dinner. But maybe, with a little bit of that luck that seems to be eluding me at the moment, the fatigue will return as soon as I'm dressed and my teeth are brushed. After all, six hours of sleep would be better than nothing, right?"

If he answered, she didn't hear him, but that was okay. It gave her time to put on her shirt, slip into her shorts, and secure her hair with a headband. When her face was washed and her teeth brushed, she stepped back into the bedroom and mustered the closest thing to a smile she could find for her husband. He, in turn, didn't smile back. In fact, his expression appeared as if it were officially frozen in the aforementioned two-heads position. "Hey! What's with that look, mister? You're going to give me a complex if you don't cut it out."

"I can't decide if Leona is livid or devastated."

"If you saw the way she looked at Georgina and Beatrice when they failed to vacate Dixie's home, you'd have no trouble picking one. Then again, that said, I'm sure she has to be hurt, as well. I mean, she likes to pretend she's at odds with Margaret Louise, but the way she stuck up for her and Jake tonight? It was"—she gave in to a budding yawn—"impressive, I'll tell you."

"I'm not talking about Leona's reaction to Georgina and Beatrice, Victoria."

She yawned again. "You're not?"

"No, I'm talking about her reaction to you."

"Me?" Tori rubbed her eyes and rolled onto her side for a better view of the man still propped against their headboard. "I don't understand."

"You said you stayed."

"Because I did," she said around yet another yawn.

"That had to kill Leona."

"Kill Leona?"

"Yeah. I mean, she may tolerate Beatrice most days. And she might enjoy a few of the perks that come from dropping Georgina's name when she doesn't want to wait in line at Bud's Brew Shack, but you're different. She loves you."

She had to laugh. "*Loves?* Aw c'mon, don't you think that might be overstating things just a little bit?"

"When it comes to Leona's feelings for you? No. I don't." He interlaced his fingers behind his head. "But what you did tonight? I can't imagine that not changing things for Leona where you're concerned."

All yawning and eye rubbing stopped. "What are you talking about?"

"You stayed."

"Okay . . ."

"You stayed with *Dixie*."

She sat up tall. "Wait a minute. I didn't stay with Dixie because I think Jake may have had a hand in Noah's murder . . ."

"Are you sure about that?" he asked. "Because last night, during one of the very brief times you actually drifted off to sleep, you kept mumbling the same thing over and over again."

"I did?"

He nodded.

"What was I saying?" she prodded.

Milo unlocked his fingers and reached for hers. "*Why*, Jake? *Why* did you kill him . . . ?"

Oh, how she wished she could refute his words, assure him that it had been *he* who was dreaming and not she. But she couldn't. She looked down at her hand inside his and gave it a squeeze. "Last night, I wasn't so sure. Margaret Louise had just told me about that contract clause and, I'll admit, it sounded pretty damning at the time— still does, in some ways. But today, when I was talking to Jake at the police station, my gut finally took over and I *knew*.

"Jake is no more responsible for Noah's murder than I am . . . or you are. It's just not in him to take a life."

"Then why did you stay with Dixie?"

"Until tonight, I didn't know anyone who was Team Noah. So I guess I was hoping that getting a different perspective might be helpful in trying to figure out who *is* responsible for Noah's death."

"Does Leona know that?" he asked.

"Of course she . . ." Her answer faded away as she found herself standing in the middle of Dixie's living room once again. To her right were a frightened Beatrice and a clearly defiant Georgina. In front of Tori stood Dixie, her face bright red with rage as Charles and Debbie followed Leona toward the hallway.

"Sugar lips? Aren't you coming?"

"No, Charles. I'm going to stay here. With Dixie."

She covered her mouth as a sudden burst of nausea racked her body. "No, no, no . . ." she murmured against her skin.

"Tori? Are you okay?" He tried to pull her hand from her face, but it was no use. The horror of her own words kept exploding inside her head.

"I'm going to stay here. With Dixie. . . ."

"I'm going to stay here. With Dixie . . ."

"I'm—"

Lunging to the side, Tori grabbed her phone off the nightstand and began to dial.

Chapter 13

Tori had thought nothing of the first kick to voice mail. It had been nearly eleven o'clock at night and Leona was a firm believer in the eight-hour-beauty-sleep rule.

She'd even tried to chalk up the second kick to voice mail in the morning to Leona's affinity for starting each day with yoga stretches. If Tori's call had come in during a particularly difficult maneuver like, say, downward-facing dog, answering the phone may not have been top on Leona's list of priorities.

But as her calls continued to go to voice mail after a ring or two, she had to consider the fact that Leona was, indeed, furious. Especially when she factored in one important thing: Leona wasn't returning her calls.

"Ugh. Ugh. Ugh!"

Nina looked up from the stack of newspapers she was

neatening and offered an empathetic shrug. "Ms. Leona still isn't answering?"

"Nope."

"Do you think she could have fallen again?"

It was a logical question considering Leona had, in fact, broken a hip in the days leading up to Tori's wedding. But Leona wasn't in the doghouse like she'd been at the time of her fall, and therefore wouldn't need to keep such an incident to herself. Tori said as much to Nina.

"Maybe she's just busy. At her antique shop or Sew-Tastic."

A glance at the clock removed that possibility from the table, as well. "You know Leona. She stops for her veggie bowl every day at this time. Without fail."

"Maybe she doesn't like to talk and eat at the same time?"

"Maybe . . ." But Tori didn't buy it. She'd had lunch with Leona countless times over the last few years, and while Leona would never lower herself to the level of talking with her mouth full, conversation had always been appreciated.

"There's also the possibility she's helping out with the kids in light of what's going on with Margaret Louise's son."

Tori leveled a knowing look at her assistant and waited.

"You don't think she'd help with the kids for something like this?" Nina asked.

"The only way I could ever see Leona looking after anyone's kids is if she could do it remotely. With at least an entire continent between her and her charges."

Nina laughed. "Is there a particular reason Ms. Leona doesn't like children?"

Tori cleared her throat, wiggled her own un-manicured version of Leona's fingers in the air, and then brought them to the base of her neck. "'Victoria, hear me now . . . If you and Milo make the mistake of having a baby, know that I have no interest in hearing endless tales of every silly little milestone. And I do not babysit. For any reason. Those horrible little people always have things coming out of their noses, they don't use the restroom, they shriek, and they're . . . *sticky*.'"

"Then she wouldn't like Lyndon," Nina declared as she moved on to the pair of reading chairs tucked into an alcove to the side of the mystery section. "My little boy is always sticky from something—mud, Kool-Aid, sweat, Duwayne's homemade Play-Doh, and the list goes on and on. In fact, the only time he isn't is for about ten minutes after his bath."

More than anything she wanted to lose herself in the lightness of the moment, but she couldn't. There was only one reason Leona wasn't taking or returning Tori's calls, and no amount of wishful thinking was going to change that. The thing she needed to focus her energy on was how to make amends.

"Hey, would you mind if I made a call from my office? It won't take long. And I'll be back before the genealogy group arrives for their program."

Nina stacked the handful of books she'd found in and around the various reading nooks and carried them over to the information desk. "I can handle things out here, no problem."

"Thanks. I won't be long." Tori stepped out from behind the desk, crossed the library's main room, and made her way down the hallway that led to both the children's room and the office she shared with Nina. At the doorway to the former, she took a moment to make sure the costumes were in the dress-up trunk and the carpet squares in their usual easy-to-reach location. When she was satisfied that all was as it should be, she continued on to the office and the answer she knew she needed but didn't necessarily want.

Bypassing her desk chair, she stopped in front of the picture window and willed the view of the trees and the picnic benches to work its calming magic.

Nothing . . .

She turned back to her desk, pulled her phone from her pocket, and dialed the number for Debbie's Bakery. It was answered on the second ring.

"Debbie's Bakery—how can I help you?"

"Hi Emma, this is Tori. Is Debbie not busy by any chance? I just need to ask her a quick question."

"I'm sorry, but Debbie stepped out for a quick bite to eat with Colby. I can have her call you when she gets back if you'd like."

Tori noted the time on the wall clock and did her best to mute her answering sigh. "Actually, there might be someone else who can help me, so I'll give that a try first. If that doesn't work out, I'll try Debbie back in about an hour if that's okay."

"Sounds good."

She ended the call and moved on to Charles. He answered halfway through the first ring.

"Snap. To. It. Books & Café."

"Were you sitting on the phone?" she teased, lowering herself onto the chair.

A beat of silence was followed by another.

"Charles? Are you still there?"

"I am."

She strained to make out any background sounds, but there were none. "Are you with a customer?"

"No."

"Is something a customer in the store?"

"No."

"Did I catch you eating lunch?"

"No."

Alrighty then . . .

Clearing her throat, she moved on to the next most obvious question. "Is something wrong?"

"You mean beside the fact I'm still in utter shock?"

The chair creaked as she leaned forward. "Did something happen?" she asked.

"The unthinkable. In fact, truth be told, I (*snap*). Can't (*snap*). Even (*snap*)." He stopped, made a series of huffy breaths, and then continued. "Sugar lips, since the day we met, I've admired the way you stand by your friends. If someone isn't feeling well, you rally the dinner patrol. When Rose and Leona hosted that tour group, you made sure we were all there to help roll out the red carpet. With what's going on with Rose right now, you have a spreadsheet to keep track of who is looking after her and when. When I moved in, you were the first one at the door with a welcome-to-Sweet-Briar hug and an army of well-built men ready and able to help me unload that hideous orange rental truck. I could go on and on, of course, but this is all merely lead-up to my point."

She waited.

"You surprised me last night, Victoria." Charles took a sip of something, marveled at its peachy taste, and then returned to the conversation at hand. "Now, don't get me wrong, I think it says a lot about the kind of person you are that despite Dixie's treatment of you when you first moved here—and trust me, I've heard all about it from Leona—you're willing to be her friend. But to pick *her* over *Leona* and *Margaret Louise*? I just don't understand that. Not"—the trio of short snaps returned—"one. Little. Bit."

Tori propped her left elbow onto the desk and dropped her head into her hand. "I didn't pick Dixie over Leona, and I didn't pick Dixie over Margaret Louise."

"You chose to stay with Dixie instead of leaving with us," Charles protested. "And sugar lips? I've never seen Leona so shaken by anything. Not even news of her cosmetic surgeon's upcoming *two-week* vacation to Bali."

"My staying had absolutely nothing to do with taking Dixie's side and everything to do with trying to learn more about the people who still identify themselves as being Team Noah."

"Go on . . ."

The beginning of a headache sent her in search of a pain reliever from her purse and a handful of pretzels from the bottom-right desk drawer. When she'd secured both, she picked up where she'd left off. "Someone went to great lengths to set Jake up as the fall guy for Noah's murder. And while I might be barking up the wrong tree, it stands to reason Jake was picked because of their infamous rivalry. Like you, I'm not from Sweet Briar. I don't know all the ins and outs of who picked which person—Jake or Noah—to cheer for and why. And I don't know who is still lingering in that mind-set to this day. And *that's* why I stayed last night. Because I was hoping Dixie could help fill in some of those holes for me."

"You stayed to *investigate*?"

She groaned. "I wasn't trying to leave you out, Charles. I really wasn't. But I knew Leona was going to need someone to talk her out of the state she was in. I also knew you were the best person for the job. Likewise, I knew that Dixie was every bit as fired up as Leona. And if I've learned anything in my accidental role as sleuth these past few years, it's that people tend to lose their filters when they're angry. It's probably some sort of human nature thing."

"You really weren't picking Dixie over Leona?"

"C'mon, Charles, do you really think I'd do that?" She helped herself to another pretzel. "Yes, I consider Dixie a friend—a *hard-won* friend, sure, but a friend nonetheless. That said, you know that Leona and Margaret Louise are like family to me at this point."

"But just yesterday, you said you thought Jake did it."

It wasn't one of her prouder moments, nor was it one she could deny. Not to Charles, anyway. "I was afraid he *could* have. But you also know I changed my mind after Jake and I had a chance to speak at the station."

"I thought maybe you'd changed it back."

"You thought wrong." She stuffed what was left of the bag of pretzels back into her drawer and stood. "Where is Leona today? Do you know? I've tried to call at least a dozen times and I keep going straight to voice mail."

"She's angry, Victoria. Very angry. But underneath that, she's hurt. She really thought you'd turned your back on her."

"Then *she* thought wrong, as well." Tori listened at the door of her office but heard no sign of the genealogy club. "I need you to do me a favor. I need you to track down

Leona wherever she's hiding and bring her here at six o'clock."

"For?"

"Our first stakeout."

Charles sputtered, coughed, and then sputtered some more. "Did you . . . did you say *stakeout*?"

"I did."

If she were a gambler, she'd lay good odds on the fact that the sound she was detecting in the background of the call was Charles's hands flapping wildly. "A stakeout of what? Or, should I say, of whom?"

"I'll fill you both in when you get here. In the meantime, fifteen members of the Sweet Briar Genealogy Club should be walking through the front door any minute now, and I can't let it all fall on Nina. She's done enough covering for me the past few days as it is."

"Nina adores you, Victoria."

"That's not the point. I have a job to do. And so do you."

"Six o'clock?" Charles confirmed. "Your office?"

"Let's make it the back parking lot. In your car."

"Roger that. And I'll bring the sandwiches."

"Sandwiches?"

"For the stakeout." The hand flapping was back along with a near-ear-piercing shriek. "It'll be just like last week's episode of *The Detective*. Minus the pickle, of course."

Tori laughed.

"Oh, and sugar lips? Does that hunky husband of yours happen to have a trench coat in either mauve or mint green? Black washes me out."

Chapter 14

Tori was waiting on the library's back step when Charles pulled into the lot in his brand-new neon green Prius. Grabbing her purse from its resting spot at her feet, she stood and met him at the base of the walkway.

"Am I good or what?" Charles pointed at his dashboard clock and smiled triumphantly. "Five fifty-nine."

She rested her forearms against the open window and flicked her own hand in the direction of the empty passenger seat. "I take it we're picking Leona up at the shop on the way?"

Charles's smile faded. "She's not coming."

"Is Margaret Louise okay?"

"I think so . . ." He shrugged. "I haven't heard anything new."

"Then why isn't Leona coming?"

The answering jump of his Adam's apple, in conjunction with his sudden inability to hold her gaze, told her everything she needed to know. "She didn't believe you about my reason for staying last night, did she?"

"I can't really say since the second I uttered your name she disconnected our call."

Tori didn't even bother trying to stifle her groan as she walked around the hood of the car and slid into the vacant seat beside her friend. "I'm sorry if she let her anger with me spill out onto you. I won't ask you to play middleman again."

"Maybe you can write her a letter and put it in a plain envelope so she doesn't know it's from you."

"It's that bad?" she asked.

"Worse." He pointed at the glove compartment and wiggled his fingers. "I've got Pixy Stix in there in all the best flavors and"—he stopped wiggling to hook his thumb toward the backseat—"our sandwiches and cold waters are in the cooler on the floor behind my seat."

She made herself smile despite the image of an angry Leona playing in her head. "Sounds good. Thank you."

Wrapping his hand around the gearshift, Charles slowly shifted the car back into drive, made a wide U-turn in the now-empty parking lot, and headed toward the Main Street entrance from which he'd just come. "So, where first?"

"You sound excited," she teased.

"Duhhh . . . We're going on a *stakeout*, aren't we?" At the stop sign, he paused and awaited direction.

"Make a right toward the Green." When they were safely on Main Street, she brought him up to speed. "Our first stop is Bud's."

"As in Brew Shack?" At her nod, he made a face. "But they *have* food."

"We're not going inside. In fact, I think we should park in front of the bookstore. It'll be easier to pull off a casual stroll that way."

His left brow rose nearly to his hairline. "Care to fill me in?"

"If we hit it right—and we'll make sure we do—Bud sits out back behind the restaurant enjoying a cigar at about six fifteen every evening, give or take a few minutes."

"And you know this because?"

"Milo and I have walked past the restaurant enough times over the past year or so that we sort of noticed a pattern." She felt the car slow as they approached Charles's bookstore. In a nod to his lack of experience behind the wheel, however, he headed toward the back alley and its more traditional parking spots rather than the parallel ones in front. "Now we just have to hope it holds true today."

"If we want to talk to Bud, why don't we just sit at the bar?" He found a spot, pulled in, and parked.

"Because I'd rather do it when there's less chance of being overheard. By anyone."

He followed her over to the walkway connecting the alley to Main Street and then fell into step beside her. At the corner, they headed east past Shelby's Sweet Shoppe and Brady's Jewelry. Next came Elkin's Antiques and Collectibles. Wordlessly, they both slowed, but a peek inside the front window revealed a darkened interior and nary a sign of its agitated owner.

When they cleared the shop, they proceeded to the end of the block and crossed the street. As they walked, Tori shared the bits and pieces of information she'd managed to assemble the previous evening. "According to Dixie, Bud was the assistant football coach at Sweet Briar High during the time Jake and Noah were on the team."

Charles flapped his hands. "Oooh, he might know some really good stuff!"

"We can hope." She paused mid-step and sniffed. "He's outside. I can smell the cigar."

His hands flapped harder. "Oooh, oooh, what do you want me to say? Should I pretend I'm trying out for a park league or something and ask for pointers?"

"Actually, let's not do that." She planted a kiss on her friend's cheek and then pulled back, smiling up at his sunshine yellow–tipped hair. "I'm not sure he'd buy that."

"Oh. Right." He touched his finger to his chin, his face scrunched in thought. "Hmmm . . ."

"We're going to cut through his parking lot to get to the Green via the access path in the back right corner. That way, when we stop to talk to him, it'll look a little less planned."

"What should I ask?"

"I think we should see where the conversation goes and follow along." Tori pointed ahead and, at Charles's nod, resumed their previous pace, the scent of Bud's cigar growing stronger with each new step.

When they cleared the front of the restaurant, they turned left into the parking lot and, sure enough, there was Bud, sitting on a fold-and-go beach chair with a cigar in one hand and a can of beer in the other. He lifted the beer in a makeshift toast at first Tori and then Charles. "Perfect night to be out and about, ain't it?" he said in lieu of a more standard greeting.

"That it is." Tori flashed what she hoped was a normal

smile and closed the gap between them with several long strides. "The clouds are almost whimsical looking, aren't they?"

Bud lifted his gaze to the sky, took a quick puff of his cigar, and then used it to guide their collective attention to an oddly shaped cloud. "That one there looks like a sports car, don't it?"

She tried to see it, but she couldn't. Charles, however, didn't seem to have that same problem.

"From the side, yes?"

Bud nodded. "Yep. See, there's the front tire"—he moved his cigar to the right a smidge—"and that there's the back tire. And that narrow snippet right there? That's the antenna, though most cars these days don't seem to have 'em, do they?"

"I'm not the one to answer that question," Tori said around a smile. "My car isn't exactly new."

"Or running."

Bud lowered his chin, took another puff of his cigar, and then looked from Tori to Charles and back again. "Something happen to your car?"

"It was fine Friday night when I got home. But come Saturday morning, when I was leaving for work, it started making a terrible racket."

"Was Milo able to smoke out the problem?" Bud asked.

"He tried, but he couldn't figure it out."

"And now it's just sitting at Jake's Garage," Charles added. "Waiting."

Bud pulled the cigar from his mouth and leaned forward to address Tori. "If it's drivable, you and Milo might want to think about taking it into Tom's Creek to get it looked at over there."

She could feel Charles's eyes on the side of her face, waiting for some sort of *atta boy* for the opportunity he'd dropped in her lap, but she kept her focus where it needed to be. "We'll just wait for Jake."

"I hate to say it, Victoria, but you might be waiting a long time if the banter I've been hearing around the bar today holds any truth."

"I don't understand."

"Seems Chief Dallas came across some pretty damaging evidence that doesn't bode too well for Jake."

She considered disputing the manner in which the so-called evidence had come to light, but she held her tongue. After all, knowing things that others didn't had its upsides on occasion.

"Mason Wheeler, Johnny Duckworth, Jessa Thomas, Tawny Wright, and Old Man Skinner—they're all having a field day at Jake's expense as we speak," Bud continued. "Hell, he's already been tried and convicted by half the people sitting in my bar right now."

"I don't know those names."

"I know Jessa Thomas." Charles waved at a gnat flying around his face and then ran to the other side of Tori when he failed to scare it away. "Jessa comes into the bookstore every few weeks. She's a big thriller reader."

"And she doesn't like Jake?" Tori asked, directing the conversation back to Bud.

"Now she don't, but back then, she liked him too much."

Interesting . . .

Bud took a long puff of his cigar and then blew a perfect smoke ring. "Mason Wheeler and Johnny Duckworth grew up here. Played football with Jake and Noah. Johnny was even considered pretty good before those two came along. But Jake's shadow—and to some extent Noah's, too—was pretty large. Not much sunlight left for anyone else. Nowadays, Mason owns that new gym down the road that everyone seems to belong to even if they don't actually use it. Johnny Duckworth just purchased a big chunk of that land out by Ramey Pond that he's getting ready to turn into a paintball field, much to the chagrin of a few developers. Tawny Wright is the one behind that new paint-your-own-pottery place at the end of the road, and—"

Charles did a little jig where he stood. "I sooo want to do that, Victoria!"

"Do what?"

"The pottery place," Charles fairly squealed. "I'm a veritable master with a paintbrush."

She gave him what she hoped was the nonverbal equivalent to a cease-and-desist and returned her focus and the conversation to Bud. "And the other one you mentioned?"

Bud leaned back, pointed up at a jet trail in the sky overhead, and burped. "Old Man Skinner. His allegiance to Noah is purely about kinship on account of him being Noah's stepfather."

"Noah's stepfather is in the bar now?" she asked, stunned. "Two days after Noah was murdered?"

"People grieve in different ways. Some cry. Some stay silent. And some drink."

It was more than she could process at the moment, but later, when she had more time, she would. Still, she needed more. "And you? What do you think about all of this?"

"There was a time when I knew Jake Davis maybe even better than I knew my own son." Bud took another, longer puff of his cigar, then leaned forward and ground it out in the simple glass ashtray at his feet. "Same went for Noah, too.

"Didn't intend for that to be the case, but coaching football is a full-time job all on its own. More so when you're in contention for a title as we always were." Reaching behind his back, he pulled a cloth from the belted waistband of his well-worn jeans and wiped his hands. "But my boy doesn't hang that over my head. Instead, he makes it sound like all those evenings and weekends he got dragged to practice were fun. It's a claim I don't believe, but he insists it's true."

"Sounds like you had a good kid," Tori said.

"They were all good kids." Bud returned the cloth to its holding place and stood, his voice taking on a faraway quality. "More or less, anyway."

Tori and Charles exchanged glances as Bud continued. "I always said if the adults hadn't taken sides, those two boys would have been fine—would've supported each other like teammates are supposed to."

She was afraid to move, afraid to break the spell that had Bud talking to them like they were old friends. But she needed more. "I gather it got pretty bad around here back then?"

"You say that like it stopped."

"Didn't it?" she challenged.

Bud set his hand atop his chair, his answering smile one of sadness rather than joy. "No. It didn't stop." With one shove, the chair folded in on itself and Bud leaned it against the wall. "Folks wouldn't let it stop then and they won't let it stop now. It's like these two boys—men, now—were commodities instead of people. And I reckon I'm partly to blame for that."

"I don't believe that," Charles gushed in true Charles-like fashion.

"But it's true. Not only was Jake one heckuva good kid, he was also the better player—a fact I was all too willing to share with reporters, visiting coaches, recruiters, groundskeepers, fans, you name it." Bud returned to the spot where his chair had been and retrieved the ashtray from the ground. "Looking back, I see how that kinda talk probably bred Noah's resentment."

There was so much she wanted to ask, so much she wanted to know, but every movement he made indicated her window of opportunity was rapidly coming to a close. Still, she had to try. "You can't blame yourself for the way the adults around them behaved."

Bud shrugged. "You're right—I can't. But maybe if Jake and Noah had stayed close, the way they were when they were younger, there wouldn't have been a chink in the armor for people to sink their teeth into, if you know what I mean."

"But why would a high school football rivalry from almost twenty years ago matter to anyone now?" Tori asked. "It just doesn't make any sense."

"If you knew where the lines were drawn, you'd understand." Bud set the ashtray on a small plastic table underneath the eave and tapped his watch. "I've gotta head back inside. Enjoy your evening."

"You, too, Bud."

Chapter 15

They were barely on the walking track around the Green when Charles, mumbling some sort of cadence, stuffed his hand inside Tori's purse and fished out a notebook and pen.

She smacked at his hand. "Hey! Get out of there!"

"Trust me, love, you'll thank me in about five seconds." He broke stride at the first park bench they passed and sat, uncapping her pen with his teeth as he did. "Let me get all of these down and then we can start divvying them up, or"—he looked up briefly—"we can vet them together if you prefer."

Vet?

Stepping off the walkway and onto the grass, she circled around the wooden bench until she had a fairly unobstructed view of the notepad, save for what was blocked by his yellow-tipped hair, of course.

Mason Wheeler

Johnny Duckworth

Jessa Thomas

Tawny Wright

Old Man Skipper

"I'm impressed. But"—she reached around him and pointed at the last name—"I'm pretty sure that's supposed to be *Skinner.*"

Charles tapped the pen to his chin—once, twice. "Oh my skip . . . oh my—Wait! You're right." He scratched out *Skipper* and wrote *Skinner.* "It was supposed to be *oil my skin.* Not *oh my skip.*"

"Oil my skin?" She wandered back around to the front of the bench and dropped down beside her friend. "What are you talking about?"

"That's what I came up with in the beginning, but then I got confused and changed it."

Lifting her hand to her brow line, she filtered the day's dwindling rays well enough to really see his face. "I have absolutely no idea what you're babbling about."

"Oh. Right." With the help of his pen, he guided her attention off his face and back onto the notebook in his lap. "When I was in high school, I had a teacher who taught us how to remember names by making up silly associations using the same first initials. Most of the kids in my class thought she was nuts, but it's always worked for me."

"Remind me to send her a thank-you note, because with each name Bud threw out, all I kept thinking was, *I wish*

I could write this down." She gestured toward the book and, at Charles's nod, pulled it onto her own lap. "Okay, so, Mason . . . He owns the gym down the road, right? The one Leona joined not too long ago?"

He handed her the pen, sans cap, and nodded. "And he played football with Jake and Noah, remember?"

"That's right. I remember thinking he could be a good person to pump." She added those tidbits next to Mason's name.

"And this one." Charles's finger moved to the second line. "He played with them, too. Might even have been the rising star before Jake and Noah came along."

Tori added that information next to Johnny Duckworth's name. After careful consideration, she added mention of the paintball field he was opening out by Ramey Pond. "I'm not sure any of these little bits will help us much, but at least it gives us a little bit of reference, you know?"

"Some information is better than no information, I say." His finger dropped another line. "Jessa is . . . how shall I put this delicately? Okay, I got it . . . She's very *into* herself. Like the other day, she stopped in to pick up a thriller she'd preordered and another customer came into the store." He pivoted on the bench, looked to his left and right, and then lowered his voice so as not to be overheard by the bird pecking at the ground a few yards away. "You remember the wind we had last Wednesday, right?"

She tried to recall wind, but came up empty. "No, not really."

"You probably had your hair in a ponytail." He waved the notion away and continued. "Anyway, this other customer opened the door and let in a huge gust of wind just as Jessa was heading in that direction."

"Okay . . ."

"*She* didn't have her hair in a ponytail." He stopped, took a breath, and widened his eyes. "And, Victoria, it wasn't pretty."

Tori waited for more.

More never came.

Finally, she broke the silence. "Can you pretend, for just a moment, that you're talking to me and not Leona?"

Understanding dawned across his face followed closely after by . . . *pity*?

Before offense could take root, though, he filled in the blanks. "Jessa Thomas is everything you'd imagine Barbie would look like if she was real and brunette." He stopped. "You *did* play with Barbies when you were little, yes?"

She nodded.

"Then you can picture what I'm—"

"Wait. I think I know who you're talking about," Tori interjected as a series of images flitted through her thoughts. "I saw her at the last Friends of the Library book sale. She spent as much time looking around to see if anyone was noticing her as she did looking through the boxes of books. And you're right, she does look like Barbie come to life."

"Makeup flawless, not a hair out of place . . ." Charles glanced at the bird and lowered his voice even more. "Leona isn't a fan."

"Why does that not surprise me?"

"It's not what you think." Again, he surveyed their

surroundings, only this time he didn't seem to care about the bird. "Leona doesn't like Jessa's games."

Tori propped her elbow on the back of the bench and dropped her head into her hand. "So this *is* about competition."

"Not between Leona and Jessa."

When it became apparent they had nothing to offer in the way of dropped food, the bird flew off. Whether that meant they could eliminate Charles's need for whispering remained to be seen. "Then I don't understand. If Leona isn't threatened, why does she care about games one way or the other? I mean, it's not like they travel in the same circles. I didn't even know Leona *knew* her, let alone disliked her."

"She doesn't want to give her"—Charles wiggled his fingers to simulate quotes—"*air time*, if you know what I mean."

"At the risk of sounding snippy, is there a chance we could move this conversation along? I'm getting pretty hungry sitting here."

Charles sat up tall. "I could run to the car and grab our sandwiches. Though, truth be told, I sort of envisioned us eating them in the car. You know, with me behind the steering wheel, drumming my fingers on the top of my door while I look in the side-view mirror for any sign of our tail?"

"Actually, we wouldn't be looking *for* the tail. We'd *be* the tail." She held her hand to her grumbling stomach and tried not to think about the hamburgers being served inside Bud's Brew Shack. "Anyway, just end the suspense and we can go eat—*in* the car, if we must."

"Deal." He sucked in a breath as if he were preparing to

dive underwater and then let it out with every bit as much drama. "From what I gather, Jessa never got over Jake."

Tori drew back. "Jake? As in *Melissa's* Jake?"

"*Melissa's* Jake, *Margaret Louise's* Jake, *our* Jake . . . yes."

"But Melissa and Jake were high school sweethearts. Surely whatever relationship Jake and this Jessa person had couldn't have lasted long."

Charles shot his fingers up in the universal peace sign. "Two months."

"Two months . . ." she repeated. And then, "They dated for two months?"

"At the beginning of Jake's junior year. Jessa was a sophomore but on the varsity cheer team." Charles looked around for any sign the eavesdropping bird had returned and, when his search turned up nothing, he jogged his feet in place. "Seems she made quite the big deal out of dating the star quarterback."

"But he wasn't yet, right? He was only a junior."

Charles shrugged off the part of the story that didn't have his preferred level of juiciness and kept going. "She left lipstick kiss marks on his locker, watched him practice, found her way into a few of his newspaper pictures, that sort of thing. Real clingy and in-your-face." He paused, pursed his lips, and scooched along the bench until their knees were touching. "So when Jake met Melissa right before Thanksgiving and fell hard and fast, Jessa was humiliated. Her attempt at revenge took the form of flirting with all of Jake's friends—even dating some of them. But from what Leona told *me*, Jake didn't care. He had eyes only for Melissa. Still does, despite Jessa's best efforts."

"Wait. You mean this woman is still trying to make Jake jealous even now?" At Charles's nod, she pulled her arm off the back of the bench, pushed the notebook off her lap, and stood. "Um, does she not see the eight kids he has with Melissa? Or the way he looks at his wife nearly twenty-four/seven?"

"Leona says it's the principle of the thing with Jessa. She—the living, breathing cheerleader Barbie—got dumped. For someone in the school's *4-H club*."

She crossed the empty walking path, took a few steps, and then turned back. "But we're talking about two months of dating. *Twenty years* ago. That's"—she searched for a kinder, gentler word, but opted for her first choice, instead—"nuts. Maybe even a bit . . . *scary*."

"I know, right?" Charles crossed his right leg over his left leg, bracing his upper thighs on the edge of the bench as he did. "Sounds a little Glenn Close-ish, doesn't it? *Eek! Eek! Eek!*"

"Well, from what Bud said, she's content to pin Noah's murder on Jake, right? That doesn't sound like someone who still has a thing for him."

Charles's left eyebrow lifted. "Remember the revenge part?"

"Yeah, but that was about making him jealous. Not trashing him."

"Twenty years ago, yes. Ten years ago, yes. A few weeks ago, yes. But I guess things have changed."

"She was still trying to make him jealous a *few weeks* ago?"

This time when Charles shrugged there was an aura of boredom. Like he'd gotten every last drop of his favorite cookies-and-cream milkshake out of the glass and was left with nothing but the cherry—the one part of the whole milkshake experience he detested. "That's what Leona told me. Granted, we were shopping when this came up, but I hadn't yet found the purple sneakers I was looking for, so I was actually paying attention."

"So what changed?" she asked.

"Changed?"

Tori stopped in front of the bench but let her gaze drift across the Green to an elderly couple just beginning their evening walk. "Why after *twenty years* of trying to make a person jealous would you suddenly abandon that quest and start trashing him? It doesn't make any sense."

"Twenty years isn't exactly *sudden*, sugar lips."

She resisted the urge to reach out, grab him by the shoulders, and shake him. Instead, she tried a different tactic. "Let's pretend you really like someone, shall we? You like him, you like him, you like him, and then— *wham!*—you despise him. Why?"

"That's easy. He did something to make me hate him."

Finally . . .

"Like what?"

Charles tapped a finger to his chin, narrowing his eyes on the walking trail as he did. "He said something mean either to me or about me, he hurt me, he hurt someone I cared about—something like that, I guess."

"So what did Jake do?" Tori prodded. "Do you know?"

He started to answer but leaned back flush against the bench instead. "I don't know."

"Well, that's something we need to find out." She thought about that for a moment and then took it a step further. "Maybe, if it was bad enough, our life-sized Barbie doll may have decided to do more than just *verbally* trash Jake."

Charles's gasp was followed almost immediately by a flurry of motion involving the notebook and the pen. "Oooh, Victoria. If you're right, and Jessa killed Noah to frame Jake, this is better than any Hallmark movie ever. I mean, think about it. By framing Jake, she gets revenge on him for dumping her all those years ago . . . but she also gets revenge on the person she was dumped *for*."

He snapped out an oh-my-gosh and then set his hands on his hips. "We need to take this little hussy down, Victoria. *Now*."

She signaled a time-out with her hands. "Whoa. Slow it down a little. Right now, this is just something we need to look into a little bit more. See if it leads us somewhere. If it does, great. If it doesn't . . . well, it doesn't. But we can't go trying and convicting this girl based on what would make a really good movie."

He tried to recover his answering slump, but hiding emotion was for Charles what ignoring the male persuasion was to Leona. It simply didn't happen.

"So what do you suggest?" he finally asked, sweeping his hands toward the sky as if he still couldn't quite grasp the reins Tori had slapped into place.

She hooked her thumb over her shoulder, mouthed the word *food*, and then walked beside him as they made their way back through the opening in the fence between the Green and Bud's parking lot. "As I see it, there are really only two options. We either ask Jake or we ask Jessa."

"We could stake out her place. I have sandwiches, you know . . ."

"Gee, really? I wasn't aware." She ducked out of swatting range and then frantically grabbed his arm as the parking lot began to spin. "Whoa. Can we stop a second? I—I don't feel so well."

Instantly his feet stopped moving. "What's wrong, love?"

"I don't know. I just got a little dizzy there for a minute." She took a few deep breaths and, when the light-headedness had passed, she released her hold on Charles. "Okay, that's better. Payback, I'm sure, for picking at my lunch *and* my breakfast."

Charles looked less convinced. "How's your head doing?"

"It's fine, why?"

"I don't know. Milo said you hit it pretty hard when you found the body." Charles looked her over from head to toe, and then, declaring her okay enough to walk with his assistance, he set their pace at slow and easy. "Maybe you should let the doctor take another peek. Just to make sure you're okay."

"I'm fine, really. Just hungry is all."

They followed the sidewalk until it was time to cross, and then made their way back to the alley the same way they'd come. While a few of the shops had still been in the process of closing up when they arrived, they were all dark now, their respective owners likely happy to be off their feet after yet another long day.

When they reached the front of Snap. To. It. Books & Café, she pointed at the front window and its impressive display of mysteries. "So, are you glad you did it?"

"The store?" At her nod, his face broke out in a no-holds-barred smile. "Best. Move. Ever."

"You don't miss your friends? Your neighbors? The hustle and bustle of the city?"

"Sometimes, I guess." He released his hold on her arm

and guided her down the side alley and over to his car. "But here, thanks to you and Leona and Rose and Margaret Louise and everyone else, I have a family."

"And you get to drive now," she reminded as he aimed his key fob at the car and hit the unlock button. "Which should cut down on your paper bag usage whenever Margaret Louise is part of the mix."

His eyes rounded just before they dipped below the roof of the car. When they were both settled in their respective seats, he held his hand to his chest and slumped back against his seat. "That woman is a menace behind the wheel. Why none of you saw fit to warn me that first time still wakes me up at night on occasion. Even now."

"You still drove with her even after you knew . . ."

"It was that or miss out on all the fun." He reached through the opening between their seats and grabbed the soft-sided cooler off the floor. With the efficiency of a man on a mission, he unzipped the top, doled out the contents, flung the empty cooler in the back, and slipped the key into the ignition. "So where to now, sugar lips?"

"Sweet Briar PD."

Chapter 16

For the second time in as many days, Tori peered at Jake across the small metal table, the only other pair of eyes in the windowless room belonging to the police officer stationed by the door.

"Did you find something?"

She shook her head quickly and watched as Jake's shoulders slumped in response. "Nothing yet. But I'm working on it. With Charles."

"You'll be sure to thank him for me, won't you?"

"Of course."

Now that she was there, she wasn't sure how best to frame her questions, but after a little mental ping-pong, she decided to cut straight to the chase. "Tell me about Jessa Thomas."

He drew back as if he'd been slapped. "*Jessa Thomas? For real?*"

"Yes."

Cupping a hand across his face, he hesitated a moment and then leaned forward against the edge of the table. "Jessa moved to Sweet Briar at the start of my junior year at Sweet Briar High. She was a sophomore. Came from someplace up north—Jersey, maybe." He stopped, stole a glance at the bored police officer, and then looked back at Tori. "I don't understand why you're asking about some girl I dated for just under two months more than half my life ago."

"This thing with you and Noah started back then—during a time I know nothing about. I'm trying to learn about it now."

His jaw visibly tightened and she could see him working to remain calm. "There was no *thing* with Noah and me," he hissed through clenched teeth. Then, seeming to realize who he was talking to, he took a deep breath and released it slowly. "Not for the last ten years or so, at least. And even back then, it was Noah's thing with me. I didn't have an issue with him."

"Even when he played and you didn't?" she asked.

"I was a kid. Of course it bothered me when he got put in and I didn't, but that was twenty years ago, Victoria. Again, half a lifetime ago."

"Doesn't Lulu's bike and Leona's window suggest someone is still hanging on to those days?"

His chair creaked as he shifted backward, earning him a quick look from the officer. "Sadly, yes. But I can't change other people. All I can do is keep my head held high the way my daddy taught me."

"If it stopped with a stolen bike and a broken window, I'd have to agree that's the best course of action. But someone is framing you for Noah's murder, Jake. Holding your head up high isn't going to be enough against a legal document that gives you motive and the location of the body that gives you means." Tori tucked a runaway strand of hair behind her ear and then splayed her hands—palms up—on the table between them. "Someone is living in the past, Jake. Someone who has no qualms about setting you up to take a murder rap. I need to know who doesn't like you and why."

Crossing his arms, he let his gaze drift up to the ceiling. "Jessa doesn't fall into that category."

"What category?"

For a moment, she wasn't sure he'd heard her, but, eventually, he spoke, his voice sounding much farther away than the other side of the table. "No matter how often or how hard I wished she would hate me, she didn't. Breaking up with her after six weeks didn't do it, chasing and then dating Melissa didn't do it, marrying Melissa didn't do it, having eight kids with Melissa hasn't done it, even my mama saying something to her a time or two—or five hundred—hasn't done it. So that's why I finally sat down with her about two weeks ago."

Tori snapped up so fast, her chair leg thumped hard against the table. This time, the police officer actually took a step forward.

"I'm sorry. My chair just bumped the table."

She followed the officer's eyes down to the floor and then back up to her face. He nodded and reclaimed his single step while she looked back at Jake. "You talked to Jessa two weeks ago?" she echoed. "Where? About what?"

"Jake Junior noticed her at the park the other day."

"What do you mean, he noticed her?"

Slowly, he dropped his chin back down, only to scrub at his face like he might a spot on one of the cars he worked on at the garage. "He noticed her watching me . . . trying to get my attention . . . that sort of stuff. He's at the age where he's picking up on cues from girls, I guess, and he asked me who she was. I told him it was someone I knew from high school, but when he wanted to know why I didn't go say hi, I knew it was time Jessa and I had a heart-to-heart. So I arranged to meet her at Bud's a day or so later."

"How did you do that?"

"She came into the garage the day after the park under the guise of needing me to put some air in her tire." He traced his finger along the edge of the table and then shrugged. "Normally, I have one of the kids who works with me address her needs, but this time I took it. So I could suggest a drink at Bud's."

"You sat at the bar?" At his nod, she leaned forward again. "So what did you say to her?"

"In a nutshell? I told her I'm sorry I hurt her feelings all those years ago by breaking it off with her, but that Melissa is my soul mate. I knew it then, and I know it now."

"And? How did she take it?"

"She tried to sway me by pointing out all the ways she thinks she's better than Melissa, but I didn't let her get past the second one before I ended the meeting. Told her she was wasting her life mooning after me because there's nothing—and *no one*—in this world that could ever change how I feel about my wife."

She tried to swallow, but it was as if her throat was frozen. "You said it like that? With that *no one* part?"

He repeated his earlier shrug, sans fidgeting. "Of course. Because it's true. And she, of all people, needed to hear that."

"Needed to and wanted to are two very different things," she murmured, only to have a thought rise up out of nowhere like an unexpected smack. "Wait. Do you know if anyone overheard you saying this to Jessa?"

"I tried to be sensitive to that," he said, his hands splayed. "But she's not one to give up easily, you know? So it's possible one of the guys overheard. I really can't say one way or the other."

"The guys? As in people you knew?"

His laugh was perfunctory at best. "This is Sweet Briar, remember? Everyone knows everyone—everywhere. That's just the way it is. Unless you're the rare soul who moved here from somewhere else in the last year or so."

"Point taken." Still, the subject gave her pause. Hell hath no fury and all that. The question was whether the public nature of that scorning had propelled Jessa into getting even. She considered posing the theory to Jake, but a glance in his direction left her silent. Jake was drained. She could see it in every crack and crevice of his being.

"Any chance you might remember who some of those guys were?" she asked instead.

"What difference does it make?"

"Just humor me."

He drew his arms up until his elbows were on the table and his hands were available to help keep his head level. "Tawny Wright was there. Mason, too. Heck, even Noah was there, though I'm pretty sure he was wrapping up his meeting with Tawny as Jessa and I were just getting our drinks. Doubt he heard anything beyond the initial basic pleasantries."

"What kind of a meeting?" she asked, sitting forward.

Jake looked a question at her, but before she could respond, he did a half nod, half shrug combination. "Oh, you mean between Noah and Tawny? A business meeting, I imagine. Noah favors the relaxed atmosphere in Bud's rather than his office. But really, it was just more of the same with him—he liked being seen as successful. It was an ego trip."

"Do you have any idea the nature of this business between Noah and Tawny?"

"Sure. Same as mine."

She rolled her fingers in a keep-going motion. After a moment or two, he did. "Noah is"—he stopped, fisted his hands beneath his chin, and blew a raspberry (sans noise)—"or *was* co-owner of Tawny's pottery place."

"Were they friends?"

Another shrug. "Back in high school, no. He used to tease her mercilessly. But something drew them together in the years following graduation. Maybe it's because Tawny slimmed out or because Noah grew up a little. I don't really know."

"Are *you* friends with Tawny?"

With the help of a long sigh, he dropped his arms back down to the table. "Not really. She was Jessa's shadow through most of high school, including the brief window Jessa and I dated. When I broke up with Jessa, Tawny got all protective and actually smacked me. I let it go on account of knowing a man never hits a woman, but, between you and me, she had a heckuva left hook back then." He rubbed his jaw at the memory and then continued. "Anyway, we got past it, more or less. Meaning, I gave her a wide berth all the way up until I graduated."

"And after high school?" she prodded.

"I think on some level she kind of understood Jessa's lingering interest was more than a little over-the-top. At least that's why I imagine she got to the point where she'd actually grunt at me if we happened to be in the same place at the same time. In fact, that grunt resembled more of an actual hello when I walked into Bud's with Jessa that day. Might have been for Jessa's sake, might have been the fact that others were within earshot and she didn't want to appear rude. Don't know. Don't really care."

He reached up, scratched at the stubble along his jawline, and then gestured toward the wall clock above and slightly to the left of the guarded door. "It's almost eight o'clock, Victoria. Which means you've wasted more than enough of your evening sitting here talking to me." He swept his tired, if not apologetic eyes onto her. "Don't get me wrong. I appreciate the fact that you're actually trying to figure this mess out, I really do. Every time I try to play it out in my head, it feels like I'm going to explode. And *I* don't have to try and learn twenty years of another person's life. But, honestly, if I could be anywhere in the world at this exact moment, it would be home—with Melissa and the kids. I reckon you feel the same about Milo."

"It's Tuesday night. Milo's at the Men's Club meeting at church." She reached across the table and patted his hand. "You'll be there again, too . . . soon. I—"

The officer stepped forward. "No touching, please."

Jake pulled his hand out from under Tori's and scooted back his chair. "It's time to wrap this up, Victoria. Really. I'm feeling kind of tired."

Her heart ached for the man now standing on the other side of the table—a man whose fatigue was overshadowed only by an overwhelming and palpable sadness. "I'm gonna figure this out, Jake. I promise."

The police officer stepped in beside Jake and followed him over to the door. Just before they disappeared through it, Jake turned back. "Tell Melissa I don't want her to come here anymore. She needs to focus on the kids. Mom, too."

"Jake, you know I can't do that. They love you."

"Then they need to stay away."

And then he was gone, the sound of his footsteps mingling briefly with the guard's before fading out of earshot completely.

Chapter 17

They drove for blocks before she realized she hadn't seen a single building they'd passed. Not the gazebo, not the library, not Debbie's Bakery, not the firehouse. She knew Charles was talking, but what he was saying, she had no idea. The images and sounds playing in her thoughts took her well beyond the confines of her friend's new Prius.

So far, though, Charles hadn't noticed. Or if he had—

"Have you heard a thing I've said since we pulled out of the parking lot?" Charles asked, his tone approaching injured.

She focused her eyes on the row of houses outside the passenger-side window and made herself nod. A second later, she changed it to a shame-ridden shake. "I'm sorry, Charles. I didn't mean to check out on you like that, but I've got a lot on my mind."

"I think it's the overprotective friend, Tawny. It makes the most sense. I mean, can you just imagine how Margaret Louise or Leona would have reacted if they'd known you when that ex-fiancé of yours took up with your friend in that coat closet—which, in case I haven't mentioned it before, was sooooo tacky."

"Ancient history." And it was. She hadn't known it at the time, of course, but Jeff had done her the biggest favor of her life. Without that moment in time, she never would have moved to Sweet Briar and, as a result, she would have never met Milo, the man she was destined to spend her life with.

"If I'd been around when he ended up dead right here in Sweet Briar a few years later, I'd have wondered if Margaret Louise or Leona had done it." Charles stopped at the four-way intersection and, after a lengthy stop and no sign of a single car for miles, he turned right. "Heck, I might have thought *I* did it."

"I'm not sure Leona's inclusion on that list would be the case any longer." She heard the tremor in her voice and did her best to breathe it away.

Charles slowed the car from his normal twenty miles an hour to something a little closer to ten. "She'll come around, sugar lips. Once she realizes you stayed back to help Jake, she'll be fine."

"She needs to listen in order to hear it, and listening isn't always one of Leona's strongest skills." She turned back to the window and pressed her forehead to the glass. "Do you know what Jake said to me as he was leaving just now?"

"Do tell."

"He told me to tell Melissa and Margaret Louise not to visit him anymore."

The car came to a complete stop. "No!"

Her head slid up and down ever so slowly against the window. "He said they need to focus on the kids."

"Are you really going to tell them that?"

"I don't know. He wants me to. But I'm not sure I can. You know how they are about him." As they inched up to the next cross street, she pointed to their left. "Can we stop and check on Rose? I've been so caught up in all this stuff, I didn't call her like I wanted to, and I didn't check in with Beatrice to see how their breakfast visit went, either. And, to top it all off, I can't even remember who was at bat for delivering dinner this evening."

"According to the spreadsheet, it was Debbie." Slowly, he moved the steering wheel counterclockwise and then settled his speed somewhere between five and ten miles per hour. When they reached Rose's home, he pulled up to the curb, shifted the car into park, and cut the engine, his grin triumphant. "I'm gifted at this driving thing." He readied his fingers. "Am. I. Not?"

She considered mentioning the fact that Rose moved faster with her walker, but she refrained. Besides, Charles's snap-accompanied question had been rhetorical, thus saving her from having to lie and open the car door at the same time.

They met on the sidewalk with Charles carrying his cooler. "Why are you bringing that?" she asked.

"I had an extra stakeout sandwich in case Leona called back," Charles said as they made the short walk to Rose's front door. "She didn't, so now it belongs to Rose."

"Her appetite hasn't been great lately. I doubt she'll eat it if Debbie brought her dinner."

Charles pressed the doorbell and then held his ear to the door. "I can always put it in her fridge."

"True enough."

"She's coming!" he whispered. "I hear the sound of her house slippers!"

"Get your cheek off my door, young man!"

Rose's command was muffled but no less effective at garnering the same reaction: Charles moved. Swiftly.

A deep breath (his) later, the door swung open. "You two weren't on the spreadsheet."

Tori swallowed and looked at Charles. Charles fanned his cheeks with his left hand. "Spreadsheet?" he quipped. "What spreadsheet?"

Rose's eyes narrowed to near slits. "I may be old, but I'm not stupid. I've signed my name to a few of those spreadsheets myself over the years. I know a pity parade when I see one." Then, without waiting for a response, she pointed at the cooler. "Debbie already brought me dinner. A plate of lasagna, in the event you didn't know."

Charles blocked Rose's view of his mouth with his hand and leaned to within inches of Tori's ear. "Lasagna? I thought she was bringing pot roast."

"I don't like pot roast," Rose hissed.

Ignoring Charles's gulp, Tori stepped into the house and kissed Rose on the cheek. "We're here because I need to pick your brain on this stuff with Jake."

"And that?" Rose asked, pointing, yet again, at the cooler.

"It's an extra stakeout sandwich." Tori waved Charles

inside and then turned back to Rose. "We thought Leona was going to come with us, but—"

"She thinks you're a traitor."

Tori felt her mouth gape as Rose headed back toward the living room and the TV game show playing on the standard-sized screen. She followed in a daze. "Wait. You know about that?"

"Check your spreadsheet, Victoria." When Rose reached her favorite chair, she lowered herself down to its worn cushion, each movement accompanied by a wince she tried to shield from view. "Though, scratch that. Leona met Beatrice on the sidewalk and shooed her off.

"I saw the exchange myself, Victoria. Leona just walked up, snatched the plate of blueberry muffins and fresh fruit from Beatrice's hand, and sent her off with an irate eyeroll." Rose peeked at the TV, yelled something about peach pies, and then shut it off with a click of her remote. "I don't know how some of these people get on these shows."

Tori waved Charles into the room and then sat beside him on the overstuffed couch. "So Leona told you about last night's sewing circle."

"Told me? It's all she talked about." Rose looked from Charles to the cooler and back again. "What kind of sandwich?"

Charles brightened. "Ham and cheese."

"Who were you staking out?"

"No one, actually. But"—he sat up tall—"we *did* net ourselves two suspects that we'll surely be needing to tail, isn't that right, Victoria?"

Tori dropped her hands onto her knees and leaned forward. "Leona read the situation wrong."

"I want to hear about these suspects." Rose took a sip of her water and then motioned for Charles to hand her a sandwich. Once it was in her possession and unwrapped, she stared at Tori pointedly.

"I didn't stay because I was taking Dixie's side," she protested. "I stayed because I knew Dixie could provide me with some much-needed background on the history between Jake and Noah. That's it."

"Then why didn't you tell her that?"

Tori slumped back against the sofa. "I tried. She wouldn't answer the phone."

"So have Charles tell her."

"She hung up on him when he said my name."

Lifting the sandwich to her thin lips, Rose took one bite and then a second. Before she went back for a third, her thin shoulders rose and fell beneath her cotton sweater. "Well, at least I know we're talking about the same Leona."

"*You* believe me, don't you, Rose?" Tori asked, her voice raspy.

"I knew there was something off about Leona's story the moment her mouth started moving. I know how you feel about Margaret Louise and her tribe."

"Thank you." She smiled at the elderly woman. "It's good to see you eating."

Rose took another bite. "So, tell me about these suspects."

Charles took point, walking Rose through the conversation with Bud and the people apparently celebrating Jake's arrest. When he was done, he moved on to their stop at the police station and Tori's visit with Jake.

"How's he doing?" Rose interjected.

"He told Victoria he doesn't want Melissa and Margaret Louise visiting him at the jail anymore; isn't that right, Victoria?"

Rose eyed Tori over the top of her sandwich. "Is that true?"

"He's having a tough time, Rose. I can see it in his eyes and on his face and even in his hands. They actually shook a few times while he was talking." She pulled a nearby throw pillow onto her lap and hugged it to her chest. "He tried to hide it by messing with his hair and the table, but I saw it. He's worried."

"Don't know why. He didn't do it."

"You sound so sure," she said.

"Because I am. I've known Jake since he was born. He was in my kindergarten class at Sweet Briar Elementary. Watched him grow up right in front of my eyes. I know the way he was raised. He wouldn't take another man's life."

"But the body was in a car he was working on," she offered.

"Don't matter. Jake Davis isn't a murderer."

It wasn't a conclusion Tori hadn't already reached on her own, but to hear it echoed by someone she treasured as much as Rose was comforting. She said as much to Rose.

"You'll figure out who did this, Victoria. I have no doubt."

"I wish I had your faith," she mumbled.

"I have enough for the both of us."

A warmth spread through her body and she released the pillow. "You'll help us, won't you?"

Rose took one more bite of her sandwich and then set it down on the end table to her left. "It's like I told Leona this morning when she stopped by with that handsome fella. I'm not sure what I can say that'll help, but I'll do my best."

"Handsome fella?" Charles clapped his hands. "Oooh, do tell . . ."

"His name was Frank. Tall. Gray hair and—"

Tori's gasp was so sudden and so loud it nearly drowned out Charles's. "Wait. He had gray hair?"

Rose nodded. "Looked to me to be about Leona's age—the one we all know darned well she is, even if she denies it like there's no tomorrow." Rose considered a second go-round on her sandwich but waved it off in the end. "Now, I don't think they were together in that way. In fact, Leona was more focused on me than she was on him."

This time, if Charles gasped as well, Tori definitely couldn't hear it over the sound of her own. "Leona was more focused on *you*?"

"She wanted the same information you want."

Tori looked at Charles to see if he was as perplexed as she was, but he was on his phone texting something to Leona that included a whole lot of exclamation points and question marks. Undaunted, she turned back to Rose. "You mean about Jake's history with Noah? Doesn't she know that?"

"She knows bits and pieces told to her over the phone at the time, but she wanted more." Rose grabbed hold of her armrests as a cough gripped her frail body. After a moment or two, the woman closed her eyes. "I don't know if Frank is used to working with a partner, but he's getting one whether he wants one or not."

"I don't understand."

Slowly, Rose opened her eyes until they mingled with Tori's. "Frank is the private investigator Leona has hired to find Noah's killer."

Chapter 18

Tori wanted to feel the same way Milo did, to laugh and see the humor in the situation, but she didn't. Maybe, if Charles hadn't reacted the way that he had when Rose let the cat out of the bag, she could have cracked a smile, at least. But she'd never seen the point in *what if*s and *could have been*s and she wasn't about to start now. Futility and all that . . .

"So Charles was really fired up, eh?" Milo slipped interlaced fingers between his pillow and his head and chuckled.

"You know how he is when there's a chance to investigate something. Sometimes I'm not sure who loves it more, him or Margaret Louise. But, I'm telling you, when he heard Leona had hired a private investigator to help her, I seriously thought his head was going to loosen right off his neck with all his indignant sass." She tried to focus on the humor in the memory, but it was no use. The incessant churn in her stomach made it so all she could see was the message Leona's actions sent. "She's lost faith in me, Milo. And it hurts. A lot."

Hearing the emotion in her voice, he pulled his hands out from under his head and scooted closer to her on the bed. "If that's true, it's not based on anything real. The second Leona hears your side of the story, she'll realize you're as loyal as ever. And when she does, she'll call off this detective. Unless, of course, he's attractive?"

Her cheek moved against his chest with her nod. "According to Rose he is. But Leona won't date him."

"Is this because he doesn't wear a uniform?"

"That might give her pause, but no."

"I take it he's married?"

She thought back to the answers Rose had given to Charles's parade of questions, his need to best a real live private investigator not even close to being restrained. "I don't think so. Rose didn't really say. But she did say this man—Frank is his name—couldn't keep his eyes off Leona for long."

"Then why wouldn't Leona get a dinner or two out of him before she broke his heart? It's kind of her trademark."

"Because he's her age—her *real* age."

"Ahhh. I see."

She felt him shift forward a half second before he held his lips to her head. The gesture, while simple, helped calm her nerves and allowed her to think in a way she hadn't been able to at Rose's or in Charles's car afterward. "I guess part of what's throwing me right now is the fact that Leona would even go there in her mind. I mean, she knows how important both she and Margaret Louise are to me."

"True. But you have to take into account where her mind is at right now, too."

Leveraging her hand against the center of his chest, she sat up and pivoted her body until she could see her husband's face. "Meaning?"

"Leona talks a good game about things. We know this." When she nodded, he kept going. "Sure, she likes to tell everyone and their brother how much she despises kids." He stopped, squinted in thought, and rolled his finger in a what-comes-next motion. "What is that term she always uses when she's talking about anyone under the age of sixteen?"

"Germ packers."

"Yes—germ packers." A smile tugged at the corners of his mouth, bringing with it a hint of the dimples she adored. "And she loves to make it sound like Margaret Louise drives her insane most days. But you and I know it's a façade. Leona loves her sister and she loves her sister's family. If she didn't, she never would have moved here and she certainly wouldn't have stayed."

Tori took a moment to absorb everything Milo said even though it wasn't anything she didn't already know. Leona was pretty transparent if she let you close enough to see. "Okay . . ."

"Her family is under attack, Tori. She's worried about her twin, she's worried about Melissa, she's worried about Jake, and, yes, she's worried about those eight germ packers."

There was nothing to dispute or weigh in on yet, so she stayed silent.

"So her stress level is pretty high. And, if you think about it, you're the one she reaches out to when she's upset. She breaks a nail, she calls you. She thinks Paris isn't feeling well, she calls you. She has a fight with her sister, she calls you."

Tori splayed her hands toward the ceiling. "I already know this."

"Then you know she counts on you in stressful times." He reached for her hand and held it close. "And it doesn't get much more stressful than what's going on with Jake right now."

His words and their meaning were like a bucket of ice water being tossed at her on a hot summer day. She had, indeed, let Leona down. Leona had needed to know she wasn't alone in her grief over what was happening to Jake and the rest of her family, and Tori had let her down.

"Oh, Milo," she said on the back of a groan. "What have I done?"

"Whoa, whoa, whoa." He tightened his hold on her hand until her eyes were on him instead of the ceiling. "I'm not saying you need to take on some sort of blame here. I'm just saying this so you can understand why her head was too clouded to know you'd never turn your back on her and Margaret Louise. It's not that she doesn't think as highly of you as you do of her. She was just drowning in stress at that moment and lashed out at what her unclear mind saw as a betrayal."

She breathed in his words and, when she was pretty sure she could speak around the lump in her throat, she returned his squeeze with one of her own. "When did you get so wise?"

Tori wasn't sure exactly how long she'd been standing at the kitchen window. She knew her reason for doing so had returned her wave and pulled out of the driveway a long time ago. And she knew the baby bird thrashing around in the birdbath that had kept her there even after Milo's car disappeared from sight had long since moved on, his feathers clean. Yet there she still was, no longer seeing much of anything.

Murmuring to herself about wasted mornings, she made herself step away from the window and return to the English muffin that had lost its appeal the second she plucked it out of the toaster and began to spread butter across its nooks and crannies. Even Milo's good-natured teasing about starving children in Africa hadn't reclaimed the hunger pains that had accompanied her into the kitchen in the first place.

But that was the thing about those first few moments after waking, when you're too groggy to really think. A trip to the bathroom, slipping on a bathrobe, and eating breakfast were all part of a routine. Unless, as the lingering fog of sleep lifted, your brain became so cluttered with thoughts and worries that the thought of food suddenly became just another thing to attend to on top of a dozen other things.

Giving up, she pushed the plate into the center of the table, lowered herself to her chair, and wrapped her hands around the semi-warm mug of hot chocolate she'd made for herself just as Milo was collecting his lunch. She sagged back against the chair. "How do you get yourself into these messes?" she mumbled.

When the sky failed to open and provide an answer, she pitched forward, pulled her hands from around the mug, and buried her face inside her palms. Trying to get to the bottom of Noah Madden's murder was daunting all on its own. Add in Rose's declining health, Margaret Louise's heartache over Jake, and Leona's sense of betrayal and, well, yeah, she was feeling a wee bit overwhelmed.

Seconds turned to minutes as she remained there, face in hands, willing her breath to slow, her head to clear.

"Take it a little at a time, sweetheart—a little at a time . . ."

She squeezed her eyes closed in an attempt to hear her great-grandmother's voice again, but the welcome sound was gone. In the beginning, when those flashes had come and gone, they'd sent her running for a tissue box. But now she saw them as little gifts sprinkled into her days— a sprinkle of motivation, a sprinkle of warmth, a sprinkle of memories, a sprinkle of wisdom.

Her great-grandmother's "take it a little at a time" mantra had guided Tori through learning her alphabet as a young child, learning to sew, studying for a particularly rough test in high school, picking the best college, and so on. Heeding that advice had allowed her to be successful in just about everything she'd done thus far in life. So why it wouldn't work now was beyond comprehension.

Pushing her chair away from the table, Tori claimed her mug and carried it into the living room. Breaking things down into manageable chunks had taken many forms over the years, dictated, of course, by the problem at hand. When she'd been trying to learn her ABC's, her great-grandmother had painstakingly gone over them with her—a few letters at a time. Sewing lessons had come in bits and pieces—threading the needle . . . knotting the thread . . . learning one stitch before moving on to another. By taking it a little at a time, she'd felt less overwhelmed.

It was a sound way of doing things that had proven itself again and again throughout her life. There was no reason to think the same tactic couldn't work now.

Her mind made up, she crossed to the end table on the far side of the couch, retrieved a pad of paper and a pen from its lone drawer, and settled down on the couch. The key was finding a way to break everything down into those small, manageable parts—a to-do list of sorts to help chart her way out of the suffocating clutter that had amassed itself inside her head.

Uncapping the pen, she drew a line down the middle of the page. To the left of the line, she wrote names . . .

Margaret Louise

Melissa

The kids

Jake

Jessa

Tawny

She stopped, tried to recall the other names Bud had mentioned, but when she couldn't, she found them on a scrap of paper in her purse and added them.

Mason

Johnny

Old Man Skinner

When she'd recorded everyone associated with Noah Madden's murder, she added two more names in the interest of the whole manageable-pieces thing.

Rose

Leona

The list she'd made with Charles had been a way to record the limited bits of information they knew on each person—bits she needed to add to now that she'd learned more about both Jessa and Tawny. But that could wait. Right now, her focus was on *actions*.

She tapped the end of the pen against her chin for a moment as she looked at the first name on her list. Knowing the normally jovial woman was hurting was hard. Painful, even. Trying to figure out who was trying to frame Jake for murder was a big thing she could do for Margaret Louise. But in the meantime, she wanted—*needed*—to do more. Something to let the kindhearted woman know that she was loved . . .

Returning the pen to the paper, she brought her attention to the right-hand column and, specifically, the space next to Margaret Louise's name.

Stop by Debbie's for M.L.'s favorite apple pie. Cheerful flowers, too.

Her gaze moved down to the second line and Melissa's name. This one would be a little trickier. Yes, Margaret Louise was on the go all the time, too, but Melissa was perpetual motion. The mother of eight made juggling look easy. Her life was her husband and her kids. If they were happy, she was happy. But if they weren't . . .

Call after the kids are asleep. Be a listening ear. Keep her apprised of what I'm doing/what I find.

She moved on to the third line and allowed herself a moment to savor the smile that came with thoughts of the Davis kids. Were they a handful at times? Sure. There were eight of them. But handful or not, they were the nicest, sweetest, most polite kids Tori had ever met—the kind of kids she hoped to have with Milo one day.

Stop by with popsicles and bubbles. Follow it up with hide-and-seek so Melissa can rest.

Even without a mirror, she knew her smile faded away as her attention moved to the fourth line and the reason the list was necessary in the first place. Everything traced back to Jake—Margaret Louise and Melissa's heartbreak, the kids' confusion about where exactly their dad had gone, the need to look into two women Tori didn't really know, and Leona's sense of betrayal.

Well, everything traced back to Jake except Rose . . .

Her problems had been mounting for the last several months. Now, instead of simply walking a little slower than everyone else, Rose seemed to prefer isolating herself at home. Now, instead of going through the charade of pretending as if Tori's nightly good-night calls were silly, Rose had actually stopped picking up most nights. Now, instead of obsessing over her garden, Rose turned her back to the weeds threatening to choke the life from her once-beloved flowers. Now, instead of setting her alarm so she'd be at SewTastic in time to hang the OPEN sign, Rose hadn't stepped foot inside the store in weeks. And the occasional winces that had been a normal part of the arthritic woman's life for years now appeared much more intense.

The practical side of Tori knew it was all part of the aging process. She'd watched it happen to her great-grandmother. She knew the steps. But the feeling part of her—the part that had grown to love Rose as an almost surrogate great-grandmother—hated to see it happening. So many nights over the past few months, she'd forsaken sleep to play the maybe game . . .

Maybe, with a little extra sleep, Rose's energy would return.

Maybe, if everyone agreed to walk a little slower when Rose was around, Rose wouldn't feel like such a burden.

Maybe, if Milo explained to Rose that the nightly phone call was out of love and not an obligation, Rose would start picking it up again.

Maybe, if Tori asked Rose for help in planting flower beds outside the home she now shared with Milo, the sparkle that once lit Rose's eyes would return.

Maybe, if she could just get Rose to agree to see a doctor in one of the bigger cities, they might have a better solution for the pain.

Maybe, if she could talk Leona into setting aside the whole germ-packer thing for a few hours, SewTastic could host a workshop to teach little ones how to sew and Rose would be in her glory.

"Like Leona would listen to anything I had to say right now," she mumbled.

Skipping over the names immediately following Jake's, Tori readied her pen next to the final one on the list.

Show you're loyal. Leave no doubt.

Chapter 19

Tori was passing Leeson's Market when she heard the chirp of her phone from inside her purse. She considered letting it go to voice mail, but, on the off chance it was important, she transferred the powder blue bakery bag to her opposite hand and fished out her phone with the other.

"Hi, Charles."

"Get Nina to cover you—stat!" he whispered.

"I'm not due at the library until one o'clock today," she whispered back, only to stop and shake her head. "Why are we whispering?"

"Because she's here. Right now. In the thriller aisle."

She tightened her hold on the bag and felt her stomach lurch in response. "Leona is reading thrillers now? Since when?"

"Not *Leona*, sugar lips. *Jessa*." A beat or two of silence gave way to more whispering. "This could be our golden opportunity to find out if she's the setter-upper."

"The setter-upper?"

"Of Jake."

"I'm not sure *setter-upper* is a real word, Charles."

Three distinct taps filled her ear before her friend's voice returned. "Yes. It. Is."

"Wait. Were those snaps? Because if they were, they most certainly lacked their usual pep."

"I'm trying not to call attention to myself, sugar lips. Not when there is a potential *murderer* in aisle three."

"Charles, I—"

"So how fast can you get here?" he asked.

She stopped, looked from the SewTastic shingle to the bakery bag and back again, and sighed. "I can be there in less than a minute, I guess."

"Are you serious? But how . . ." His words drifted off, only to return on the heels of a muted squeal. "Oooh, I see you! I see you! I had no idea you were so close!"

"I was actually planning on stopping at—"

"See you in two."

"Charles, I . . ." But it was no use. He'd already ended the call. This time, she followed up a glance at the blue bag with one at her watch.

Twelve thirty.

If she hurried, maybe she could still stop in at SewTastic . . .

Her mind made up, Tori picked up her previous pace, her feet guided as much by the hand waving at her from the front window of Snap. To. It. Books as the sign itself.

She'd barely made it to the front door when it opened and Charles pulled her inside, the excitement on his face matched only by the excitement in his continuing whisper. "Hurry, hurry, before she finds her book and tries to leave! But"—he poked his head up and to the side in an attempt to gain a better view of aisle three—"play it cool, so you don't scare her off."

"Oh. So you don't want me to sidle up alongside her and ask her, point-blank, why she's trying to frame Jake for murder?" She tapped her finger to her chin in mock thought. "You think that would be a bad tactic?"

Charles lowered the periscope that was his head and rolled his eyes. "Leona is sooo right. Sarcasm doesn't become you."

Her gaze dropped to the bag in her hand and lingered there for a moment before she thrust it into Charles's hand. "Set this aside, okay?" At his nod, she made her way in the direction of the mystery section and the life-sized Barbie doll looking through the thriller titles.

Jessa looked up as Tori approached, gave her a once-over from head to toe, and then resumed her inventory of authors toward the first half of the alphabet.

"Have you tried Jeremy Brightwell yet?" When Jessa looked over her shoulder to see who Tori was talking to, Tori stepped closer, located the author's first book, and pulled it from the shelf. "He's relatively new, so he's not getting the shelf space of the big authors. But if this book"—she extended it toward Jessa—"is any indication, that won't be the case for long."

"Really? It's that good?" Jessa took the book and immediately turned to the back cover and the synopsis, her eyes darting back and forth as she took it all in. When she reached the end, she flipped the book over and studied the cover more closely. "Wow. It sounds great."

"It is." Tori leaned her shoulder against the shelf and gestured toward the book. "My husband loved it, too. In fact, he's the one that told me this guy has another book coming out in July. Same protagonist."

"Oh, so it's the first in a planned series?" Jessa asked.

"It looks that way, yes."

"Hmmm. I think I've found my winner of the week." Jessa gave the book a little wave and followed it up with a smile. "I take it you're a thriller reader, too?"

Tori nodded. "Thrillers, cozies, women's fiction, romance . . . I pretty much read everything I can get my hands on. It's a sickness, really."

Jessa's laugh mingled with Tori's. "There could be worse things, right?"

"Indeed." Tori parted company with the shelf on which she'd been leaning, walked across the aisle to the cozy section, and plucked a title from the third shelf down. "I read the first in this series last summer and it was so much fun."

"That's a cute cover . . ."

"It's a cozy. Perfect for those days when I want to escape into a different world for a while."

Jessa pulled her book against her chest and gave Tori another, less judgmental once-over. "What *is* your world?"

"I work at the library."

"Oh? What do you do there?"

"I'm a librarian."

Jessa's eyes widened. "Wow, so you get to be surrounded by books all day long."

"Best. Job. Ever."

"So why are you here? At a bookstore? You surely have access to anything you want to read at the library, no?"

Uh-oh . . .

Caught off guard, she searched for something that would sound natural, believable, but Charles beat her to the punch as he stepped around the corner and pointed at the book in Tori's hand. "Remember, I can ship that to Chicago free of charge for you."

"Oh. Great. Thanks." Tori held up the book and smiled at Jessa. "I think my friend would really love this one, and it'll be a nice just-because present."

"Especially after everything you told me she's been through," Charles said, continuing the ruse. "I mean, the way that guy shut her down like that? After the relationship they had? It's . . . it's"—he placed one hand on his hip and readied the thumb and middle finger of the other—"just. So. Wrong."

Jessa's eyes widened as they came to rest on Tori. "What *happened*?"

"I—I—"

"It was so sudden." Charles stepped all the way into their aisle and flailed his hands around. "One minute *Aaaa . . .*" He looked to Tori for help but, at her answering shrug, he squeezed his eyes closed briefly, made an O with the thumb and index finger of both hands, and then opened them all. "A-*manda* thought things were great between her and—and Stavros, and the next thing she knew he was moving on to someone else."

Stavros?

"Oh, I *so* know all about that," Jessa said, her voice breathy. "You have *no* idea."

Charles drew back, topping the gesture with what could qualify as a bone-chilling gasp. "Tell me someone did *not* do the same thing to you, Jessa!"

It took everything in Tori's power to resist the urge to clap. But really, she had no idea Charles could be so— Wait. Yes she did . . .

"For years. *Decades*, even," said Jessa. "And then, out of nowhere, he tells me to have a nice life."

Out of nowhere?

She tried to gauge Charles's reaction, but if he had one, he was disguising it behind empathy. For Jessa.

Jessa, in return, strode past them and over to the pair of mirrors Charles had deliberately placed to give him a view of the shop as well as a not-so-discreet view of himself. When she reached the one best suited for her to see into, she turned to her left and then her right, swinging her long, silky brown hair back and forth across her back as she did. "He had *this*. And he tossed it aside for the absolute plainest of Janes."

"I wouldn't call Mel—"

Charles stopped Tori's protest with a fast-moving palm and something that sounded a lot like a hiss before making his way—complete with clucks of understanding— over to Jessa. "Amanda and Stavros dated for three years before he up and moved on. How long were you and . . ." He stopped, tapped his finger to his chin, and then nodded at Jessa's reflection. "I didn't catch your guy's name."

"That's because I didn't say it." Jessa stopped preening and carried her book over to the register. "What's the point?"

Tori stepped over to the counter and pretended to rummage through a few of the bins Charles had filled with various impulse items—reading lights, magnetic book clips, notepads, etc. "My friend A-Amanda? She said it helped to talk through what happened with . . ."

Her words drifted off as she tried to remember the name Charles had pulled out of the air. When nothing came, she tried again. "What happened with . . ."

"Stavros!" Charles volunteered.

But it didn't matter. Jessa had fished her wallet out of her purse and plunked a twenty-dollar bill atop the book Tori had recommended. When Charles took it, Jessa glanced back at the mirror for yet another self-inspection. "I used to be that way, too. But not anymore."

Tori matched Charles's swallow and raised it with a quick I've-got-this look. "Oh? If you've got some pointers I can share with my friend, I'd appreciate it. I want to help her move past this guy, but sometimes I'm at a loss for what to say or what to do, you know?"

"Tell her to believe in karma."

"Karma?" Charles paused his hand inside the register just long enough to exchange a raised eyebrow with Tori.

Jessa turned back to the counter and held out her hand. "You know, the whole what-comes-around-goes-around thing."

"And waiting for that is enough?" Tori asked.

"For some, I imagine it is . . . or could be." Jessa took her change, nudged it around her palm with her thumb, and then, when she was sure it was correct, she dumped it into her purse and took her shopping bag from Charles. "For someone like me, though? Who lacks patience? Giving it a helping hand can be *oh* so very therapeutic . . ."

Chapter 20

Somehow, Tori got through her afternoon shift at the library. She sorted returns, printed overdue notifications, helped an elderly woman set up an e-mail account, pointed a gaggle of high school kids toward the resources they needed for an upcoming history project, and fixed a button on one of the costumes in the children's room.

Still, no matter how busy she was, her thoughts never strayed far from Jessa Thomas or the ominous words the woman had spoken just before leaving the bookstore. On the surface, they were probably innocent enough. But in light of the information Tori had already amassed, *innocent* wouldn't be her first choice of adjective.

The key was knowing whether they had enough to go to Chief Dallas . . .

Tori looked from the high school students to the overhead clock and back again. But it didn't matter. Watching the trio of girls and matching trio of boys thumb through the pile of historically relevant materials was like watching and waiting for a pot of water to boil. It didn't change anything.

Instead, she reached for a piece of scratch paper and a pencil and began to write the incriminating things they had on Jessa.

Infatuated with Jake for twenty years.

Jake told her to stop two weeks ago.

Several peers may have overheard.

In regard to karma, Jessa said: "Giving it a helping hand can be oh *so very therapeutic."*

Everything about Jake being framed for Noah's murder made sense with Jessa as the culprit. Especially when you factored in the timing of Jessa and Jake's conversation in relation to Noah's murder . . .

She scanned her way down her list, stopping on the final point. There was no getting around the fact that carrying a twenty-year-old torch for someone you only dated for six weeks as a teenager was strange. So, too, was the part about Jake having to sit down with Jessa to point out the obvious—like his wife of nearly eighteen years and their eight children. But even with that kind of track record of strange, one thing still didn't sit right . . .

Why kill Noah just to lash out at Jake?

Sure, a murder rap would mess up Jake's life, and have a lasting impact on his marriage to Melissa—both attractive outcomes for someone hell-bent on revenge. But wasn't killing an innocent person rather extreme?

And, taking that a step further, why Noah Madden?

Because there was history between Noah and Jake. History that would bode well in setting Jake up for the fall . . .

The thought was barely formed before another, more troublesome addendum mumbled its way past her lips. "History Jessa knew as well as anyone."

"Huh?"

Startled, Tori fixed her gaze on the sixteen-year-old boy grinning back at her from the other side of the information desk. Her cheeks flushed warm in response. "Oh. I'm sorry. I hope you weren't standing there long."

"Just long enough to hear you talking to yourself." He tightened his hold on his backpack strap and hooked his opposite thumb in the direction of the now-empty table where he and his classmates had been sitting. "Just wanted to tell you I put the books back. They were really helpful, thanks."

"My pleasure."

A slice of fading sunlight enveloped the information desk mere seconds before the teenager's peers appeared in the door, motioning for him to move faster. He waved them away and turned back to Tori. "So, how do you know my aunt Jessa?"

She drew back. "Excuse me?"

"My aunt Jessa. The one you were talking about when I . . ." He stopped, smacked his hand to his head, and then let it slide slowly down his face. "Okay, I'm an idiot. There's like four Samanthas in my grade, so there's probably other Jessas in the universe, too, right?"

The voice in her head told her to answer, to marvel at life's odd coincidences at a later date, but her mouth wasn't cooperating. Instead, she simply continued to stare at the blond, blue-eyed teenager on the other side of the counter as if he'd been teleported into her library from some unknown dimension.

Eventually, after an awkward shrug, he gestured toward the door. "Okay, well, have a great—"

"Is your aunt Jessa *Thomas*, by any chance?"

The boy stopped, mid-step, and turned, his nod giving way to a knowing smile. "So you *do* know her."

Under normal circumstances, she'd probably refute the teenager's statement—pointing out that she and Jessa had just met. But considering the person in question and her possible ties to a murder, Tori simply offered a passable nod of her own.

"Cool." Then, "I'm Ben, by the way. Ben Thomas."

"Hi, Ben." She tossed her pencil into the pencil basket, took one last glance at her notes, and then shoved the slip of paper into the front pocket of her slacks. "I'm going to venture a guess, based on the way you're smiling, that you're close to your aunt?"

"Everyone loves Jessa." He untucked his hands from his backpack straps and used them, instead, to scoop a pile of books off a nearby table and carry them over to the counter. "How could you not? She's funny, super sweet, and cool to hang out with, you know?"

Rather than risk admitting she didn't, Tori merely volleyed another question while putting on a show of sorting the pile into smaller ones. "You see her often?"

"Let's put it this way—if I don't see her, I know something is up. Dad calls it my Jessa radar."

"Your Jessa radar?" she asked, looking up.

"I always knew when something was off between them

even before she said anything. Mom said it's because I'm observant and I pick up facial expressions really well. Dad always said it was because the odds were in my favor when it came to there being an issue between the two of them. But it wasn't either of those two things. It was more a sixth sense. Jessa is always around—stopping by with cookies, or swinging by school to give me a ride home, or cheering for me at a track meet. When she's not, it's because there's something wrong."

"Oh?"

"You know Aunt Jessa. You know how she was about that guy."

She didn't need a mirror to know she'd reacted. She felt her brow lift, her eyes widen, the whole nine yards. Fortunately, Ben had chosen that exact moment to make a beeline for a stray book he'd spotted on a reading chair near one of the floor-to-ceiling windows along the southern wall, giving her time to recover her expression and formulate a response.

When he returned with the book, she was ready. "I know. As pretty as Jessa is, I don't know why she wasted so much time on Jake. I mean, surely, there had to be—"

"You mean *Noah*?"

"Noah?" she echoed, stepping back.

"Yeah. The guy that mechanic dude offed and threw in a trunk." Ben backed against the nearest table and lowered his backpack onto it. "The rich one."

Her thoughts rewound back to the moment the conversation she thought was about Jake turned into one about Noah. Then, like a dog in search of a bone, she put her sniffer into high gear and hoped it wouldn't show behind the house of cards that was her supposed friendship with Ben's aunt.

"It makes sense. They'd known each other since, when? Like, her sophomore year in high school, right? She must be taking this whole thing really, really hard."

"Mom thought that, too. That's why she invited her over for dinner last night—to make sure Aunt Jessa was okay. But I already knew she was. She'd picked me up at school yesterday and if she was upset, she wouldn't have done that." Ben tapped his temple. "See? My Jessa radar is never wrong."

It was official. Tori was beyond confused. Still, she thrashed about for an entry point that would make things a bit more clear. "So why do you think she isn't more upset?"

"She was sick of him."

"Sick of *Noah*?"

Ben gave a half nod, half shrug combination. "Dad says they dated for the wrong reasons in high school. And every single time thereafter."

Tori tried not to react, but in light of the book that was now on the floor, she knew her attempt had been largely unsuccessful.

Noah and Jessa had dated? Multiple times?

"Mom said it was going to keep on happening until Aunt Jessa figured it out," Ben continued. "But at least she finally did, you know?"

Tori leaned forward. "Why do you say that?" she asked.

"Jessa *told* me she did."

She opened her mouth to speak but closed it in favor

of shielding her eyes from a second, wider blast of sunlight.

"Yo, Ben. Are you coming or not?"

She sidestepped a crack in the sidewalk and continued counting rings.

Three . . .

Four . . .

Five—

"Hello, Victoria."

Pulling the phone from her ear, she double-checked the name on the screen and felt an odd mixture of validation and disappointment. On one hand, she was glad she'd dialed the right number, but hearing the pervasive sadness in Margaret Louise's normally cheery voice made her wish she hadn't.

"How are you holding up?" she asked, returning the phone to its resting spot against her cheekbone.

"I tried to see him today. But he refused." Emotion choked the woman's words and made Tori swallow in response. "Can you imagine? A boy refusin' to visit with his mama?"

"I'm sorry, Margaret Louise. I—I know how hard that must have been."

Silence filled the space between them for several seconds before Margaret Louise broke it with a labored sigh. "He did the same thing to Melissa a few hours later. She came home cryin'."

"He loves you both so very much. He just"—she took a deep breath and released it slowly—"doesn't want to be any more of a burden than he already is."

"A burden? Jake ain't no burden!"

She rushed to explain. "He doesn't want this to affect the kids. He wants things to remain as normal for them as possible."

"That's why Melissa and I were tryin' to visit in shifts! But those kids aren't foolish. They know somethin' is wrong. Jake is always home for dinner. He always plays with them b'fore bed. And Jake Junior? He's hearin' things at school."

"I'll talk to Milo. He'll reach out to the faculty at the high school."

"Can't keep these kids in a bubble, Victoria. The longer this goes on, the more likely one of my grandbabies is goin' to hear somethin'."

Margaret Louise's words bowed to a sob-like sound that nearly brought Tori to her knees right there in the middle of the sidewalk. She hated hearing her friend so upset. It was as if the whole world had slipped off its axis.

"Margaret Louise?" she said, quietly. "I—I need to ask you a few questions."

A few sniffs and a hiccup later, Margaret Louise's voice reemerged. "I'm listenin', Victoria."

"Tell me everything you can about Jessa Thomas and Noah Madden as a couple."

Another sniff.

Another hiccup.

"Why we talkin' 'bout that one?"

"You mean Jessa?"

"I knew, the first time I laid eyes on that one, she was goin' to be trouble." Margaret Louise sniffed again. "Mamas know that sort a thing, Victoria. You'll see when you become one. You just know things."

"But she and Jake dated for a little while, yes?"

"Not more 'n a month or two. Why, I tell you, that one was practically plannin' their weddin' after the first date. Went on and on 'bout how addin' his name would make them the same."

"Make them the same?"

"Jessa Thomas . . . marryin' a Jake Thomas . . . and addin' a Davis at the end."

She stared at her friend. "You can't be serious."

"That's bein' sixteen for you."

It was interesting stuff, really, but they were getting off track. "So how did Jessa end up with Noah, then?"

"Jake found Melissa that fall, and he was smitten in a way his daddy and I had never seen him. Jessa, of course, was fit to be tied. She tried beggin' and cajolin' and doin' everything she could think of to get Jake's eyes back on her, but Jake was havin' none of it. So Jessa tried somethin' new. She thought datin' Noah would make Jake jealous. But it didn't. Jake had eyes only for Melissa."

Tori tried the words on for size. They fit. "Okay, and how long did this thing last between Jessa and Noah?"

"Off and on right up until graduation. Jessa kept thinkin' Jake was gonna come runnin' back, but anyone with a brain in their noggin would've known that wasn't goin' to happen. Not then. Not now. Not ever."

"And after graduation? Then what?"

"Jessa and Noah broke up."

"Okay . . ."

"They got back together when Jake and Melissa got engaged. Came to the weddin' together, too."

Tori stopped walking. "Wait. Noah came to Jake's wedding? I thought they weren't friends."

"That's my Jake. Always tryin' to do the right thing. Always tryin' to prove he had no bad feelin's 'bout Noah."

"How long did Noah and Jessa date that time?"

"'Bout a month or two. But they got back together again when Melissa got pregnant with Jake Junior. You should've seen that little thing struttin' 'round in just 'bout any scrap of fabric she could find that would hug her body like a glove as soon as Melissa started showin'. Why, she'd be sashayin' herself 'round on Noah's arm at every festival and outin' there was. But my Jake never looked her way. The only one he was seein' with his eyes was Melissa."

"When did they break up *that* time?"

"After Jake Junior was born and Melissa had her little figure back again."

"And they got back together again after that?"

"Every single time Melissa got pregnant. And they broke up after each baby was born and Melissa was back to bein' the way she is."

Tori processed the information and moved on. "I get why Jessa dated Noah. She was hoping to make Jake jealous. But I'm not really getting why Noah played along. Wasn't he smart enough to realize he was being used? I mean, if his ego was as big as I'm hearing, why on earth would he have kept getting back together with her?"

"I'm guessin' because he, like Jessa, had convinced himself it was botherin' Jake even if Jake didn't show it." Margaret Louise sniffed again. "But more 'n that, I reckon he liked squirin' 'round the kind of woman most men stop to look at. Noah was 'bout appearances. Always. Jake used to say Noah only started mindin' Jake bein' better when folks started sayin' it was so. And seein' the man Noah became, my Jake was right. Noah liked bein' fawned over. He liked bein' envied. It's why he had to have his hand in so many pies in this town. He liked people knowin' he was important, liked people droolin' over what he had."

"Hence dating Jessa—someone who looks like a real live Barbie doll," Tori mused. "Hmmm. Did you know they broke up again recently?"

"I didn't. But I reckon that makes sense on account of Melissa's figure bein' back again."

She found her thoughts rewinding back to the library and the bits and pieces she'd gotten from Jessa's nephew, Ben. "I think this breakup might have been different. More final, maybe."

"Can't get much more final than one of 'em dyin', Victoria."

Chapter 21

With Milo's car safely in park, Tori's gaze traveled across the street and up the wide steps that led to Leona's condo. Like the four units to its right, and the single unit to its left, the brick face of the building was a ruddy red color with a half-glass/half-mahogany front door.

More than anything, she wanted to grab her purse off the empty passenger seat, get out of the car, and take the steps two at a time as she so often did when she dropped by to see her friend. But if she'd learned anything in their nearly three-year-long friendship, Leona wasn't a fan of unexpected visits. The official explanation put the reason on a lack of manners. The unofficial (read: unspoken) reason was a lack of preparation time (read: reapplication of lipstick, et al.). Regardless of the true reason, though, the last thing Tori wanted to do was go into an apology situation with an even bigger black mark.

Still, maybe if she launched into her explanation for staying behind at the last sewing circle meeting before the front door was even fully open, her failure to call ahead would go unnoticed.

"And if pigs could fly, yada, yada, yada," she murmured, shifting her focus to the large bay window and the lamp Leona had brought back from a recent jaunt through Italy. Movement just beyond the lamp was followed, a few seconds later, by the front door opening and a gray-haired man stepping out and onto the welcome mat Leona had purchased in Spain. Behind him by not much more than a footstep or two was Leona herself.

Tori scooted down in her seat so only her eyes and the top of her head cleared the steering wheel. It wasn't an ideal pose, but it was the best she could do while still having a vantage point from which to observe the pair.

Two things struck her in the immediate. One, the man who had preceded Leona onto the front stoop was classically handsome, with the height of Clint Eastwood and the endearing realness of George Clooney. Dressed in a pair of khakis with a navy blue blazer, the stranger exuded a quiet confidence Tori found both calming and oddly reassuring—like all would be well under his watch.

The other thing she couldn't help but note was her friend. To say Leona looked off her game was being kind. Her fingers were pressed against her lips, her shoulders were sagging, and—gasp!—she wasn't wearing shoes.

The man was saying something to Leona who, in turn, was looking down at her stocking-clad feet, her shoulders hitching upward every few seconds as if she was . . .

Crying?

Tori sat up so fast she bumped the top of her head

against the upper doorjamb, eliciting a moan she rushed to stifle with her palm. But it didn't matter. The window was closed and the two people in her field of vision were oblivious to their surroundings.

The man stepped forward, cupped Leona's upper arm with his left hand, and gently lifted her chin with the index finger of his right. When their eyes were level, he pulled his finger from the base of Leona's chin and gently wiped first her left and then her right cheek. When he was done, he said something that earned him a slow nod in return.

Tori held her breath as he took Leona's hands in his, gave them a gentle squeeze, and then turned and made his way down the stairs and over to a silver four-door sedan parked directly in front of the condo. Leona waited as he started the car, watched as he pulled away, and then remained on the stoop, visibly lost, as his car disappeared from sight.

Even from across the street and two car lengths away, she could sense a sadness in Leona she'd never witnessed before. It was, in a word, heartbreaking. It was also motivating . . .

Reaching into her purse, she pulled out her phone and dialed Leona's number. One ring turned to two as Leona, still standing on the stoop, reached inside her open door, pulled her phone off the entryway table, consulted the screen, and put it back down as her voice simultaneously filled Tori's ear.

"I'm sorry to say I'm not here to take your call right now. But if you leave your name and number, I will be sure to return your call just as soon as I can. If you're calling to arrange a date, please know there's a long

waiting list and I'll get to you just as soon as possible."
The voice turned decidedly purr-like in time to add, "I've
been told I'm more than worth the wait. Ta-da!"

Tori heard the beep, even considered leaving what she
was pretty sure would be her twentieth message in nearly
forty-eight hours, but, in the end, she simply hung up, her
heart heavy.

Tori hiked her purse strap onto her shoulder and
took a deep breath, the promise of a much-needed
pick-me-up no more than twelve steps away. Yet even
after the breath had been gathered and released, she continued to stand there, staring up at Rose's front window,
waiting for the calm she'd come to equate with her elderly
friend—a calm she desperately needed at that moment.

It didn't come.

Maybe if she actually went up to the door and
knocked . . .

Tightening her grip on her purse strap, she climbed
the single step up to Rose's front porch and knocked on
the door. When there was no response, she knocked
again, adding a slight urgency to her effort.

A glance at the living room window showed snippets
of blue light flickering around the edges of Rose's blinds.
A check of her watch confirmed it was time for the woman's favorite evening game show.

She knocked a third time and, when there was still no
answer, tried the door and found it unlocked. "Rose?" she
called before launching into an oft-repeated (and ignored)
reprimand. "You left the door unlocked again . . ."

Using the canned cheers and applause of the game

show to guide her steps, Tori crossed the narrow hallway into the living room and stopped in her tracks as her gaze fell on Rose's chair.

No Rose . . .

Aware of the dread starting to rise up in her throat, Tori tried to will it back down by cocking her ear toward the hallway bath.

No sounds . . .

"Rose?" she called again. "Are you—" the rest of her inquiry faded away as a faint thump from the far end of the hallway claimed her attention and sent her running for Rose's bedroom. "Rose? Rose?"

The thump gave way to Rose's weak voice. "I'm . . . in . . . here . . . Victoria."

Tori stopped just inside the doorway and looked around.

"I'm . . . down . . . here . . . next . . . to . . . the . . . bed."

There was no mistaking the roar of fear that filled her ears, the taste of bile that rose in her throat, or the way her feet barely touched the ground as she ran around the foot of the bed. There, between the nearly made bed and the mint green colored wall, was Rose, lying on the ground, looking up at Tori with hooded eyes.

"Rose!" She dropped to a squat and reached for Rose's hand. "I'm here, Rose. I'm here. Don't move, okay? I'll have an ambulance out here in no time."

"You'll do no such thing, Victoria Sinclair Wentworth," Rose groused.

"But Rose, if you broke something, I could make it worse by trying to move you myself."

"I didn't break anything."

She smoothed a strand of white hair from Rose's

narrow face and tried to steady her breathing. "We can't be sure."

"Yes, we can." With painstaking effort, Rose lifted her hand from its resting spot atop her stomach and pointed at her partially tucked sheets. "I was trying to make my bed is all."

"At eight o'clock at night?"

"Better late than never, as they say."

She resisted the impulse to make a face and, instead, got back to the part that mattered. "So that's when you fell? While you were making the bed?"

"I didn't fall," Rose snipped. "I . . . I just couldn't stand up again."

Tori leaned closer in case she hadn't heard correctly. "You couldn't stand up again?"

Rose closed her eyes and nodded.

She tried to make sense of what she was hearing, but she couldn't. And before she could fire off any more questions, a lone tear escaped from between Rose's lashes and slid down her age-spotted face.

Not sure what to say or do, Tori simply guided Rose's hand back down to its starting place and covered it with her own. "Did you get dizzy?"

Rose shook her head.

"Did you get confused?"

Rose's eyes flew open and pinned Tori's. "No!"

"Then why—"

"Because I didn't have the strength to get back on my feet." Rose closed her eyes again, took a long, deep breath, and then met Tori's questioning eyes with conviction. "I just need you to help me off this floor. Then you can check me off your to-do list and I can get back to my game show before the big money round."

"You aren't on my to-do list, Rose. Never have been, never will be." She maneuvered herself next to Rose and then, using the wall for leverage, helped her friend sit up, collect her bearings, and then rise slowly onto her slipper-clad feet. "Whoa . . . whoa. Not too fast. Give yourself time to adjust."

"I might be weak, Victoria, but I'm not a buffoon."

"I know that, Rose. I—I'm just worried is all." When Rose was steady on her feet, Tori offered her arm and was surprised when it wasn't swatted away. She waited for that fact to give her comfort, but it didn't. Instead, it resurrected the crushing fear she'd felt as she rounded Rose's bed and found the elderly woman lying on the floor.

Now, step-by-step, they made their way back out of the room, down the hall, into the living room, and over to Rose's favorite chair as the closing credits of the game show flashed across the television screen.

"I haven't missed a big money round in years," Rose said, her voice hushed.

Tori made what she hoped were sympathetic sounds, but her thoughts were already sifting through a mountain of *what if*s . . .

What if she had opted to go home after leaving Leona's house?

What if Rose had remained on the floor through the night?

What if Beatrice had gotten busy and failed to check on Rose in the morning?

What if—

She stopped, shook her focus back onto Rose, and then laid claim to the corner of the couch closest to her friend's chair. "Why didn't you call me when you realized you were having trouble?"

Rose pointed to her phone atop the television cabinet.

"It's supposed to be with you at all times," Tori said, looking from Rose to the phone and back again. "It won't do you any good if you're in one room and it's in another."

"I left the room to make my bed, Victoria. It should have taken five minutes."

"But that's why you need to keep the phone with you, Rose. Because you can't know what's going to happen at any given moment."

Propping her elbow on the armrest of her chair, Rose winced her forehead into her hand and sighed. "I never wanted to be like this. Ever."

"Be like what?" she asked.

"Weak. Needy. A"—Rose's voice cracked—"charity case."

Tori launched off the couch and into a squat beside Rose, claiming the woman's hand as she did. "First of all, you're not weak. Not by any stretch of the imagination. You are, in fact, one of the strongest women I've ever known."

"That's not the kind of weak I'm talking about, Victoria."

"Well, it's the kind of weak *I'm* talking about. The kind of weak *you're* talking about is outside your control."

"And therein lies my point." Rose squeezed Tori's hand

once, twice, three times, and then disengaged herself once again. "I wanted to go out of this world strong—on my own terms."

Her stomach flip-flopped. "And you will. When it's time. Which it's not." Then, not wanting to leave any room for Rose to argue, she moved the conversation forward. "As for needy, you're the least needy person I've ever met."

"I have a spreadsheet devoted to my care, Victoria," Rose groused. "That spells needy in my book."

Tori bobbed her head to the left until Rose was all but forced to return her gaze. "It spells *we love you* in my book."

"You've barely been married six months. You should be home, spending your evening with that handsome husband of yours, not here, adhering to a spreadsheet." A flash of pain zipped across Rose's face, but for once, Tori doubted it was physical.

She shifted her weight more evenly across her squatted legs and then gave up and lowered herself to her knees. "First of all, Milo loves you, too. So it doesn't matter how long we've been married—you're important to both of us. Period." When Rose opened her mouth to protest, Tori silenced her with a raised palm. "Second, Milo has parent-teacher conferences this evening. I'm picking him up at the school at nine thirty. So if I wasn't here, I'd be twiddling my thumbs at home—alone.

"And third, I'm not here because of a spreadsheet. Tonight was Georgina." She paused, weighed the question that came to mind against the wisdom of asking it, and opted to go for broke. "She did come, right? With dinner?"

"If you call pot roast that tastes like shoe leather dinner, then yes."

She nibbled back the urge to laugh and, instead, took a moment to savor the positive sign that was Rose's feisty response. Then, aware of a faint gurgle emanating from her stomach, she motioned toward the kitchen with her chin. "Um, any chance you have a little of that shoe leather left over? I'm pretty hungry all of a sudden."

Rose's head was shaking before Tori had uttered her last word. "It was in the trash before Georgina hit the sidewalk."

"That's okay." She shifted her thoughts off the promise of food and back onto the woman seated in front of her. "As for why *I'm* here, that's easy. I need you—I need your ears, your wisdom, and your opinion. And somewhere in there, if it's okay, I could use a hug, too."

Chapter 22

Noting the time on the dashboard clock, Tori slid the key into the ignition and listened as Milo's six-year-old car purred to life. If she'd had her druthers, she'd have stayed with Rose a little while longer so as not to be stuck with this awkward time gap, but there were only so many times a person could doze off mid-conversation before the writing on the wall became impossible to ignore.

She couldn't help but smile at the memory of Rose startling awake in her chair, only to deny being tired. It was a dance they'd done at least a half dozen times before Tori had made up some cockamamie story about needing to drop something off at Debbie's before picking up Milo.

Yet even with the sound (albeit completely false) reason for leaving, Tori couldn't quite shake the nagging fear churning away in her stomach as she waited for proof that

Rose had, indeed, made it from the now-darkened living room to the dimly lit bedroom in the back corner of the house. As she waited, she tried to imagine the elderly woman making her way down the hallway, into the bathroom to brush her teeth, and, finally, into the very room in which Tori had found her less than two hours earlier, on her back . . . on the floor.

Tori swallowed against the emotion she felt building in her throat all over again. She'd wanted to stick around until Rose was safely in bed, tucked beneath her sheets with no danger of falling or being too weak to move, but Rose had protested (read: glared and refused).

On the surface everything was as it had always been— Tori being overly protective and Rose wanting nothing to do with it. Beneath the surface, however, it had been a different story.

And that was the part Tori couldn't shake off—that pesky sense that Rose was starting to doubt her own strength, her own safety.

"Oh, Rose," she whispered, "don't lose your toughness . . ."

Blinking against the tears she felt forming, she willed herself to concentrate on the part of Rose's bedroom window she could make out from the car. Any minute now the light should go off . . .

She peeked again at the clock and then back at the window.

"Three more minutes, and I'm—"

Her words dissolved into a sigh as Rose's bedroom finally went dark.

Phew . . .

Resting her head against the seat back, she took a

moment to steady her breath and get her emotions under control. What exactly she was going to do with the almost-forty-minute window she had left before needing to be outside Sweet Briar Elementary, she wasn't sure, but whatever it was, she didn't need red-rimmed eyes.

A vibration inside her purse sent her scrambling for her phone. A check of the screen and the time stirred a different set of fears.

"Is everything okay?" she asked as she hit the button and held the device to her ear. "Did something happen?"

"You mean besides the fact my boy is sittin' in a jail cell for somethin' he didn't do?" Margaret Louise paused, took an audible breath, and then continued. "I'm sorry, Victoria. I know you're worried 'bout Jake, too."

"I'm worried about all of you. Jake, Melissa, the kids . . . you. It breaks my heart that you're going through this." And it was true. It was hard to watch bad things come down on the heads of good people, but to see it happen to Margaret Louise? A woman who defined the expression *happy-go-lucky*? A woman who was always thinking of others before herself?

It simply wasn't right.

"It helps knowin' you're out there, tryin' to help, Victoria." A long pause was followed by a louder, deeper breath. "Why, that's the only thing makin' it so I can get any sleep. That and knowin' in my heart that my boy ain't no killer."

"The truth will set you free," she murmured as her eyes, once again, strayed back to Rose's house. "My great-grandmother used to say that all the time. It's how she lived."

"I wish I'd had a chance to know her," Margaret Louise replied.

"So do I." She swiped the back of her left hand across her eyes, waited a beat, and then forced every ounce of strength she could muster into her tone. "I wish there was more I could do to help you and Melissa. I—I feel kind of helpless, you know?"

"Havin' you out there, nosin' 'round town with Charles, is the most important thing of all, Victoria. I'd be out there investigatin' with you if my grandbabies didn't need me like they do. Which is why I'm callin'. It's 'bout Lulu."

"Lulu?" she echoed, her gaze swinging around to the empty road ahead. "Is . . . is she okay?"

Tori loved all eight of Melissa and Jake's children. It was hard not to. They were good kids. They were funny, sweet, respectful, and happy. Yet as much as she loved Jake Junior, Julia, Tommy, Kate, Sally, Molly Sue, and Baby Matthew, there was something about Lulu, the fifth in age order, that jettisoned the now fourth grader to the top of the pack for Tori . . .

Maybe it was their shared love of the Little House on the Prairie books.

Maybe it was the little girl's gentle soul.

Maybe it was—

"I was hopin' maybe you could commandeer Milo's car and pick her up at that pottery place in town? I was s'posed to be the one pickin' her up, but Tommy is strugglin' with his math homework in the other room and, last I checked, Melissa fell asleep readin' bedtime books to Molly Sue. She's been through so much these past few days I don't have the heart to wake her if I don't have to."

"No! Don't wake her. I'm actually in Milo's car right now. He had to go back to school tonight for parent-teacher conferences and I dropped him off. I can be at the pottery place in"—she dropped her gaze to the dashboard clock once again—"eight minutes. Tops."

"You sure I ain't interruptin' your evenin'?"

"I'm actually just sitting outside Rose's house, trying to kill time before I have to pick Milo up at the school at nine thirty."

"Is Rose okay?"

She debated telling Margaret Louise about finding Rose on the floor, even considered sharing her fears regarding Rose's health, but she couldn't. Not now. Margaret Louise had enough on her plate. Tori and the rest of the sewing circle would look after Rose.

Instead, she made herself smile and hoped the gesture would find its way into her voice. "Rose is fine. She just went to bed, actually." Then, not wanting to be peppered with questions she didn't want to answer, she directed the conversation back to Margaret Louise's request. "Is Lulu at a party or something?"

"A scout meetin'. I'll give Lindy Whalen a call and tell her you'll be gettin' Lulu this evenin'."

"Is that Lulu's leader?"

"It is, bless her heart."

Before moving to Sweet Briar, Tori would have seen the answer as complimentary. But now, thanks to two-plus years in the southern town, she knew better. "I take it you don't like this leader?"

"She's a gossip." A change in background noises let Tori know Margaret Louise was on the move. "Okay, I'm back. Too many ears where I was, though four of them ears should've been in bed ten minutes ago . . . Now, where was I? Oh, right, Lindy Whalen. She was practically salivatin' when I dropped off Lulu. But I gave her a warnin' eye and she best be heedin' it."

"Are the kids still oblivious to what's going on?" Tori asked.

"The little ones are. But the older ones—includin' Lulu—know more than we were hopin' on account of flappin' jaws. We've told 'em it's a mistake and we're workin' on fixin' it, but they're strugglin'. They're missin' their daddy."

"I'm going to figure this out, one way or the other."

"And I believe that, Victoria, I really do." A cacophony of voices in the background of the call was followed by a sigh. "I'm just worried 'bout the damage bein' done in the meantime."

"Meaning?"

"Jake refusin' to see Melissa is hurtin' her. Deeply. It's hurtin' me, too. The kids are pickin' that up, Victoria. Some are cryin', some are fightin', some just aren't talkin' at all."

She closed her eyes against the image of eight sad faces sitting around a table—eight normally smiling faces now weighed down by worry and sadness. "I'm on it, Margaret Louise."

The door-mounted bell jingled in greeting as Tori stepped into the pottery shop and surveyed her surroundings.

To her right were three separate floor-to-ceiling shelving units with each individual shelf playing host to no less than a half dozen unpainted pottery pieces. The pieces themselves ranged from simple (plates and coffee mugs) to intricate (lamps and figurines) depending on taste and painting ability. To her left and beyond the register was what appeared to be a series of tiny cubbies with each section boasting a trio of bottles with numbers written in black marker on each and every lid. The numbers, she quickly ascertained, corresponded with a veritable potpourri of colors showcased across a large pegboard. Even from her spot just inside the doorway she could tell that there were at least a dozen different shades of each basic color. To the right of the pegboard were two paint-spattered sinks, a large counter with jars of paintbrushes in varying sizes, and a clothes rack filled with yellow vinyl paint-spattered smocks.

A short, stocky redhead stepped out from behind the counter and smiled. "Welcome to Pottery Place. Are you here to pick up a painter or a project?"

"A painter. She's here with a scout troop." Tori glanced at her surroundings one more time and then met the woman's eye. "I suddenly have an irresistible urge to don a smock and pick up a paintbrush."

"Which is exactly the reaction we love here at Pottery Place." The woman held out her hand. "My name is Tawny. Tawny Wright. And while I know I've seen you around town a bunch, I'm sorry but I don't know your name."

Any momentary startle reflex on Tori's part dissipated as her thoughts traveled back to the limited bit of information she and Charles had gleaned from Bud. Instead, she took Tawny's hand and returned the smile. "That's okay. I'm Tori. Tori Sinclair Wentworth. I'm the librarian over at Sweet Briar Public Library."

"That's it! The library. My niece loves that children's

room you made." Releasing her grip, Tawny tapped her chin in thought. "I think it was a few months ago. When my brother was out of town and my sister-in-law had to be in too many places at one time with the kids. So I volunteered to take Phoebe to the library. It was pretty cool."

"Thank you."

"Did you paint all those murals yourself?" Tawny asked.

"I did. But it was pretty easy. All I did was project the drawings onto the wall and then fill them in with paint."

"Still, it's pretty darn cool. The library was nothing like that when I was growing up here."

"We're pretty proud of it." And it was true. In fact, to date, the creation of the children's room, in what had once been a storage room prior to her hiring, remained the thing Tori was most proud of when it came to her career thus far. It filled her with a sense of accomplishment like nothing else. Still, this wasn't the time to get all doe-eyed about anything. She needed to be sharp, to take advantage of an opportunity she hadn't expected. But how, exactly, to do that was the problem.

"Well, last I checked, the girls were just finishing up back in party room number one. So feel free to peek in on them and claim your daughter."

Tori shifted her purse from one arm to the other, shaking her head as she did. "I'm actually picking up my friend's granddaughter—Lulu Davis."

Tawny's eyes widened. "Lulu Davis? As in one of Jake Davis's kids?"

"That's right." Then, seeing an opportunity, she propped herself against the outer edge of the counter and casually traced her index finger along its edge. "It's a shame what that family is going through, don't you think?"

"Something Jake should've thought about before he chose murder."

Tori drew back. "You really think Jake did it?"

"He's sitting behind bars in the basement of the Sweet Briar PD, isn't he?" Tawny made her way back around the counter to a calculator and pad of paper, her fingers grazing over the buttons but stopping short of actually pushing any of them. "And that's *after* Noah's body was found in the trunk of his own car—in Jake's garage, no less."

"Did you know the victim?" It was a rhetorical question, really, as she already knew the answer. But, considering she and Tawny didn't know each other, Tawny wasn't privy to that little fact.

"I did. And I know Jake, too. I went to school with both of them."

"Were you friends?"

Hiking up her shoulders, Tawny jogged her head a little left and a little right. "Meh. In high school, I pretty much hated both of them for different reasons."

"Ahhh, so you avoided them?"

Tawny rolled her eyes. "I wish. Unfortunately, my best friend was pretty intertwined with both of them."

"That must have stunk."

"You have no idea. But it wasn't all bad, I guess. I have this place, don't I?"

"*This* place?"

Nodding, Tawny held out her hands, palms up, and swept her gaze around the shop, guiding Tori's to do the same. "I didn't have the capital to open this place. Noah did. And it's because of him I opened this place—and now *own* this place."

Footsteps just over her left shoulder redirected Tori's attention to the pack of women and vest-wearing scouts making their way toward the counter. The girls were happily chattering with each other about their projects and the colors they'd chosen, while the mothers, walking a few steps behind them, peppered their daughters with questions.

"Did Lulu say anything?"

"Did Lulu mention her dad?"

"Did Lulu seem upset?"

On and on it went, each question feeding off the one before.

Lulu . . .

Clearing her throat, Tori hooked her thumb in the direction of the hallway and the project room Tawny had referenced earlier, and dropped her voice to a level only the pottery shop owner could hear. "I better get Lulu now. Do I owe you anything for her?"

"Nope. She just needs to come back next week and pick up her piece. It'll be in a bag with her name on it in that bin over there."

Tori followed the path forged by Tawny's finger and nodded. "Great. I'll be sure to let both her mom and her grandma know that."

Then, squaring her shoulders, she made her way down the hallway and into the open room denoted by a colorful number one. Sure enough, seated at a table toward the back of the room was Lulu—the child's head bent low, her face covered from view by her long dark hair.

Curious, Tori stepped farther into the room, her gaze falling on the table directly in front of the fourth grader.

No project . . .

"Lulu? You okay?"

Slowly, the head lifted, prompting at least some of the hair to fall back into place. Recognition dawned but failed to unearth its normal face-splitting smile. "Hi, Miss Victoria. Are you here to paint pottery, too?"

"Nope. Even better." Tori slid into the chair next to Lulu and planted a kiss on the child's cheek. "I'm actually here to pick you up."

"Why?" Lulu burst out, her eyes welling with tears. "What happened?"

Tori pulled Lulu's hands from the table and held them tight. "Nothing, sweetie. Nothing at all. Your mom fell asleep with the baby, Mee Maw is working with Tommy on his math homework and trying to get the younger ones off to bed. So she asked if I'd pick you up." She released her hold just long enough to tuck a strand of long, silky hair behind the child's ear, their gazes locked. "I, of course, jumped at the chance because . . . well . . . it's not often I get a little alone time with my special little friend, is it?"

She waited for the smile—the one that could spread across Lulu's face faster than wildfire. But it didn't come.

"Please tell me the truth, Miss Victoria. Please?"

This time, when she brought her hand back to Lulu's she followed it up with a squeeze. "Your mom is asleep, Lulu. And Mee Maw is working on math. You have my word."

Relief sagged Lulu against the back of the seat but failed to dissipate the tears Tori saw hovering at the corners, waiting. "What's wrong, sweetie? Did you not have a good time tonight?"

Lulu's chin dropped nearly to her chest, taking her voice and her gaze with it. "It was okay. I—I made a coffee mug," Lulu mumbled, flicking her hand to the left. "For Daddy."

Leaning forward, Tori spied the rainbow-colored mug and let out a little squeal. "Oh, Lulu! That is fantastic. Your dad is going to absolutely love that mug. In fact, I bet it becomes his very favorite—the one he'll drink his coffee out of every single morning before he heads out to the garage."

Once again, Lulu's hair fell forward, blocking Tori's view of the child's face. "Bonnie says Daddy won't be able to use it."

"Well, that's silly. Of course he'll be able to use it. I don't think they'd sell coffee mugs here if you couldn't drink out of them when they're done being painted."

Silence gave way to an answer so quiet Tori had to practically lean into Lulu's lap to hear it.

"Bonnie said Daddy won't be able to bring anything with him. Not even his wedding ring."

"I—"

Lulu lifted her chin ever so slightly as the tears finally made their escape down her wide cheeks. "Not even a picture of us. Because then he might try to use it to"—Lulu stopped, swallowed, and then swallowed again—"*break out* . . . and if he *did*, Bonnie said he'd get in really, really, *really* big trouble."

Reaching down, she turned Lulu's chair so it was facing her instead of the table and gently raised the child's focus back to her own. "Whoa, whoa, whoa. Stop right there, young lady. I don't know who this Bonnie person is, but she's got it all wrong."

"Bonnie is in my class at school and my scout troop, too. And she's really, really smart. She gets a donut for every subject, and she *takes math with fifth graders*!"

"A donut?" she asked.

"Miss Debbie gives a free donut for every A you get on your report card. Last report card I got four. But Bonnie got all six!"

She tried not to laugh and, instead, forced herself to focus on the parts that had Lulu looking so lost and so sad. "And that's wonderful, Lulu. It really is. But just because Bonnie takes advanced math and gets really good grades in everything doesn't mean she *knows* everything—especially things that deal with adults, like this stuff with your dad."

Lulu swiped at the tears rolling down her cheeks and sniffed. Hard. "You mean Daddy really can take my mug to jail with him?"

"Who says your dad is going to jail?"

A matching set of tears raced their way down Lulu's face, only to drop from her chin onto her lap. "Bonnie, Shelby, Jana, everyone. Even . . . Mrs. Whalen and Mrs. Larkin."

"Who are they?"

"My scout leaders. I—I heard them talking while I was picking out the colors for Daddy's mug. They said Daddy isn't going to come home anymore, and Mommy is going to have to get a job and put Baby Matthew and Molly Sue in day care so we don't go broke."

Tori fisted her hand at her side and did her best to rein in the anger she felt raging just below the surface. Right now, Lulu needed her to be calm and reassuring. Later, once she knew Lulu was okay, it would be time to have a chat with the little girl's leaders.

"Daddy hasn't done anything wrong, Lulu. I believe that with my whole heart."

Lulu's head jerked up. "You do?"

"Of course I do. I know your daddy. I know how much he loves you and your mom and your Mee Maw and all the kids. And I know he's a good person, with a really big heart." She reached out, wiped yet another round of tears from Lulu's face. "He wouldn't hurt anyone."

"That's what I said!" Lulu said. "But Bonnie said he wouldn't be in jail if he didn't do anything wrong."

She made a mental note to ask Milo about Bonnie and then pulled Lulu's chair still closer. "Remember that time Molly Sue knocked over that little unicorn in your room? And it broke?"

Lulu nodded.

"Do you remember how it happened?"

"I left it on the ground and Molly Sue kicked it with her foot. But she didn't mean it. She's too little."

"So it was a mistake, right?"

Lulu nodded again.

"Well, sweetie, babies aren't the only people who make mistakes. Big people make them sometimes, too. You know that."

When Lulu said nothing, Tori continued. "Your dad is in jail because the police believe he did something he didn't really do. And as soon as they realize they've made a mistake, he'll be back at home with you, and your mom, and the rest of the kids. You'll see."

Lulu seemed to consider Tori's words, the tangible

tension in her young shoulders relaxing a smidge. But just when Tori had thought she'd calmed the waters enough to coax the child from her chair, Lulu dropped her head into her hands.

"Lulu?"

"Didn't Daddy tell them they made a mistake?"

"He did."

Slowly, Lulu popped up her head. "Then how come he's still in jail, Miss Victoria?"

More than anything, she wanted to ignore the question. But this was Lulu.

Lulu was bright.

Lulu was inquisitive.

And Lulu trusted Tori.

Gathering her emotions into something resembling even keel, Tori tapped the little girl's nose. "Because sometimes people like the easy answer more than finding the right one."

"But I want Daddy to come home."

"I know, sweetie." She relocated the tip of her finger to the underside of Lulu's chin and lifted the little girl's gaze until it was firmly on Tori. "And that's why I'm going to do everything I can to show them they've made a mistake arresting your daddy."

Chapter 23

The moment she'd gotten word Milo had secured a ride home from a fellow faculty member, Tori knew she was going to walk Lulu into the house and stay to help Margaret Louise corral the little girl and any of her still-awake siblings toward their beds for the night. The process, in and of itself, was lengthy, delayed by requests for a pre-bedtime drink (Tommy), a quick shower (Jake Junior), a few more minutes of reading time (Lulu), and on and on it went.

But now that it was over, Tori wished it wasn't. Had it been chaotic? Sure—mind-numbingly so. But it had also been fulfilling in an odd way.

"You're a natural with them kids, Victoria. A real natural."

She lifted her chin off the resting zone her palm

provided and took in her friend across the homework-strewn table. "You really think so?"

"I don't think so. I *know* so." Margaret Louise surveyed the mess between them and then, doing her best Moses impression, parted it down the middle with her arm. Textbooks went to the right, scratch paper to the left. "You're goin' to make a wonderful little mama when you and Milo get 'round to havin' some babies."

"I hope so. I really do. But sometimes, when I watch Melissa and Debbie, I wonder if I can even come close to having Melissa's patience and creativity, or Debbie's seemingly endless energy."

When the table between them was clear, Margaret Louise reached across it and patted Tori's hand. "You will. And you'll bring your own specialness to it just like you do with Lulu."

She didn't mean to sigh, but the mere mention of the woman's grandchild jettisoned her back to the pottery shop and Lulu's sad eyes. Removing her hand from beneath Margaret Louise's, she traced a faint pencil mark across the table while she gathered her thoughts and figured out how best to share the reason behind the gnawing worry in her stomach.

Margaret Louise beat her to the punch. "Quit holdin' back, Victoria. Tell me what happened."

"Happened?" she parroted.

"With Lulu on the way home. Why, I saw the frettin' in your eyes the moment you two walked through the front door."

Part of her wanted to deny there was anything wrong. After all, Margaret Louise had entirely too much on her plate already. But the other part of her, the part that loved Lulu with all her heart, knew staying silent wasn't a good option.

Still, she tried to temper her words and her tone so as not to cause unnecessary alarm. "She's worried about Jake. And it seems her peers are only adding to that angst."

"They're whisperin' 'bout her, ain't they?" Without waiting for a response, Margaret Louise shook her head. "I was hopin' the adults in this town would watch their tongues 'bout all of this, but I've been livin' in this town long 'nough to know that kind of hopin' and thinkin' is like spittin' into the wind."

"She's afraid Jake isn't coming home." Tori stopped, leaned back in her chair, and slowly lifted her gaze to Margaret Louise's. "Ever."

For a moment, Tori wasn't sure Margaret Louise had even heard her, but just as she was preparing to repeat herself, the grandmother of eight dropped her chin to her chest. "That makes two of us."

Margaret Louise's words were akin to a smack across the face. Yet even as she fought to recover from the un-expected, her sense of right and wrong took over. "You can't believe they're going to convict him—there's no way."

"People have been locked away with far less evidence, Victoria."

It was her turn to reach across the table, to find and cover her friend's hand with her own. "You can't talk like that, Margaret Louise."

"I'm just repeatin' what the attorney told Melissa and me on the phone this evenin'."

"How long was Noah's car in that bay?" she asked.

Margaret Louise's shoulders rose and fell with a painful shrug. "I'm not sure. Maybe a couple hours at most. My Jake is quick at fixin' cars."

She considered the woman's words, trying them on for size with everything she knew about that day. "We drove past the garage that day, remember? You wanted to tell him something, but he wasn't there."

"He was at home, havin' a quick dinner and fittin' in a little playtime with the kids b'fore headin' back to the garage to finish up a few things, just like he always does." Margaret Louise stared down at Tori's hand as if she'd just realized it was there. "That's the way his daddy was. Finish what you start, he was always tellin' 'im."

"How long was Jake at the house with Melissa and the kids that evening?"

The shrug was back, only this time it came and went a little faster. "I don't know. Maybe an hour? Maybe two?"

"And this is something he tends to do often?"

"Just 'bout every night 'cept Sunday."

"Okay, so let's err on the conservative side and say he was home for an hour. Don't you think that would be enough time for someone to open up Noah's trunk, dump his body inside, close it, and take off?"

Rising onto her feet, Margaret Louise crossed to the built-in desk in the far corner of the kitchen and yanked open the top drawer. A few quick movements and a grunt yielded a sheaf of papers held together by a giant clip. Less than a minute later, the woman was on her way back, the sought-after paperwork in her hand.

"What's that?" she asked.

"Jake's contract with Noah. 'Bout their partnership."

Margaret Louise came around to Tori's side of the table and laid the document in front of her. "Page three. Last paragraph."

With a quick glance at the front page and Jake's full name in bold print near the top of the contract, Tori moved on to the noted item. Even knowing it existed, there was no denying the way her mouth went dry at the legalese that was nothing short of damning for Jake when it came to serving up a motive for murder on a bright, sparkly silver platter.

She read it once, twice, and then looked up at her troubled friend. "We already knew this. It doesn't change anything."

"I keep hopin' Robert will find another lead—one that will take his mind off my Jake—but that means Robert would have to be lookin'."

"I thought you said the chief is Team Jake?"

"He is, for the most part. But more 'n that, he's Team Easy, which I reckon you know probably better 'n anyone, Victoria."

And it was true. She did. If a person was new in town and something happened, that person was the immediate (and only) suspect. If someone was old, yet still died unexpectedly, it was chalked up to age. If—

She shook her thoughts off the memory parade warming up in her head and forced them back to the present. "This is the paragraph that was left for the chief?"

"That's what Robert said on the phone."

"And he doesn't find it odd that someone would make a copy of this one paragraph, slip it in an unmarked envelope, and leave it where he could find it, rather than deliver it by hand?"

Margaret Louise opened her mouth to respond but closed it as Tori sat up tall, smacking her hand atop the document as she did. "I mean, think about it. Doesn't that seem odd to you?"

"I hadn't given that part much thought."

"Then think now. *Who* would do that?"

"Just 'bout anyone on Team Noah, I reckon."

"Not to mention the person who killed him."

Margaret Louise looked from Tori to the contract and back again, her mental wheels practically clacking out loud as she processed the possibility. When her eyes widened, Tori knew her friend had caught up.

"The killer is framin' my boy."

"Again, we knew that. But what we *don't* know is how he or she got ahold of this contract. I mean, is this something Jake would have shared with other people? An accountant? An attorney? A friend?"

"Jake hated the thought of partnerin' with Noah," Margaret Louise said between scratches of her scalp. "He wanted to expand the garage another way—*any* other way. But when it came to Noah or not expandin' at all, he chose Noah."

"Which brings us back to my question. Who knew about this agreement?"

"In the beginnin', just me and Melissa. But once the expandin' started, Noah crowed 'bout it to everyone. Jake said it was because Noah was excited. But I think it was more 'bout lettin' Team Jake know that *he* was on top now."

She let that simmer for a moment until she realized it changed nothing. "Okay, so others knew. But who would have had access to a copy of this contract?"

"Why, I don't know, Victoria. Never really did much thinkin' 'bout that."

Tori returned her attention to the contract and casually flipped through each initialed page until she got to the one bearing two distinct signatures—Jake's and Noah's. Something tickled just below the surface of her thoughts, but try as she did to coax it out, it remained elusive.

"Victoria?"

She looked up at her friend and waited.

"Can we talk 'bout somethin' else for a little while? My heart has had all the achin' it can hold for one night."

"Margaret Louise, we're going to get this figured out. I'm positive of it."

The woman rocked back on the heels of her favorite Keds, closing her eyes briefly as she did. Then, like a curtain parting, her lashes opened to reveal a hint of desperation. "Please, Victoria. Just somethin' happy or silly or . . . just *different*."

"I—"

"Tell me 'bout your visit with Rose."

She tried to hold her reaction in check, but Margaret Louise, although compromised by her own grief, was still Margaret Louise. Which, translated, meant she missed nothing where Tori or any of their friends were concerned. The majority of the time, it was an immensely appealing trait. Now was just not one of those times . . .

"You have to be tired, Margaret Louise. You're running all day long now with the kids, trying to keep Melissa's spirits up, and likely not sleeping much, if at all. So why don't we table this discussion for another day? When things are less crazy, okay?"

Margaret Louise shot her finger up in the universal

I-have-a-thought gesture, her expression unreadable. "My daddy always used to tell my twin and me that if it looks like a pig and oinks like a pig, it's a pig."

"Okay . . ."

"You're avoidin' my question 'bout Rose, Victoria. And don't go denyin' it, neither. My antenna is pingin' something fierce."

She thought about denying it anyway, but, in the end, she knew the effort would be pointless. Margaret Louise's antenna was legendary.

"Okay, you win." Tori pulled out the empty chair beside hers and gave it a quick pat. Margaret Louise, in turn, heeded the invitation.

"I hate dumping anything else on you, I really do."

"Rose is my friend, too, Victoria. The stuff goin' on right now with Jake don't change that."

She fiddled the seam of her slacks between her fingers and then released it with a sigh. "I'm worried about her, Margaret Louise. Whatever this slump is that she's in isn't going away. In fact, it's getting worse. Much worse."

"She stayin' put in her chair all day?"

"Not enough."

Crossing her arms in front of her polyester-clad chest, Margaret Louise quirked an eyebrow at Tori. "How 'bout we quit all this banterin' and tell it like it is? We'll both get to bed a lot sooner if you do."

"Touché." She pushed at the air and then slumped back against her chair. "I found Rose on the floor of her bedroom this evening."

Margaret Louise's gasp echoed around the kitchen. "Did she break her hip?"

"No. She claims she didn't actually fall."

"Then what was she doin' down there?"

"She'd gotten onto her knees to tuck in her sheets and was too weak to stand back up again." She heard the emotion building in her voice and could do nothing to stop it. "If I hadn't needed a Rose fix when I did, it's likely she'd have still been there, in that same spot, when whoever is on for tomorrow morning's visit showed up."

"That would have been Beatrice." Like one of Molly Sue's wind-up toys at the end of its wind, Margaret Louise sagged against the table. "What's goin' on 'round here, Victoria? It's like the world has gone mad. My Jake is in jail, Melissa is lost without him, my grandbabies are askin' questions I don't know how to answer, Rose is slippin' toward the grave right in front of our eyes, and you're not lookin' too good, neither."

She drew back. "Nothing is wrong with me, Margaret Louise. Except worry, of course. I don't like seeing what's happening with Jake, either. And Rose? I think she's going through a rough patch right now, but I don't think that means we're losing her!"

And then the unthinkable happened. Margaret Louise began to cry. It wasn't that Tori had never seen the woman cry, because she had. Quite a lot over the last three days, in fact. But this time the woman's tears were powered by a despair so raw, and so powerful, Tori could barely breathe.

Chapter 24

Three things struck her as she opened the door of Sweet Briar Fitness Station and breathed in a veritable potpourri of scents including body odor, excessive perfume, a hint of chlorine, and . . . *mint*?

First, the part of the gym visible through an interior glass wall was packed.

Second, the folks working out ran the gamut when it came to age.

And third, she felt like a bum in comparison.

The twentysomething male perched atop a stool behind a nearby counter pulled his attention off the health magazine in his hands and smiled around the red-and-white-striped mint clenched between his back left teeth. "Welcome to SB Fitness. Are you ready to start your journey?"

"My *journey*?" she echoed.

Max, as his name tag read, pointed to the illuminated

sign just over his right shoulder. "At SB Fitness, we believe that healthy living is a journey, not a destination, which is why our new membership plans reward commitment. You stay for six months, we discount your monthly fee by ten percent. Stay a year, we knock it down by twenty-five percent."

Fortunately, she was saved from responding by the sudden yet persistent ring of a nearby phone. Max shot his index finger into the air and, after her answering nod, took the call. "Good morning, SB Fitness—where healthy living is a journey, not a destination."

She took advantage of the distraction to conduct a more thorough inspection of her surroundings. Up ahead and through the glass wall, she counted twenty elliptical machines in use. Roughly half of the members stared straight ahead, their expressionless faces giving an almost robotic feel to their movements. The other half watched TV, listened to music via headphones, or chatted with a fellow elliptical machine user. Beyond them and to the right were stationary bikes, rowing machines, treadmills, and a section devoted entirely to free weights.

Swinging her attention to the left, she noted another glass door and what appeared to be colorful pennants attached to a rope across the ceiling.

"Sorry about that interruption," Max said as he replaced the phone into its cradle. "Normally there's at least two of us manning the desk, but my partner, Leslie, is covering a Zumba class at the moment. And Rachel, one of our coworkers, is spotting Tina with weights."

Tori pulled her gaze off the pennants and fixed it, instead, on the muscular Max. "I've never taken a Zumba class, but I've heard it's fun."

"One of our most popular classes at the moment," Max said by way of agreement. "Membership at SB Fitness includes unlimited classes, and we offer a wide variety to suit just about any taste. Spin classes, yoga classes, Pilates classes, tai chi, kickboxing, stretch classes, and butt and gut classes. Basically, if you can think of it, we likely have it. And if we don't, all you have to do is put it on this sheet"—he turned, plucked a clipboard off the wall, and set it on the counter between them—"and we'll do our best to get it on the next month's schedule."

He returned the clipboard to its hook and then crossed to a bin with colorful tri-folded brochures in an eye-catching yellow with purple block lettering across the front. "Our brochures detail everything we have here at SB Fitness in terms of cardio and weight machines, as well as the pricing breakdown. We don't believe in a one-size-fits-all membership at SB Fitness. You know your schedule better than we do, so we offer different levels in the hope you'll want to start your journey toward better living right here with us."

She took the brochure, glanced at it, and then tucked it in her purse. "Thank you. I look forward to giving it a good once-over after work this evening."

"I'd offer to give you a tour, but I can't leave the desk until Leslie gets out of Zumba."

"That's okay. I'll just get one the next time." She pointed up at the photograph of the dark-haired, blue-eyed man smiling down from the wall behind Max's head. "By any chance is Mason available?"

"You know Mr. Wheeler?" Max asked, as he offered a friendly wave to a trio of men on their way out the door. When they were gone, he reached under the counter for another stack of brochures, and added it to the display from which Tori's had come. "I feel like I learn something from him every day, you know?"

Since she didn't really know the man, she couldn't really say one way or the other, but still, she offered something resembling a nod. "I was hoping maybe I could have a few minutes of his time?"

"I can check." Max turned, craned his neck around the brochure display, and peeked down a long hallway Tori hadn't noticed until just that moment. "He said he had some work to do when he came in, so I probably shouldn't just send you back. But I'll give him a call and see if it's okay."

"That would be great, thanks."

Max picked up the phone, reached for the buttons, and then stopped, his face taking on a crimson color. "Oh, wow, I just realized I never asked your name when you came in."

"That's okay. My name is Tori—Tori Sinclair Wentworth. I'm the librarian over at Sweet Briar Public Library."

"Oh. Okay. Yeah. I'll let him know that." Max paused his hand atop the first button and cleared his throat. "You won't tell him I forgot to ask your name, will you? Because I'm usually real good about that."

"I won't say a word." She took a few steps back as he waited for his boss to answer and again let her gaze drift through the glass, past the elliptical machines, past the stationary bikes, past the treadmills and—

Leona?

On cue, Leona Elkin looked up from the control panel of her chosen treadmill and met Tori's eye, her expression changing from one of determination to disdain in short order. Without thinking, Tori started to step through the recessed door but was thwarted, mid-step, by Max.

"I'm sorry, Mrs. Wentworth, but you can't go in there unless you're a member or on a tour. But if you can wait around for another twenty minutes or so, Leslie will be out of class and able to cover me."

"No, I just . . ." The words drifted away as Leona stepped down off her treadmill and disappeared from Tori's view. Then, as she continued to watch, Leona returned with a woman clad in the same yellow and purple color scheme as the brochure in Tori's purse. After a few words and a finger point in Tori's direction, the fitness center employee crossed to the wall and drew closed a large theater-style curtain.

She steadied her emotions as she turned back to Max. "Is Mason available?"

"He said you can come right back." Max motioned her to come around the far side of the counter and then pointed her down the hallway. "Mason's office is the last one on the right. He said you can just go on in."

"Thanks, Max. I really appreciate your help."

At the mouth of the hallway, she squared her shoulders and took a deep fortifying breath. Somehow, seeing Leona had thrown her off her game. Sure, she'd known Leona was angry. Charles and Rose had both made that crystal clear. So, too, had the bird's-eye view of Leona's reaction to Tori's call the previous day. But somehow, today's reaction had ratcheted up the sting factor. She needed to make things right with Leona, to make the woman understand that Tori wasn't siding with Dixie against Jake. But not now. Now she had bigger fish to fry.

Mason was waiting as she approached his office, a curious smile tugging at the corners of his mouth. "I didn't know librarians made house calls." He held out his hand, his smile widening across his face as she returned the gesture. "Mason Wheeler. I know I've seen you around town these last few years, but it seems we've never crossed paths quite close enough for a proper hello."

"Tori Sinclair Wentworth." When his grip loosened, she removed her hand and crossed to the chair he indicated. "Thanks for seeing me this morning."

He perched on the edge of his desk and nodded. "My pleasure. But I must admit to a little curiosity, seeing as how I can't remember the last time I was in the library. Fifteen, twenty years . . . at least. So if this is about an overdue book, I'm in trouble . . ."

The shake of her head was met with a sigh of relief that echoed around the tiny office—a sigh so loud, in fact, she couldn't help but laugh. "No, you're safe."

"Phew." He returned to his feet and wandered around the desk to his leather chair. "So what can I do for you this morning, Tori?"

She cast about for something to say that would net her the kind of information she needed without putting him on the defensive. But just as she was realizing how contrived her options were, her gaze fell on a series of framed photographs lined up along the windowsill. "I see you have a student at Sweet Briar High School?" she asked, pointing to the second picture from the left.

"My son, Ryan. He's a sophomore."

"I take it he's an athlete?" She looked from the team baseball picture to the team football picture and then back to Mason.

Mason beamed with pride. "Baseball and football. Just like his old man. Only he's far better at both than I ever was."

"Did you play for Sweet Briar, too?"

"I did. Though I was more of a benchwarmer when it came to football, truth be told."

She slid her gaze down the row of pictures until it landed on the proverbial jackpot. "Is that from your time on the team?" she asked, rising to her feet and moving closer to a photograph she'd seen many times before—in Margaret Louise's house. "Oh, hey, I recognize a few familiar faces in this picture."

The farce tasted bitter on her tongue, but she considered it a necessary evil.

"Just about everyone in this picture still lives right here in Sweet Briar. Some still look the same, more or less."

"Some?"

His chair creaked beneath his body as he, too, stood and ventured over to the windowsill. "Paul Riker"—he pointed at the teenager in the back row, far left—"is bald now . . . and Tanner Smythe's nose is more crooked now on account of more than a few bar fights along the way."

His finger paused on his younger self. "Of course, I haven't aged much in the last twenty years. My wife claims that's because of her, naturally. But honestly, after seeing the way"—his finger moved one face to the right of his own—"*Big Johnny* here has aged the past few years, she might actually be onto something."

"Johnny Duckworth? As in the one who'll be opening up that new paintball field out by Ramey Pond soon?" She sent up a mental thank-you to Bud for the information and to her late great-grandmother for all the memory games they'd played together. "I heard he was a pretty good football player back in the day."

"Quarterback on the rise until Jake Davis and Noah

Madden made varsity. After that, there was a whole lot of humble pie being passed around, as my mother used to say."

"That must have been hard, huh?"

"Sure, sometimes. Being seen as one of the stars had its definite advantages—especially with the cheerleaders. But Big Johnny? It was really hard for him." Mason lingered his finger on the glass front for a moment before setting the frame back down on the sill. "Every time he tried to shake it off, though, his old man was right there to remind him of the way he'd been replaced. And it wasn't done nicely—I'll tell you that much."

"His dad was tough?"

"Tales involving the backside of his hand were legendary around here."

She drew back. "You mean he hit Big Johnny because he wasn't the star of the team anymore?"

"Nah, he was already doing that for things like leaving a soda can around or sleeping in too late on a Saturday, but it got worse when the old man couldn't brag about him on the football field anymore."

"And no one stopped him?"

"Big Johnny never told."

"Then how did you know?" she asked.

"Big Johnny was my best friend, way back when. Until Tina decided we were spending too much time together."

She couldn't help but hurt for the teenager she hadn't known. "I guess that kind of pressure would age anyone."

Mason crossed his arms in front of his chest and rocked back on the heels of his workout shoes. "Things weren't easy with his old man, that's for sure, but they got through it, eventually. Even have a relationship to this day—or as much of a relationship as they can have when the old man doesn't know who Johnny is anymore."

"Wow."

"I know, right? And as tough as that was back then, it was a picnic compared to his time with Tina Lynn Murdock. *That's* what's aged him."

"Tina Lynn Murdock?"

"One of those cheerleaders we all thought were so wonderful back in high school."

"I take it she broke his heart when he got sidelined for Noah and Jake?" she probed.

His laugh was without humor. "Nah, Big Johnny wasn't that lucky." He paused, looked up at the ceiling, muttered something about wisdom, and then looked back at Tori. "I can't imagine you came here to talk about my days as an almost football stud, so tell me what I can do for you."

She weighed the benefit of arguing against the very real possibility of raising unwanted suspicion, and came down on the side of caution. After all, Mason did admit that Jake and Noah had caused problems for him and Johnny. But was it enough of a reason to murder Noah and frame Jake almost twenty years later?

"Tori?"

Lifting her gaze to his, she realized he was waiting for her answer—an answer she didn't really have, unless . . .

"I, uh . . . I know it's still a very long way off, but I was wondering if SB Fitness might consider donating something for a possible raffle basket at our Friends of the Library sale in the fall."

Chapter 25

The click of her heels against the tiled floor barely registered in her thoughts as she passed one artwork-strewn bulletin board after the other. The artwork, like the students who'd made it, progressed in ability with each passing classroom.

On the kindergarten bulletin board there were brightly colored rainbows in non-rainbow colors. On the first grade bulletin board there were oddly shaped paper tulips popping out from paper vases. And on the second grade bulletin board there were—

"I was hoping that was you clickety-clacking in my direction." Milo stepped out into the hallway and pulled her close. "And what a sight for sore eyes you are."

"Rough day?" she asked, disengaging herself in favor of eye contact.

"The part with the kids was great. But the after-kids part? Not so much."

"Uh-oh. Bad staff meeting?"

He pulled her in for one more hug and then turned to face his empty bulletin board. "I spent the past half hour taking down pictures of bunny rabbits adorned with cotton balls. In their place, I need to display a writing assignment the kids completed yesterday. Want to help?"

"I've been told I'm a pretty good stapler . . ."

"You're hired!" Milo held up his index finger and then disappeared into his classroom, returning in mere seconds with a pile of loose-leaf paper and a black stapler. He handed the stapler to Tori but held on to the essays. "Jimmy says he'd put a playground on every street if he had Georgina's job."

"What?"

"Jimmy Larkin." Milo retrieved the first essay from the pile, held it up for Tori to see, and then tapped the upper left corner of the bulletin board. "Let's put his up here."

She looked down at the large letters and misspelled words that covered the paper and grinned. "Ahhhh, the old If-I-Were-Mayor essay . . . I remember writing one of these when I was in second grade, too."

"I'll tell you what I wrote if you tell me what you wrote . . ."

"I said my town should have a bookmobile just like my school did. Only it would stop on each street and if you were a good kid, you could get free books and keep them forever." She held Jimmy's paper in place, positioned the stapler along the top edge, and pushed, the click of the staple barely audible over her laugh. "I guess I didn't really understand the concept of a business back then, huh?"

Milo grinned. "I should've known yours would be about books."

"Ha-ha. Now it's your turn."

He looked from Tori to the top of the pile and back, a sly smile inching his mouth upward. "I said there would be mandatory kickball parties in front of my house each and every night."

"Mandatory, huh?"

"Man-da-to-ry." Tapping his finger atop the next essay, he began to read. "If I were mayor, everyone in Sweet Briar would get to stay up until ten o'clock on school nights. And get to have chocolate ice cream. With hot fudge. And sprinkles, too."

She leaned across the gap between them and eyed the name scrawled across the upper right corner. "Caroline Walters sounds like my kind of kid."

"Which is exactly what I told her when she read her essay to the class this morning." He held the paper out with one hand and pointed to the area just below Jimmy's paper with the other. "So, how was your day?"

"Mildly productive," she said, taking the paper and stapling it onto the board.

"Care to elaborate?"

She took the third paper, skimmed the student's big plans for a new town swimming pool, and attached it to the bottom edge of the bulletin board. "I got my first donation for the next Friends of the Library sale. From SB Fitness."

Milo handed her the next paper, narrowing his eyes

on her as he did. "I didn't know you were working on that already. Isn't that in October or November?"

"It is, and I'm not. In reverse order."

He glanced down at the next essay in his pile and then leaned against the wall, his shoulders sagging beneath an invisible weight.

"Milo?"

She watched his eyes move from left to right across the paper before lifting to meet hers. "I'm sorry, can you bring me back up to speed?"

"I can, and I will. *After* you tell me what's brought on that face."

"What face?" he asked, returning his attention to the paper in his hands.

"The troubled one you're sporting right this minute . . ."

Again, his eyes skimmed left to right before disappearing for a few seconds behind closed lids. When he opened them again, he did so with a labored shrug. "Most of the things my kids want to do as mayor are funny. But Hannah's"—he pulled the paper off the slowly decreasing pile and handed it to Tori—"is just sad."

"How so?" She took the paper, noted the penciled words that were so lightly written, and then stepped forward until the afternoon rays from Milo's classroom enabled her to read it aloud.

"Hannah Duckworth. Age eight. If I were mayor of Sweet Briar, I would make flowers for all the mommies and sunny days for all the daddies. It would be a happy town. With lots of smiles." She couldn't help but grin at the image of a town filled with flowers and endless sunshine, yet as she looked back at Milo, she saw a sadness she didn't understand.

"What am I missing? I think"—she stopped, looked again at the name in the upper right-hand corner—"Hannah did a great job on this."

Milo tucked the remaining stack under his left arm and wandered across the hall to the third grade bulletin board and its display of art projects utilizing the division the eight- and nine-year-olds were learning in math. "I don't know. I guess it's just hard to read that stuff and know that no matter how much they wish for it, it's not going to happen."

"That's the point of the assignment, isn't it?" When he didn't respond, she looked back at the papers she'd already affixed to the board and gestured toward the first one. "I mean, no mayor is actually going to erect a playground on every street in Sweet Briar, or mandate kickball parties either . . ."

"But those are the kinds of things I expect to see from second graders. It's what I see, in one form or another, every year." He lingered in front of a drawing of an apple pie cut into sixths and then turned around and made his way back across the hall. "Then again, I guess I see at least one like Hannah's each year, too."

"Meaning?"

"Meaning something they think will fix things at home . . . but rarely does."

She looked from Hannah's paper to Milo and back again, his words slowly sinking in. "There's trouble in her house?"

"More like World War Three, but yeah, there's trouble." He raked his fingers through his hair, exhaling a burst of frustration as he did. "At this point, I think she'll be better off once the divorce is official and her parents are no longer living under the same roof. At least then she won't be subjected to the constant bickering."

Tori leaned over, set the stapler on the floor, and then guided his dislodged hair back to its original starting position. "I suspect you're a calming force in Hannah's life. Don't discount that. Ever."

"I know. And I'm trying to make sure I'm the same thing for Jake and Melissa's kids when I see them in the cafeteria or at recess. But I know that my hand on their shoulder or a word of encouragement in their ear as they pass by doesn't really hold a candle to what they're going through at the moment. They're worried about their dad, worried about their mom, and dodging whispers from their peers."

She felt her own shoulders sag. "So the kids around here really are talking?"

"Kids are much more aware of what's going on in the world these days thanks to the Internet, so they rarely miss a thing. Couple that with the fact that jaws are no doubt flapping across their dinner tables every night and, well, my colleagues and I have our work cut out for us in trying to minimize any fallout for the kids.

"But my eyes and ears are always open, I assure you of that." He captured her hand in his, brushed his lips across her fingers, and then, when he'd elicited the smile he was seeking, he handed her the stapler once again. "No rest for the weary until these are all on the board."

She was glad to see him smile in reaction to her laugh. "You can be a real slave driver sometimes . . ."

"There's a steak dinner in it for you later tonight if you stick with me on this."

"Did you say *steak*?"

"I did."

She reached over, plucked the next paper from his hand, and held it to the board with nary a glance at the name or its content.

Milo laughed. "You're such a pushover."

"For steak, yes. For you, even more so."

Slowly but surely, they made their way through the next dozen papers, chatting about his various students and a few funny moments throughout the day. When they were down to just three, Milo stopped. "So when is this book fair again? The one you're already starting to work on in terms of donations for the raffle prizes?"

"The book sale is in the fall—the first weekend in November, to be exact. And no, I'm not working on that yet."

"So it was an unsolicited donation?" He glanced back down at the last of the papers and liberated the top one.

"Considering I asked for it? No, it wasn't unsolicited."

He started to hold out the next essay, but pulled it back at the last minute. "But you just said—"

"I said I wasn't working on the sale yet, because I'm not. But I needed a ruse for my being in Mason Wheeler's office, and the book fair was the first thing I could come up with."

"You were in Mason's office? At SB Fitness?"

She plucked the paper from his hand and added it to the board. "According to what Bud said the other day, Mason was one of the ones in the bar after Jake's arrest— one of the ones who wasn't too terribly upset at the news."

"Ahhh, I see. So? Did you learn anything that might be useful?"

"I'm not sure. Maybe." She stapled the last two papers

into place and then handed the stapler back to her husband. "Thanks to Mason, I know that he and Johnny were a year ahead of Jake and Noah at Sweet Briar High, and that they, too, played football. I also know that Johnny had been the rising star on the varsity team before Jake and Noah arrived on the scene. But what I *didn't* know was that his being cast to the side *because of them* made his already questionable home life even worse."

"Seriously?"

She followed him into his classroom, and when he veered off in the direction of his desk, she plopped down onto a chair that was a bit too small for a full-sized adult. "That's what Mason said, anyway."

"And so the lousy home life cycle continues . . ." Milo wandered over to the bins of toys intended for rainy days and added a few strays that had been left on the counter. "You'd think firsthand experience would've taught—"

The vibration of his phone cut short his sentence and redirected him back to his desk. He opened the top drawer and pulled out his phone. "It's Doug. From the men's group. I left him a message about your car earlier today, and I'm guessing that's why he's calling back."

She waited as he took the call, his warm greeting for his friend barely processing as her own thoughts rewound back through the day. If what Mason said was true, it made sense that Johnny might have some resentment toward Jake and Noah. While only one had been murdered, the other—if convicted—would be in jail for life. It would be the perfect revenge for someone who felt wronged by the pair. But even if that was true, why now? Why wait almost twenty years to exact that revenge?

"We're in business."

Startled back to the present, she made herself focus on the man smiling at her with an air of triumph. "We are?"

"We are."

"And what business would that be?"

He slipped his phone into the breast pocket of his blazer, retrieved his keys from the same drawer that had housed his phone, and motioned for her to follow. "Your car being up and running again."

"But my car is at Jake's."

"Doug and I are going to pick it up and take it back to his house to smoke out the problem."

"Doug knows cars?"

"He fixes his own when there's an issue, so he knows enough." At the doorway, Milo flicked off the fluorescent overhead lights and pulled shut the door. "Doug seems to think he knows what the issue is, based on the sound I made for him on the phone, and he's pretty confident we can get it taken care of in less than an hour. So"—he pushed up the sleeve of his blazer and consulted his watch—"assuming he's right, I should be home with your car by about six, six fifteen. And that's with a stop at the store to pick up that steak I owe you."

"If you can get my car up and running, I'll give you a pass on the steak."

He grabbed hold of her hand and turned her to him, his normal Milo smile lighting his eyes in that comforting way she treasured so much. "A deal is a deal. But first, I need you to drop me off at Doug's."

"You sure you don't want to just drop me off at the house?"

"Nope. Because if all goes well, I'll be bringing that steak home in *your* car." He tapped her nose with his index finger and then pulled her in for one last hug. "Maybe you can try and get in a nap between now and then. It might make you feel a little better."

She reveled in the warmth of his chest and wished she could stay like that forever. But she couldn't. "I didn't say anything about not feeling well."

"You don't have to. I see it in your eyes."

She drew back. "Why does everyone keep saying that? Do I really look that bad?"

"Did you eat today?"

The question caught her off guard. "I nibbled here and there, between things I had to get done."

"And what did you nibble on, exactly?"

Drat.

"A few pretzels. Maybe a piece of Nina's string cheese. You know, quick stuff."

He kissed the top of her head and then hooked his thumb toward the outer door and the parking lot beyond. When she acquiesced, he fell into step beside her, draping his arm across her shoulders as he did. "Look, I haven't pressed, but I'm well aware of the fact you've been picking at your food these past few days. And I get it, I really do. Finding Noah the way you did was rough. But not eating and not sleeping isn't the answer. If anything, it'll make new problems."

She considered telling him that the incessant churning in her stomach made it so the thought of eating made her nauseous, but she opted to keep that tidbit to herself. The last thing she needed at that moment was a trip to the emergency room for a possible concussion. If things weren't back to normal when Jake was released, she'd come clean then.

For now, though, she needed to extend something resembling an olive branch, if for no other reason than to make him stop worrying. "I'll eat something. I promise. And I'll even make a point of trying to get to bed a little earlier tonight. But right now? After I drop you off? I'd like to make a pit stop in town before I meet you back at the house."

Chapter 26

There were a few distinct things Tori had come to expect the moment she opened the door of Debbie's Bakery—the melodic jingle of the string-mounted bells that announced her arrival, the warm greeting that invariably followed from both staff and patrons, and the way her mouth began to salivate with the first whiff of baked goods. It was why, on a particularly stressful day, she often stopped at the eatery on the way home from work. Because no matter how drained she felt, those three factors always lifted her spirits.

So it was more than a little disconcerting when, after dropping Milo off at his friend's house, the detour she took in the interest of destressing was marred by a wave of nausea so strong she waved off Debbie's greeting in favor of a mad dash for the bathroom trash can. Debbie, of course, followed, arriving just in time to help hold back her hair as Tori voided her stomach of the handful of pretzels and bit of string cheese she'd managed to eat that day.

When she was done, she made her way over to the sink and met Debbie's eyes in the mirror. "I'm sorry. I don't know what came over me out there."

"Please. No apology necessary." Debbie stepped to the sink next to Tori's, pumped soap into her hands, and turned on the faucet. "Feeling any better?"

"I guess. I wasn't aware I was feeling bad when I got here. But, all of a sudden, I walked inside, breathed in something that smelled an awful lot like caramel and chocolate, and that was it." Tori grabbed a paper towel from the dispenser and leaned against the edge of the sink. "Weird, huh?"

"Not if you have a concussion, it's not."

"I'm fine." She stopped, took a deep breath, and released it through her nose until any remaining queasiness was all but gone. "Honestly, I think my stomach is just protesting the stress is all."

"Is everything okay at home? With Milo?"

"Milo is awesome. He really is. In fact, he's probably outside Jake's Garage right now with his friend, trying to get my car up and running sans strange noises." She took another breath, released it, and, when she was sure she was okay, gestured toward the door. "Which, if they're successful, will eliminate some stress right there."

Debbie led the way out to the dining area and over to a table in the far corner. When Tori was settled on one of the high-top lattice stools, the bakery owner slid onto one on the other side of the two-person table. "Have you been walking everywhere?"

"No. Most of the time I've had Milo's car. And when

I didn't, someone always seemed to magically appear with an open passenger seat."

"Good."

Leaning against the back of her chair, Tori took a moment to get a handle on her thoughts, and then addressed her friend. "When you and Colby were starting out, did you worry about stuff?"

"All the time. I worried he'd hate the way I squeezed the toothpaste in the middle; I worried my sleep talking would keep him up all night wishing he hadn't married me; I worried my cooking wouldn't be up to par; I—"

"Wait. You seriously worried your cooking wasn't good enough?" she asked.

"I bake, yes. But making the kinds of dinners Colby was used to with his mom? Yeah, I was worried." Debbie pulled a dishcloth from the waistband of her apron, folded it more neatly, and then tucked it back into place. "And then there was the worry about money."

Tori felt her jaw slacken just before the telltale prick of tears she blinked away. "You worried about money, too?"

"All the time. The last thing I wanted to do was be a drain."

"Don't I know it," she murmured. "The second my car started making that crazy sound on Saturday morning, my heart sank. I mean, we just spent way more than we should have on that weekend getaway to Heavenly, Pennsylvania, in February, and the last thing we need is for my car to conk out."

"It's life, Victoria."

"I guess . . ."

"There's always going to be expenses you didn't count

on—a broken car, a refrigerator that decides to stop working, a pipe that starts leaking, et cetera." Debbie smoothed down the sides of her apron and then leaned forward. "And that's *pre*-kids. Once kids are part of the equation, it's all that stuff I just mentioned *plus* feet that grow a full size overnight, costly field trips, birthday presents for the endless parade of parties they're invited to on a near-weekly basis, and on and on it goes. But everything has a way of working out. The key is being a team. Because when you stand as a team, you can get through just about anything. And the really daunting things that rear their heads on occasion? Even those are easier to handle with that someone special by your side."

Tori traced her finger along the edge of the table, Debbie's words echoing in her head.

"Can I get you something to eat?" Debbie asked, hooking her thumb toward the display case of baked goods. "Maybe one of those caramel brownies you smelled when you walked through the door? Or a piece of pie?"

Tori felt her stomach roil in response and immediately waved off the offer. "I'll pass, but thanks. For the offer and, more importantly, the advice. I needed to hear that."

Debbie reached across the table and covered Tori's hand with her own. "Let the money thing go. If you don't, you'll be turning down brownies for the rest of your life."

"Bite your tongue," she said, laughing. Then, leaning forward, she widened her original field of vision to include the handful of tables on the other side of the bakery. "Have you spoken to Margaret Louise lately?"

At the mention of their fellow sewing sister, Debbie's shoulders sagged. "I check in with her a few times a day just to see if there's any news."

"She's devastated, Debbie. Absolutely devastated. And last night, it was like she'd lost her resolve to keep fighting. And it was heartbreaking to see."

Debbie paused, mid-nod. "Charles said you two are looking into things. Is that true?"

"I'm trying." She traveled her attention from one table to the next, recognizing some faces and trying to place others.

"Have you found anything at all? Anything that might help get Jake out of . . ."

She knew Debbie was still talking—she could see the woman's hands moving in her peripheral vision—but the moment her gaze came to rest on the gray-haired man seated in the opposite corner of the room, everything else faded away.

"That's him!" she whispered.

Debbie's eyebrow quirked upward as she pivoted on her stool. "Who?"

"The private detective Leona supposedly hired to clear Jake." She searched her memory bank for a name and then rushed to supply it as it fell into place. "Frank. The handsome gentleman sitting in the back corner."

"Oh, I love him! He's been in here every day this week so far and he's very friendly. In fact, Emma has taken quite a shine to him. Says he reminds her of her grandfather."

Tori was pretty sure she nodded, but her focus was on Frank. Dressed in a pair of black dress trousers with a short-sleeved white button-down shirt, the private detective sat hunched over what appeared to be a notebook and an open manila folder. Whatever he was reading had his full attention save for an occasional break to take a sip from the powder blue mug to the left of his papers.

"Do you have any idea what he's drinking?" she asked.

"Earl Grey tea."

"Could you make him a fresh cup, on me, that I can deliver to his table?"

Debbie looked as if she was going to ask a question but, in the end, she simply shrugged and slid off the stool. "C'mon, I'll pour you a cup right now."

"Thanks, Deb." She followed the woman over to the counter, chatted briefly with Emma while the tea was being poured, and then carried the steaming liquid over to the man's table.

"Debbie tells me you're drinking Earl Grey?"

Startled, Frank looked up, the smile on his lips reaching into the bluest eyes she'd ever seen. "I am. Thank you." He took the mug, set it on the table next to his nearly empty cup, and then turned back to Tori. "I've met Debbie and Emma, but this is the first time I've been in while you're working. I'm Frank—Frank Porter."

"Actually, I don't work here."

His eyes crackled with surprise. "Oh?"

"I work down the road. At the public library. My name is Tori. Tori Sinclair—"

"Wentworth," he finished. Surprise turned to curiosity as he swept his hand toward the empty chair across from his. "Would you like to sit down for a moment?"

"Yes. Please." Yet as she settled in she suddenly became aware of the fact that this man seated across from her knew her name. And the reason for him knowing it dawned as bright as day.

But before she could come up with something to say, he took the lead. "From what I've been able to gather by talking to Jake, he thinks you and I are working toward the same goal?"

"If that goal is to get him out of that jail cell so the correct person can take his place . . . then yes, we're working toward the same goal."

"You really believe Jake is innocent in Noah Madden's murder?"

"With everything I am."

He studied her closely as he took another, longer sip of his tea. "My client believes otherwise."

"Your client is wrong." She heard the pleading in her voice but could do little to stop it. "I've tried to tell her that, but when she won't take my calls, she makes it impossible to do so."

"You stayed at your sewing circle meeting," he said, his tone more matter-of-fact than accusatory.

"To gather information. That's all."

"Leona is hurt by what she sees as a betrayal."

Clearing her throat of the emotion she felt building, Tori splayed her hands. "There's no basis for that particular hurt. None whatsoever."

"So you really want to clear Jake's name?"

"I really *will* clear Jake's name."

Seconds gave way to minutes as Frank took another sip or two of his tea, pushed his mug to the side, and steepled his fingers beneath his chin. "Leona is a special lady, though I suspect you already know that."

"I do. She's also pigheaded and infuriating. But I love her and I would never, ever turn my back on her." Tori scrubbed her face with her hands before dropping them back down to her lap. "I just need her to believe that . . . as she should."

Silence settled between them, but it wasn't of the uncomfortable variety. Quite the contrary, in fact. There was something about Frank that put her at ease in much the same way Milo did. It was an odd revelation.

"Maybe, if we put our heads together, we can prove it to her."

"How?" she shot back. "She won't take my calls. She— she turns her back when we cross paths. She won't listen to anyone who tries to speak to her on my behalf."

"You clear Jake's name."

"Trust me. I'm trying."

"We try together."

It was her turn to study him. "But you don't even know me."

"I've spoken to Jake. I've spoken to his wife. And I see just how much this misunderstanding where you're concerned is affecting Leona. That tells me enough."

There was no mistaking the way his eyes lit up as he spoke Leona's name, or the way his tone rasped when he did. A little voice inside her head told her to let it go. But the louder voice, the one that was fiercely protective of her friends, didn't listen.

"Did you know Leona before this thing with Jake?"

He fiddled with the handle of his mug. "I wish I could say yes, but I can't."

"I don't understand."

"Leona is . . ." He looked up at the ceiling as if searching for the rest of his sentence. When he found it, he splayed his hands atop the table. "She . . . she's mighty special. Smart, funny, motivated, creative, and sweet."

"Sweet?" Tori echoed, only to cringe at the naked shock in her voice.

Frank pulled his hands toward his body and then used them to brace himself against the edge of the table. "The other day, she spent close to a half hour calling local restaurants and arranging it so a different place will deliver dinner to Melissa's house every night for the rest of this week and all of next. She went through each and every menu, painstakingly picking out the meal she thought each kid would actually eat. And when she was done placing each order, she made sure that everything would be delivered anonymously.

"And her elderly friend—Rose? Leona is always calling her, asking her opinion on stuff at the store they share even though it's quite obvious she is equipped to make the decisions on her own."

Tori felt her mouth dropping open and was powerless to stop it.

"I'm kind of in awe and"—he stopped, cleared his throat—"enamored, truth be told. But she's hired me to clear her nephew's name, and that's exactly what I intend to do."

"You sound awfully convinced he's innocent."

"Because I am." Frank leaned back in his seat. "You see, before I accept a job like this, I research the person I'm being asked to help. If I don't turn up anything suspect, I sit down with the person—one-on-one. If my gut tells me to take the job, I take it."

There were no ifs, ands, or buts about it. She liked this man. She liked his directness. She liked his calm manner. She liked his aura. And she liked the feeling that his attraction to Leona was different—real.

Now, if only he could be, say, twenty years younger. Maybe then he'd actually stand a fighting chance . . .

Without really thinking what she was doing, she told him everything she'd learned so far, including Jessa's over-the-top obsession with Jake, the fact that Jake had insisted she back off not more than two weeks before Noah's murder, and Johnny's reportedly contentious relationship with his father, which had only grown worse because of Jake and Noah.

He listened to everything without interrupting. And when she was done, he nodded. "That's some good detective work there, Victoria. In fact, you got some stuff I missed while checking out Noah's stepfather, Hal Skinner."

Intrigue pulled her forward. "And? Anything there?"

"From what I've been able to tell, he had a decent enough relationship with the victim over the years. Came into the family when Noah was not quite ten. So it's a relationship with some legs behind it. And just to be sure, I did a little checking into whether Noah's life insurance policy lists Skinner as a beneficiary."

"Does it?"

"No. In fact, it's a pretty small policy, and it was left to his mother—whom I absolutely do not consider a suspect."

"Why?"

"Because my source says she's using just about every penny of it to buy a top-of-the-line casket, primo burial plot, gigantic granite tombstone, et al., for Noah."

Tori took it all in, but there wasn't much to process. Nothing game changing, anyway.

"What's your gut?" Frank asked.

"My gut?"

"So far. As to who killed Noah."

It was a question she'd asked herself many times over the past few days—a question that reared its head when she was working, showering, and trying—unsuccessfully—

to sleep at night. But as many times as she'd asked it of herself, it was odd to have it asked by someone else. "I don't know," she said, honestly. "I guess, based on what I know right now, I'd have to say Jessa . . . with the motive being revenge. I mean, she put her whole life on hold under the belief that she'd win Jake back. Then, two weeks before Noah's murder, he sits her down and tells her it's never going to happen. He tells her this in a place filled with people they knew from high school, upping the humiliation factor in her head. And, to top it off, since she had a relationship with Noah, she may have had access to a copy of the contract the police are now seeing as Jake's motive for the crime."

He appeared to mull that over for a while before taking another sip of his tea. "But why kill Noah? I mean, she had to have had at least some feelings for him to date him off and on for, what? Twenty years?"

"I wonder about that, too. But maybe her anger and her resentment toward Jake were stronger than any feelings she might have had for Noah."

Frank drained the last drop of tea from his mug and then set it next to the other one. "It's possible—that's for sure. But my hunch is we're missing something."

"Mine, too."

"So we keep looking," he said. "And, when we're done, Leona will know, beyond a shadow of a doubt, where your loyalty lies."

Chapter 27

"You do realize that's a *rib eye*, right? Grilled to perfection, I might add."

Tori looked up from her plate. "I do."

"Then why aren't you eating it?" Milo set his fork next to his own nearly empty plate and leaned forward against the edge of the patio table. "I even used that special seasoning you like so much."

She wanted to eat it, she really did, but her appetite had disappeared the moment she stepped out the back door and got her first whiff of the cooking meat. "I'm sorry, Milo. I really am. I just can't eat this right now."

The scrape of his chair against the wooden slats of the deck announced his rise mere seconds before the feel of his hand on her upper arm. "C'mon. Let's sit on the Adirondack chairs for a little while and just talk."

He pulled her onto her feet and led her over to the pair

of chairs they'd purchased shortly after their honeymoon in the fall. Positioned on the far end of the deck, they afforded a view of the backyard and the carefully tended flower beds Rose had helped her plan.

Lifting her chin, she savored the breeze that had kicked up over the past twenty minutes. Judging by the clouds building in the distance, she suspected a storm was on the way, but for now, the evening air was perfect.

"I'm feeling it, too, if that helps."

"Feeling what?" she asked.

"This stuff with Jake." Milo tilted his head against the back of the chair. "It's like it's sucking all that is good out of this town."

She wished she could argue, but she couldn't.

"It's all anyone can talk about in the faculty lounge. Like it's a three-ring circus that's come to town."

"I know." Tori let her eyes wander across the dusk-filled yard before bringing them back to the deck and her husband. "People aren't even trying to be subtle in the gossip department. I hear people talking about it at the library all the time. And even this afternoon, after I dropped you off at Doug's, I overheard more than a few people talking about it at Debbie's."

"I didn't know you stopped at the bakery."

Shrugging, she swung her attention back to the sky. "But you know me, and you know that's one of my go-to spots for a pick-me-up."

He squeezed her hand and then released it long enough to wag a disapproving finger. "Ahhhh, the truth behind the uneaten steak comes out . . ."

Mustering a burst of energy she didn't really have, Tori reached out, grabbed his finger, and lowered it back down to her armrest. "Actually, Mr. Know-It-All, I'll have you know I didn't eat anything while I was there."

He drew back. "No caramel brownies?"

Her stomach swirled. "No."

"No Boston cream pie?"

"No."

"No gooey butter cake?"

"No."

"No peanut butter cup parfait?"

Aware of an unpleasant taste rising in her throat, Tori merely shook her head.

"Who are you, and what have you done with my wife?" Milo joked.

She shrugged again. "I think I've found the perfect diet. I just wish my three best friends didn't have to be struggling the way that they are in order for me to stop eating."

And it was true. Seeing Margaret Louise so upset over Jake, watching Rose suffer the ill effects of aging, and knowing Leona doubted their friendship had kicked off a constant state of unrest in Tori's heart and stomach.

Milo's smile disappeared. "A diet? Are you kidding me? You look fantastic."

"I'm not *trying* to diet, Milo. I'm really not. I like treats way too much to even consider that, but this stuff that's going on right now isn't really giving me much of a choice."

"I hear you, baby, but you have to eat. You getting sick won't help Margaret Louise or Rose."

He was right, and she knew it. But for whatever reason, her head and her stomach were having difficulty getting in sync. "I just want to fix everything, you know? Get it back to the way it's supposed to be—where everyone is happy . . . and healthy."

"As do I. But right now, at this moment? I'll take sitting here with you, enjoying the night air, and knowing that you're my wife."

She pushed through the sleepy fog she felt descending and laughed. "A wife who no longer needs to hijack your car."

"So true." When their laughter faded, he cocked his head and studied her closely. "All joking aside, I hope you know how much I treasure you. Treasure this relationship. It's based on love and respect—the kind of relationship I wish all my students could see in their homes."

"You're talking about that little girl who would give flowers to all the mommies if she was mayor, aren't you?"

"Hannah."

"Maybe her parents will surprise you and get their act together."

"That's not going to happen." Milo raked a hand through his hair and released a long, weighted sigh. "But I'll settle for her getting out of that war zone sooner rather than later."

Despite the subject matter at hand, she couldn't help but smile. "Hannah will be okay, one way or the other. After all, she's got a really awesome teacher looking out for her."

A comfortable silence settled between them as they watched the approaching storm. For Tori, it was a chance to think back on her day—to relish the good parts, to think through the not-so-great parts, and to take stock of the parts that had been unexpected.

"I met Leona's private investigator this afternoon. At Debbie's." She tugged her feet from her sling-back shoes and then tucked them next to her on the chair. "I like him.

A lot. He's very"—she stopped, looked up at the sky, then looked back at Milo—"genuine."

"But he's her age, right?"

"I can't say for sure, but I'm putting him in his early to mid-sixties. But he's handsome in the way George Clooney is handsome."

"I'm sorry," he said, and leaned his ear toward her chair. "I think I misheard. You did say he's handsome in the way Milo Wentworth is, yes?"

It felt good to laugh. Like, for at least a little while, life wasn't so hard.

Milo grinned. "Okay, good. That's what I thought I heard." He scooted forward and off his chair and then hovered his hand above hers. "Come with me for a second. I want to show you something."

She stood and followed him over to the edge of the deck, her curiosity aroused. But when he stopped, he swept his hand out across the same backyard she'd seen every day since they'd returned from their honeymoon. "Okay . . ."

"Remember that pergola Diane Weatherly was talking about putting in behind Sleep Heavenly?"

As nice as the laughter had been, there was no denying the instant calm that came over her as she thought back over their weekend getaway to Heavenly, Pennsylvania. Everything about that trip had created the kind of memories she knew she'd treasure for years to come. She'd loved the pace, the tone, the Amish tours, and the hours spent poking in the shops along Lighted Way. But more than all of that, she'd loved their time with Diane Weatherly, her niece, Claire, and Claire's boyfriend, Jakob Fisher, most of all.

"Do I ever," she whispered. "Those plans were amazing, weren't they? I could just see sitting out there, after dinner, watching the sun set over the Amish fields. And the little white lights she said will come on at nightfall? Can't you just imagine how magical that will be?"

"I wish you could see yourself right now."

She looked up at Milo. "Why?"

"Because then you'd understand why I want to see you like this all the time."

"See me like what?"

"Happy. And at peace."

Reaching up, she bookended his face with her hands and kissed him softly. "Milo, being here with you is what makes me happy. Never doubt that. Anything you're seeing to the contrary right now is because of everything else—Jake, Margaret Louise, Leona, Rose . . ."

"I get that. I have things that weigh on me, too. But when we're here, with each other, I want it to be the one place where we can detox from all the things we can't fix in life. A safe spot, for lack of a better word."

"And it is." She kissed him one more time and then snuggled into her favorite spot against his chest. "Just sitting out here with you has made things better."

"For me, too." He rested his lips atop her head for a moment and then stepped back. "I was thinking that maybe we could make that safe spot even nicer—more magical."

"Oh?"

"I saw Diane's drawing."

"I know that. You and Jakob talked about it for nearly an hour that one night . . ."

"That's why I'm confident I can build one just like it."

He gestured toward the yard again. "Right here. There's plenty of room. And I could even bring in an electrician so you could put up those same little white lights Diane was talking about."

She wanted to protest, to point out the fact that a pergola was something they didn't need in the grand scheme of things, but she couldn't. Not with this. "Milo, I love it. I really do."

His smile was back, along with the dimples she loved. "Then it's settled. I'll start drawing up some plans so I can figure out the materials we'll need to make it happen."

"When it's done, we'll have to send a picture to Diane so she can see it."

"I agree." Milo pulled her close once more, his breath warm against the top of her head. "I love you, Tori."

"I love you, too."

Chapter 28

Tori looked around the Green, half expecting to see one of the hundred or so people flocking toward the road to be holding a plate of fried dough in their hands. But despite the tables strewn with food to her left and to her right, and the volume of cars parked around the entire perimeter, the floral easels standing sentry beside the poster-sized picture of Noah Madden removed any doubt as to what had just transpired.

She'd hoped to make it to the memorial, but a snafu with the computers at the library had made that impossible. Still, she couldn't stay away completely.

Wandering across the open space, she tried not to stare at the hearse or the mourners now seated in their cars waiting to follow it to the cemetery on the outskirts of town. She hadn't really known Noah beyond his name and an occasional sighting around town, but there was no denying the utter silence that hung heavy in the air. It was as if the birds and squirrels that normally frequented the Green in the hopes of finding a scrap from someone's picnic lunch sensed there was something different about today.

"They were all here."

Startled, Tori spun around, only to slump in relief as her gaze came to rest on Frank. "You scared me," she said, pressing her hand to her chest.

His smile disappeared, wiped away by tangible regret. "I'm sorry, Victoria. I figured you saw me when you first walked up." He wedged a manila envelope between his elbow and his body and pointed toward the gazebo and its view of both the temporary stage tasked with housing Noah's picture and flowers and the parade of cars now on the move. "I found a bench before things officially kicked off, and stayed there through the whole thing."

"I intended to come, but we had an issue at the library and I couldn't get away until now." When she was sure her breath had returned to normal, she took in their surroundings one more time. "Looks like a lot of folks turned out to say good-bye to Noah."

"And all the players were here. Jessa Thomas, Noah's stepfather, Tawny Wright, Johnny Duckworth, and Mason Wheeler."

She swung her focus back toward the funeral procession and watched as the last few cars turned left and disappeared from sight. "They always say in movies and books that it's not unusual for a murderer to show up at the funeral of his victim. Do you think that's really true?"

"I'm here, aren't I?"

"Anything strike you as odd about any of them?" she asked.

"The on-again, off-again girlfriend wore sunglasses the whole time, so I couldn't get a good gauge on her emotions."

"You mean Jessa?"

Frank nodded. "Once or twice, I thought I saw her shoulders hitch as they might if she was crying, but I can't be sure. She could've sneezed for all I know."

"Was she with anyone?"

"Her friend—the pottery store owner . . . Tawny. And a whole group of people that reacted whenever Noah's high school years were mentioned."

"Former classmates, I'm guessing?"

"That's my guess as well. And the bigger fellas? That all sat in a row behind Jessa? Were likely former teammates based on the fact Johnny and Mason were in that same row."

"Anything jump out at you about either of them or Tawny?"

"Not really. I saw Mason looking over his shoulder a few times, but I couldn't tell what he was looking at. Though, at one point, he jabbed Johnny in the side, said something to him, and he, too, looked in the same direction, but just once and only for a split second."

She took it all in, processed it quickly, and then plopped down onto one of the folding chairs. "The key to all of this has to be that contract that was sent to the police station. If we could just figure out who had access to it, we'd have a starting place. But Margaret Louise keeps insisting Jake wouldn't have given it to anyone."

"But he did." Frank dislodged the envelope from its holding place and handed it to Tori. "I managed to get a copy of what was sent to the chief."

Tori unhooked the clasp and opened the flap, her eyes darting between the envelope and Frank. "They just gave it to you?" At his half shrug, half nod, she reached inside and pulled out a single sheet of paper. "Margaret Louise wasn't kidding, was she?" she asked, flipping it over on her lap. "It really is just this one paragraph."

"Why send more when that one does such a great job of handing the chief a motive?" he said. "With Jake Davis as the perfect suspect?"

"It's literally the most damning provision of the entire contract." She read and reread the paragraph—every word, every sentence exactly as she remembered it. "With Noah's and Jake's initials at the bottom, to boot."

Frank took the chair next to hers and waited until her eyes were on his. "I know it's not looking good right now, Victoria, but you've got to keep the faith. Someone other than Jake killed Noah. Right now, he's lying low, watching his steps. But with Noah's body about to be lowered into the ground, and Jake sitting in jail for the crime, our guy is going to get sloppy. And when he does, we're gonna nail him."

"Charles is on the phone."

Tori looked from the computer to the fall book catalog and added yet another title to her handwritten order list. "Please tell him I'm busy right now, but that I'll give him a call on my way home from work."

"I'll take care of this; you take his call," Nina said.

Looking back at the computer screen, Tori shook her head. "No, really, I'll call him as soon as I can. I need to figure out what we're ordering for fall." She scrolled down to the next batch of holds. "Oh, and tell him my car is fixed, so if he's calling to see if I need a ride, I'm—"

"Victoria, you want to take his call. *Now.*"

A chill skittered down her spine as she finally looked up at her assistant, the woman's dark face grave. "What's wrong? Is it"—she stopped, took in the clock at the bottom of her screen, and swallowed—"*Rose?*"

Nina's shoulders rose and fell with great effort. "I don't know. He didn't say. But I know he doesn't sound good."

If Nina said anything else, she couldn't be sure. All she was conscious of in that moment was the near-deafening roar in her head as she abandoned her stool and ran for her office. Once inside, she dropped onto her desk chair and lifted the phone from its cradle. "Charles?"

"Rose cried today," Charles half whispered, half sobbed.

The chill that had reared its head by the information desk performed an encore so strong she actually shivered. "Is she hurt?"

"No."

"Did she get stuck on the floor again?" She closed her eyes against the image of Rose lying on her back between the bed and the wall, her body too weak to move on her own.

"No."

She felt her head beginning to pound. "Did she lose one of her friends?"

"No."

"Then why did she cry?"

"Because she wants to keep living by herself," Charles said between sniffles. "But she's afraid of what could happen if she needs help and no one is nearby."

"Did something happen to kick this conversation off?"

"I called her a little while ago, just to check in, see if she wanted anything from Debbie's on my way home from work. She asked what was going on with Jake and I told her there was nothing new to report." Charles paused, said something to someone in the background, and then continued. "I mentioned the memorial service on the Green for Noah and how all of Sweet Briar seemed to be there to bid farewell to one of its own. And that's when the crying started. She said she should have been there, that she's known Noah his whole life. But her stupid body was changing everything—stupid being *her* word, not mine, sugar lips."

She dropped her head into her free hand and groaned. "Ugh. I should have thought about that, that she'd want to go. Where is my head these days?"

The sniffling ceased in her ear. "Are you really asking that question, sugar lips? Because I can answer that. Your head is in too many places, that's where. It's on Jake and trying to clear him of a murder he didn't commit, it's on Margaret Louise and how much she's hurting about Jake, it's on Leona and the fact that she's cut you out of her life, it's on whatever made you turn down *chocolate* at Debbie's yesterday, and it's on your car being on the fritz and the expense you're afraid that's going to—"

"Milo fixed my car. It's sitting in the parking lot as we speak."

"Well, well, well, that's one off the list."

"And how did you know I turned down . . ." She let the sentence die as she remembered where she was living and who was on the phone. "I'm going to stop by and see Rose on my way home. I'll keep you posted."

Chapter 29

She tried the usual topics—gardening, the previous night's TV game show contestants, and sewing, but nothing seemed to reach Rose. It was as if the elderly woman's occasional nods and grunts were part of some autopilot setting more than anything resembling genuine engagement.

Finally, when it became apparent she was getting nowhere, Tori gave up her spot on the floral couch in favor of the floor beside Rose's favorite chair. "Rose, I know you're having a tough time right now, and it breaks my heart to see you so upset. But you have me. I'm not going anywhere. And neither is anyone else. We love you."

Rose reached up, removed her bifocals from the bridge of her nose, and placed them atop her folding snack tray. "I never wanted to have children of my own. I liked teaching, and watching my students learn and grow, but I was just fine when the end of the year came and it was time for them to move on to first grade."

"You impacted a lot of lives in this town," Tori said, only to have her sentiment waved off with a dismissive hand.

"When I was a young woman, there were really only two acceptable professions—teaching and nursing. Aside from that, it was being a mother." Rose tipped the back of her head against her chair and lifted her gaze to the ceiling. "I embraced the teaching part, but never the mother part."

Not sure how to respond to the unexpected turn in conversation, Tori simply stayed quiet and waited.

"That's why I never got married." Rose paused. "That and the fact I was content on my own and never felt as if a man was necessary. And until you came along, I had no regrets."

"Until *I* came along?"

"Having you here is like having a granddaughter of my own. Only you're not mine."

Rising up onto her knees, she sandwiched Rose's hand between her own and squeezed. "A long time ago, while out shopping with my great-grandmother, I came across an expression that I thought was kind of silly. It was on this really pretty wall hanging with flowers and butterflies. In the center, in fancy black lettering, it said, *Friends are the family we choose for ourselves.*

"I thought it was silly because my family was my family. Period. But since moving here and meeting you, I get it loud and clear. Because you, and Margaret Louise, and Leona are my family. When you're happy, I'm happy. When you're sad, I'm sad. And when you hurt, I hurt."

She took a breath, cleared her throat, and did her best to power through the emotion now hanging on her every word. "When something good happens in my life, I want to pick up the phone and tell you all about it. When I'm worried or feeling blue, I have this need to come here—to simply be here. It's as if, by your very presence, I know I'm safe.

"You get angry when I call you before I go to bed because you're convinced I'm checking up on you. And maybe there's some truth to that. But the main reason I call is because I like to hear your voice, to know you're there . . . because you *are* my family, Rose. Don't ever, *ever* doubt that."

Rose closed her eyes, but not before a tear escaped down her weathered cheek. "I don't know what I did in life to deserve you, Victoria."

"You're you." She wiped the woman's tear away while blinking back a few of her own. "I know you're having a tough time right now, Rose. But I'm no more than a phone call away—twenty-four/seven."

"I don't want to be a burden."

"You're not now, nor will you ever be, a burden. I love you. We just need to build up your strength and get you back to your happy place. When we do, I think you'll—"

"It's time to sell the house."

She sucked in a breath. "Sell your house? C'mon, Rose, you don't mean that."

Slowly, Rose lowered her chin until her gaze mingled with Tori's. "I can and I do. It's time I look into one of those assisted-living places in Tom's Creek."

"You don't need that! You're fine. This is just a speed bump is all."

Rose hooked a trembling finger beneath Tori's chin and held it there. "Even if you're right, and I certainly pray that you are, this place is just too much for me now. When I have energy, I want to use it on things that matter."

"You . . . you could move in with Milo and me!"

Rose laughed softly. "I may not have any firsthand experience at being married, Victoria, but I'm quite sure opening your day-to-day life to someone my age isn't high on the list of smart ideas."

"We can make it work. I know we can."

"No, Victoria. All my life I've lived on my own and I intend to keep it that way."

"But you're talking about—"

"An assisted-living facility. Where I'll have my own apartment and my independence . . . with someone nearby in case I need them." Rose retrieved her glasses and slid them into place. "Now, if you don't mind, I think I'd like to eat that hamburger you brought with you. And I'll even take a few of those fries I'm smelling, while you're at it."

Tori was drying the last of the dinner dishes when she heard the knock at the back door. "Milo? Are you expecting someone?"

"No."

Shrugging, she added the final plate to the stack and then crossed to the door to find a familiar face peeking back.

"Margaret Louise!" Tori swung open the door, stepping back as she did. "Come in! Come in! Isn't this a wonderful surprise!"

"My twin is always tellin' me it's rude to stop by

without callin' first, but I wasn't really plannin' on comin' by." Unzipping the jacket of her polyester running suit, Margaret Louise let out a sigh. "I just started walkin' and this is where my feet took me."

"And I'm glad they did." She kissed the woman on the cheek and then directed her toward the table. "Would you like some tea? Or some soda?"

"With as much walkin' as I just did, I reckon a water would be nice."

"Coming right up."

She filled three glasses with water, poured some pretzels into a bowl, and carried everything to the table as Milo's head popped around the corner.

"Margaret Louise—this is a nice surprise."

"That's what Victoria here just said."

"That's because it's true." At Milo's nod, Tori took his chair and studied their guest, noting the dark circles under the woman's eyes and the uncharacteristic slump to her shoulders. "Tell us."

Margaret Louise helped herself to a pretzel but stopped short of actually eating it. "Noah was buried today."

"I know."

"On one hand, I can't imagine what his mama is goin' through, knowin' she ain't never gonna see her boy again." Margaret Louise stared down at her pretzel even though it was painfully obvious her mind was seeing something completely different. "Her cryin' ain't never gonna end."

Unsure of what to say, Tori scooted her chair closer to her friend's and waited.

"But I get that cryin' part. Every single time my grandbabies are lookin' the other way, I'm wipin' my eyes 'bout

Jake. Wonderin' if I'm ever goin' to be able to give him a proper hug again—one without some nosy guard thinkin' I'm tryin' to hand him a knife or somethin'. And that's *if* my boy will even see me at all."

Tori looked to Milo for help, but even he seemed at a loss. "Margaret Louise, I know we're spinning our wheels right now, but I think Frank is right. It's only a matter of time before whoever did this gets sloppy."

"I want to believe that, Victoria, I really do. But I feel like I'm losin' hope with each passin' day."

"Don't. Please." She tried her best to infuse her voice with some semblance of reassurance, but it was hard.

"I've been feelin' so helpless since all this started. Like I should be out there investigatin' with you, the way we do. But Melissa and them youngins need me."

"Trust me, Margaret Louise. I'll figure this out." She swung her attention back to Milo. "Could you get that manila envelope I put on the desk in the sewing room?"

"Sure thing."

When he left, she nudged the still-untouched water glass closer to her friend. "I know I've asked you this before, but I still think it's important to try and figure out who had access to Jake's contract with Noah. Even if it's someone he just shared it with over a cup of coffee or a beer."

Milo returned with the envelope and handed it to Tori.

"It's like I told you b'fore, Victoria, Jake is a private person."

Tori flipped the envelope over, unhooked the clasp, and slipped the copy Frank had given her out and onto the table. "But someone had to have had access—"

"That ain't Jake's."

"Yes it is—*see*?" She pointed to the initials at the bottom of the page. "JD—Jake Davis."

"Jake's initials are JTD," Margaret Louise said. "Like his daddy's."

"M-maybe he left off the *T* this time."

"He doesn't leave off the *T*."

She looked from her friend to the paper and back again, confusion making it difficult to think. "But he did."

"I showed you the whole contract the other day, Victoria. Each and every page, includin' this one, has the *T*."

"Then how—"

"It's from someone else's contract."

Tori turned and stared at her husband as the meaning behind his words hit with a one-two punch. "Someone else's contract?" she echoed. "But—"

And then she knew.

"JD isn't Jake Davis," she whispered. "It's . . . *Johnny Duckworth*."

Chapter 30

It made sense.

Sort of.

Johnny Duckworth had had a contentious relationship with his father—a relationship further strained by the besting of Johnny as star quarterback on his high school team by both Jake Davis and Noah Madden.

But why exact revenge now? Twenty years after the fact?

She looked at Milo across the top edge of her favorite throw pillow and then released it back onto the couch. "You look as confused as I feel."

Shaken from his own thoughts, he pushed off the couch and wandered around the living room, his path taking him almost to the mantel before he doubled back. "There's some of that, I guess. But really, I'm more worried about Hannah."

"Hannah?"

He stopped. "I really thought she was going to get the chance to be a semi-normal eight-year-old soon."

"I don't understand."

"Hannah Duckworth is Johnny's kid, Tori."

She heard the gasp around her hand a split second before a wave of guilt pushed her back against the sofa. "Oh, Milo, I didn't realize . . . I—I was so focused on figuring it out and Margaret Louise's reaction and then you driving her home . . ." The words fell away as she stood and followed him to the window overlooking the street.

"It's not your fault," he murmured. "You didn't tell him to kill Noah. You didn't tell him to stuff Noah in the trunk of his own car. And you didn't tell him to frame Jake for the crime with that contract."

Threading her arms through his, she rested her cheek against his back. "But I should have put the names together, and I didn't. Honestly, that's because Johnny was never really on my radar, for all the same reasons I'm struggling with it now."

"I remember when Hannah started at the school. She was always smiling. And from what the kindergarten teacher said, eager to learn. All of that carried into and through most of first grade." Gently, he loosened her hold until he could step away. Then, turning to face her, he leaned back against the window, his eyes hooded. "We all saw the change toward the end of last year. Hannah smiled less, played by herself on the playground, and no longer seemed to care about her work. The first grade teacher called the home and talked to Tina, Hannah's mother. Tina said only that Johnny had lost another job thanks to his dad."

"His dad?"

Milo played with the tasseled rope tasked with holding the curtain away from the window and shrugged. "Again, based on things Hannah has said, it sounds like Johnny travels to Florida every few months to visit his dad in some nursing home. When he goes during the summer, he takes her with him. When he goes during the school year, she's always extra quiet that whole week."

She found her thoughts rewinding to her conversation with Mason Wheeler and the bits and pieces she'd learned about Johnny at that time. "Actually, now that you say that, I think his dad might have dementia or Alzheimer's or something."

"Maybe. I can't say one way or the other." Milo cupped his mouth briefly and then resumed his aimless wandering. "So this year, when Hannah came into my class, I noticed right off the bat that she just wasn't the same kid. She talked back, she picked fights with the other girls, she stole things out of her classmates' desks, and on and on it went. Knowing what I did about the stuff at home, I knew it was likely a cry for attention, so I tried to be extra patient—to talk with her about her behavior and why it was unacceptable. And, after a while, she opened up a little about the fighting at home. From things she said, it sounded pretty awful."

"Poor kid."

"Talking about it helped . . . some. She wasn't the way she'd been at the start, but she was better. I tried to get her to focus on the things that made her smile—like her walks with her dad, and the bedtime stories he'd tell her sometimes. Then, when he made that deal with Noah that allowed him to purchase the land out by Ramey Pond for a paintball field, she was beside herself with excitement. She was going to get to *help her daddy* with his business."

"Help? Help how?"

"He was going to let her help package up the paintballs for his customers," Milo said as he reached the dining room and headed back. "*Hannah* was excited because it meant she and her dad were going to get to have lots of time together. *I* was excited because it had her smiling and, as a side benefit, it would also have her counting and doing simple math problems."

"So she has a good relationship with her dad?" she asked.

"From what I can gather, yes. He's very good with her." Milo took a breath and stopped. "Anyway, she walks into my classroom on Monday, and bursts into tears. I mean, she just lost it. When it became obvious this was something major, I asked the principal to cover my class so I could talk to her."

"Wait. Why didn't you tell me about this?"

"That was the night of your sewing circle meeting. When all hell broke loose between Leona and Dixie, remember?" Milo stopped in front of the mantel, adjusted their wedding photo a bit more to the right, and then lowered himself onto the hearth. "So I bring Hannah into the office, sit her down, and ask her what's wrong. She tells me she's not going to get to count paintballs with her daddy because there isn't going to be any paintball."

"Did she elaborate?"

"No, and I didn't press. She's only eight. But I imagine it's related to the divorce. I mean, assuming they have to split everything fifty-fifty, half that field wouldn't be big enough for a paintball field." He dropped his forearms onto his thighs and sighed, loudly. "I thought maybe her mother might say something on Wednesday night, but she didn't."

"Wednesday night?" she echoed.

Milo nodded down at the floor. "Parent-teacher conferences, remember?"

"Oh. Right. I forgot about that. So how bad was it?"

"It?"

"Dealing with Hannah's parents?" She returned to the couch, pulling her feet onto the cushion beside her.

He unclasped his hands and braced them against the brick hearth on either side of his body. "Frankly, I'd have rather had Johnny there, because I think he actually gives a damn about his daughter, but he was still in Florida and wasn't due back until the next day."

"I take it this Tina is pretty awful?"

Milo hesitated, his reluctance to say anything negative not really a surprise. But, eventually, he shrugged a nod. "She's . . . difficult."

"Mason seems to think she's controlling."

Milo laughed, the sound void of anything resembling humor. "Controlling, arrogant, stuck on herself, not terribly bright, take your pick."

"Does she at least get along with the other moms?"

"That would imply she embraces *her own role* as a mom."

An overwhelming sadness crashed down around her as she thought of the little girl who believed flowers and sunshine could fix things. "I feel awful for this little girl."

"So do I."

"Have I met Tina?" she asked.

"I don't know. I doubt it. Hannah would have been out of the Toddler Story Time age when you moved here, and I'm guessing that's not something Tina would have done with her, anyway."

"What does she look like?"

Milo scrubbed at his face as his gaze fixed on the wall behind Tori. "Five four, maybe. Blonde. Blue eyes. Muscular build. My female colleagues are always commenting on her clothes in relation to Hannah's."

"Meaning?" she prodded.

"Whatever money Tina saves by shopping garage sales for *Hannah's* clothes goes toward Tina's wardrobe." Milo paused, shook his head, and then pushed off the hearth and onto his feet. "I'm sorry I'm being such a downer, baby, I really am. I'm thrilled you found what you needed to clear Jake. I'm just worried about Hannah in the fallout, you know?"

She met him in the center of the room and stepped into his arms, the warmth of his breath against her head helping to settle the incessant churning in her stomach. "And that, Milo Wentworth, is one of many, many things I love about you."

It was just shy of five in the morning when her phone rang, rousing them from a slumber that, at least for Tori, was already spotty at best. Milo fumbled for the lamp while Tori hoisted herself up and onto her elbow.

Please don't let it be about Rose . . .

Please don't let it—

The thought died as she plucked the phone off her

nightstand and stared down at the smiling face on the screen. Hitting the button, she held the phone to her cheek and waited for the pounding in her chest to stop.

"You didn't wait, did you?"

Sniffle.

"Margaret Louise?"

Sniffle. Sniffle.

Tori sat all the way up, pulling the phone closer to her cheek. "You went to the station tonight, didn't you?"

"I just couldn't let my Jake spend even one more night in that jail for somethin' he didn't do. So I called Chief Dallas the second Milo dropped me off at the house and demanded he meet me at the station. He started grousin', of course, but I told him I'd make his life a livin' hell if he made me wait 'til mornin'."

"Okay, I'm listening . . ."

"Melissa called Leona to come and stay with the kids."

"Wait," Tori said, mid-gasp. "*Leona* stayed with the kids?"

"They were sleepin', Victoria. It's not like she was actually takin' care of them."

"But, we're talking about Leona . . ."

"I had no other choice."

"I would have offered if I knew you were going to take Jake's contract to the station right then instead of in the morning."

"I just couldn't wait. And you need your sleep, Victoria. You look awful."

She pulled the phone from her ear, verified she was, indeed, talking to Margaret Louise and not the woman's opinionated-to-a-fault twin sister, Leona, and then resumed the conversation. "So what happened?"

"Melissa and I showed Robert Jake's actual contract

with Noah, and we made him show us the snippet that was sent to him in the mail."

"Surely, he saw the difference, yes?"

"He did. Even had one of his officers haul Johnny Duckworth to the station for questionin'. But Johnny has an alibi for the day Noah was murdered."

"An alibi? How?"

"Johnny was in Florida visitin' his daddy. He has proof of his flights, *and* the staff at the nursin' home verified he'd been there all of last weekend."

She felt Milo pull away from his spot next to her ear, the confusion she saw in his eyes surely a mirror of her own.

"Okay, but the chief has to realize Jake didn't kill Noah, either."

"He says there's no gettin' 'round the fact Noah was found in the trunk of his car while Jake was workin' on it. And that my Jake's prints are on the murder weapon."

"But how can he discount the fact that someone deliberately sent the most damaging part of Jake's contract to him? I mean, surely that has to give him at least a little pause, yes?"

"Nothin' gives Robert pause except a can of beer and a fishin' lure."

"Did Johnny at least confirm that paragraph came from his contract?" Milo whispered.

She relayed the question on to Margaret Louise, earning them three sniffles and a whispered yes in return.

Milo dropped back down onto his pillow. "This is just weird. Who would have sent—"

She knew Milo was still talking, knew Margaret Louise was still sniffling, but at that moment, two entirely different conversations were cycling through her thoughts . . .

"Johnny Duckworth just purchased a big chunk of that land out by Ramey Pond that he's getting ready to turn into a paintball field, much to the chagrin of a few developers . . ."

"I mean, assuming they have to split everything fifty-fifty, half that field wouldn't be big enough for a paintball field . . ."

"Wait a minute," she said aloud. "Half of a whole would be better than half of a half . . ."

Milo looked at her funny while Margaret Louise sniffled once again.

"Half of a whole would be better than half of a half," she repeated.

"There's no reason to be repeatin' yourself, Victoria. I heard you the first—"

"Wait. Stop!" She pulled her hand down her face as she struggled with the last piece she needed to make her theory fit. "Milo? When you said Johnny's wife was muscular, did you mean toned?"

"No, I meant muscular. As in lifts weights."

"Could she pick you up if she tried?" Tori asked.

His pillow creased beneath his head as he drew back. "Pick me up? I doubt it. But knock me over, maybe."

"Oh my God . . ."

Milo shot upright. "Tori, what's wrong?"

"I know who did it. I know who killed Noah!"

Chapter 31

Tori pulled her forehead from its resting spot against the passenger-side window and turned to Milo. "Can you go a little faster? Please?"

"We're almost there."

"I shouldn't have said it was Tina in front of her. I should have just hung up and called the police."

"You couldn't have known she was going to do this."

"I could have, and I should have. This is Margaret Louise we're talking about . . ."

"It's okay, baby. She's going to be fine."

"You don't know that," she said, returning her attention to the houses and trees whizzing past her window. "I can't imagine someone being that desperate for money that they'd a) kill someone, and b) try to destroy a second person in the process."

"Jake was the perfect fall guy. Because of his history

with Noah—both on the field, and, most recently, as a business partner with the same contract clause that motivated Tina to kill Noah in the first place."

"And don't forget the fact that Jake left the garage for a limited time just about every night, giving her both the perfect setting and the perfect time frame in which to make her move," Tori said. "The fact that Jake picked up the bloodied crowbar and actually used it before the body was found was just the proverbial icing on the cake."

The trees and houses began to slow as they rounded the next corner. "Milo, please, I need you to go faster."

"We're here." He pulled to a stop in front of a small bungalow-style home and cut the engine. "And there's her car."

Sure enough, Margaret Louise's powder blue station wagon was parked in the driveway, the driver's-side door open with no sign of the driver anywhere. Tori unhooked her seat belt and unlocked her door.

"Tori, wait! Frank and the chief will be here any minute."

"And any minute could be too late." She threw open her door and jumped out of the car, the pounding in her chest making it difficult to breathe. "Please! We have to go inside; we have to make sure she's okay."

He met her on the curb and, together, they ran up the walkway, the familiar voice inside guiding their every step.

"Don't you move an inch, young lady, or I'll cloud up and rain all over you! I'll cut off your water and take out the meter! I'll knock a knot on your head and dare it to rise! I'll—"

"Margaret Louise!" Tori yanked open the front screen

and dashed inside, Milo close on her heels. "Margaret Louise, where are you?"

"I'm in the kitchen, Victoria. Cleanin' up the trash."

Tori rounded the corner and stopped, her mouth gaping open at the sight of the woman Milo had described bound to a chair with a . . .

Jump rope?

Standing over the woman, in what appeared to be polyester pajamas, was Margaret Louise, with a bright pink baseball bat at the ready.

"Where's Hannah?" Milo barked.

"I sent her and her daddy out for a mornin' walk." Margaret Louise thumped the top of the bat up and down against her pudgy hand, her eyes never leaving Tina Duckworth. "Told him to bring her by Melissa's and then come right back."

The sound of screeching tires wafted into the house moments before first Frank and then a handful of Sweet Briar police officers stormed inside. Frank took the bat from Margaret Louise while the officers untied and handcuffed Tina.

"She tried to ruin my boy's life," Margaret Louise wailed as she dropped into a kitchen chair and buried her face in her hands. "She tried to ruin my Jake."

Tori stepped to the side to allow the officers room to escort Tina out of the kitchen, down the hall, and outside to a waiting patrol car. When they were gone, she made her way over to her friend and squatted down beside her chair. "I wish you would have waited for the police, mama bear."

"Mama bears don't wait for nothin', Victoria."

"I see that."

Footsteps in the hall made them all turn.

"What on earth happened here?" Johnny asked, his eyes darting from Milo, to Frank, to Tori, before finally settling on Margaret Louise. "Where's Tina?"

Margaret Louise stood, took back her bat from Frank, and propped it against the wall alongside Hannah's bright pink scooter. "They say every garden has some weeds, young man. And I just got rid of yours."

Chapter 32

A week later

Tori handed the bowl of potato salad to Charles, and the bowl of macaroni salad to Beatrice, and led the way out to the deck, her own hands full with hamburger buns and the covered plate of tomatoes. "This should be the last of it."

"I'm telling you, sugar lips, I've been dreaming about Milo's hamburgers since you sent out the invite for this little soiree." Charles set his bowl on the table next to the chips, only to change his mind and move it closer to the macaroni salad. When he was pleased with the aesthetics of the table, he stole a chip from the chip bowl and popped it into his mouth. "So, inquiring minds want to know . . ."

She gave Milo the high sign that they were ready and

then turned her attention back on her spiky-haired friend. "About Leona, you mean?"

"Did you invite her?"

"Of course."

She followed his gaze across the deck and out into the backyard. "Then why isn't she here?"

"I can't answer that." She intended to sound carefree, but if the expression on Charles's face was any indication, she'd fallen short. Still, she wanted to enjoy the day, to savor time with the people who'd chosen to be there, to celebrate Jake's release and—

A kiss on her cheek caught her by surprise and she turned to find Frank holding a powder blue box with the Debbie's Bakery logo emblazoned on the front. Beside him, wearing an unreadable expression on her flawlessly made-up face, was Leona.

"Leona!" Tori started to reach for a hug but stopped. "I am so sorry I made you doubt my—"

"No, dear. It is I who should be apologizing." Leona gathered Tori's hands in her own. "You've never given me any reason not to trust you, and yet I didn't. I was wrong."

Tori felt herself start to sway a split second before Leona's hold tightened. "Victoria? Are you okay? You look a little"—she followed Leona's gaze to Frank before it came back to her with a rare and heartfelt tenderness—"peaked."

Wait . . .

Where were the unsolicited makeup tips?

Where was the reminder that *marriage* wasn't a code word for *let yourself go*?

Where was the disappointed sigh?

Where was the dreaded eye roll?

Where was the—

And then she saw it. Frank's arm was draped across Leona's shoulder.

Frank . . .

Sixtysomething, gray-haired Frank . . .

She looked around for Charles, for Margaret Louise, for Rose—for anyone who would happily offer up a pinch to prove she wasn't dreaming. Since all were otherwise occupied, she stole back her hands and squeezed herself.

Yup, Frank's arm was still around Leona.

And he was still the same gray-haired sixtysomething he'd been a second earlier.

Only now that her hands were no longer inside Leona's, Leona was slipping her arm around Frank as they moved off in the direction of Margaret Louise and Rose . . .

Tori was still standing there, staring, when Milo came up beside her with a platter of perfectly grilled hamburgers. "You look like you saw a ghost."

"Not a ghost, exactly. But definitely a different version of Leona than I'm used to . . ."

Milo stole a glance in Leona's direction and then turned back to Tori, his voice barely more than a whisper. "I'm not sure Sweet Briar can handle another Leona."

"I'm not sure *I* can, either," she said, only half joking.

He repositioned the platter in his arms and then whispered a kiss across her temple. "So, do we tell them now, or do we wait until everyone gets their food?"

She looked from Leona and Frank, to Margaret Louise and Rose, to Charles and Beatrice, to Dixie and Georgina, to Debbie and Colby, to Melissa and Baby Matthew, to Jake and the gaggle of kids happily racing their way across the yard, and took a moment to breathe in the pure joy that was her surroundings.

"Well?"

"I say we tell them now."

His answering smile, and the dimples it carved in his cheeks, warmed her from the inside out. "I was hoping you'd say that."

She waited as he set the platter onto the table and called everyone to gather around. When everyone was there, hungrily eyeing the spread in front of them, Tori held her hand out to Rose and carefully pulled her close.

"Before we eat, there's a few things Tori and I would like to say."

"Then start flappin' so we can start eatin'!"

Tori laughed. "You heard Margaret Louise, Milo. Start flappin'."

"First up, we just want to say how grateful we are for all of you. Every single one of you has touched our lives in countless ways. So thank you." He glanced down at Tori and winked. "Now it's *your* turn."

She cleared her throat of the emotion she needed to hold at bay for a few more minutes and turned to Rose. "Rose? Milo and I have been talking, and we have something of a proposition for you."

Rose's eyebrow arched above her bifocals. "For me?"

"We know you're wanting to sell your house, and we think the reasons for doing so are sound. But that said, we'd like you to consider moving somewhere closer."

"There aren't any assisted-living facilities in Sweet Briar, Victoria—you know that." Rose swept her hand toward the table of food. "Can we get to the food now? That potato salad is looking mighty good."

"In a minute." Tori took a deep breath and dove back in, her excitement over the plan she and Milo had come up with over the past few days making it hard not to squeal. "As I said, we'd like you to consider moving somewhere closer—as in right here. With us."

Rose scowled. "I told you, Victoria, I don't want to live with anyone else. I need my independence."

"And we agree. That's why our proposition doesn't involve the house, but rather, the backyard."

"You plan on puttin' her in a tent, Victoria?" Margaret Louise bellowed from her spot behind Jake Junior and Lulu. "Under that pergola Milo is goin' to be buildin'?"

"I'm not building that anymore," Milo replied.

"You're not?" Charles nibbled on his thumbnail. "But it sounded so dreamy the way Victoria described it."

"It did. But we've come up with something much better for our backyard." All eyes returned to Tori, while hers remained solely on Rose. "We're buying a Granny Pod."

A few gasps mingled amid pockets of murmuring as Rose made a face. "A Granny Pod? What on earth is *a Granny Pod*?"

Milo held up his finger, pulled a magazine out from under the Adirondack chair, and placed it in Rose's hand. "It's essentially a small house that can fit right here in the backyard."

"A house we'd like you to live in," Tori said.

There was no mistaking the tremble in Rose's lips as she took in the picture. There was also no mistaking the emphatic shake of her head as she handed the magazine back to Milo. "I don't take charity."

"This wouldn't be charity," Tori said. "It would be payment for your services."

"And what services would those be?" Rose asked, mid-glower.

"Rocking, reading. That sort of thing."

"So charity . . ."

"No, *helping*. Us."

"Helping you with what?"

Tori looked up at Milo and grinned. "Are you ready?"

"Am I ever."

"On the count of three?"

He laughed. "Works for me."

"Charles?" She leaned around Rose for a better view of her nail-nibbling friend. "Will you do us the honor?"

"Anything to end this suspense, sugar lips." Then, readying his fingers he began to snap. "One . . . Two . . . Three!"

"We're having a baby!"

Reader-Suggested
Sewing Tips

~Theresa M., via my Fan Page on Facebook

- I sewed a small pincushion to a hair scrunchy, and . . . voila, I have a pincushion I can wear on my wrist while I'm working.

~Stephanie T., via my Fan Page on Facebook

- I always keep a dryer sheet in my sewing basket. I run my thread across it to prevent tangling.

~Laura J., via my Fan Page on Facebook

- Binder clips make a great second (third, fourth) pair of hands when working with binding.

~Shirley L., via my Fan Page on Facebook

🪡 Next time you make a pincushion, use steel wool as stuffing. This will keep your pins and needles extra sharp, as it sharpens them every time you poke them back in. Stuff it even fuller with rice, which will help absorb any moisture.

~Megan R., via my Fan Page on Facebook

🪡 Want a fun way to decorate a nursery? Buy some double-sided fusible web and apply it to your chosen fabric. Cut it into the shape of whatever you want—letters, balloons, stars, etc. With an iron, fuse it to the wall. When you want to take it down, just peel it right off!

Sewing Pattern

Magic Hanky

(AS SUGGESTED BY LONGTIME SOUTHERN SEWING CIRCLE
MYSTERY READER LYNN DEARDORFF)

Magic Hanky Materials

Any white lace handkerchief, white embroidered hand-
kerchief, or color embroidered handkerchief
¼-inch-wide white ribbon
Embellishments (optional)

Magic Hanky Instructions

Iron the handkerchief flat.
Fold one edge approximately 1 inch (this will be the

back on the hanky). Depending on the size of the hanky or the way you would like the bonnet to look, you may want to adjust this fold anywhere from 1 to 2 inches.

Fold the opposite edge toward the first fold approximately 3 inches. Again, this length of this fold may depend on the size of your hanky. Make sure to leave some space between the two rows of lace.

Press both folded edges with an iron. Open the hanky and hand stitch running stitches along the first fold. Do not knot or finish this stitch off.

Refold the hanky along the pressed line.

Now with the first fold, pull on the thread to gather the hanky into a bonnet. When the desired size is reached, secure the thread and finish the bonnet off by adding ribbon at the back of the bonnet. Now, with the second fold, take each corner and fold a small edge into the hanky (this will form a small triangle inside the bonnet). Add a length of ribbon for tying onto each corner of the front of the bonnet. If desired, add small embellishments for a decorative touch.

Poem:

THE MAGIC HANKY

I'm just a little hanky, as square as square can be.
But with a stitch or two they made a bonnet out of me.
I'll be worn from the hospital or on the christening day.
Then I'll be carefully pressed and neatly packed away.

For her wedding day, so we've been told,
Every well-dressed bride must have that something old.

So what could be more fitting than to find little me?
A few stitches snipped, and a wedding hanky I'll be.

And if, perchance, it is a boy, someday he'll surely wed.
So to his bride, he can present the hanky
Once worn upon his head.

—*author unknown*

FROM NATIONAL BESTSELLING AUTHOR

ELIZABETH LYNN CASEY

-The Southern Sewing Circle Mysteries-

SEW DEADLY

DEATH THREADS

PINNED FOR MURDER

DEADLY NOTIONS

DANGEROUS ALTERATIONS

REAP WHAT YOU SEW

LET IT SEW

REMNANTS OF MURDER

TAKEN IN

WEDDING DURESS

NEEDLE AND DREAD

PATTERNED AFTER DEATH

Praise for the Southern Sewing Circle Mysteries

"Filled with fun, folksy characters
and southern charm."

—Maggie Sefton, *New York Times* bestselling
author of *Purl Up and Die*

elizabethlynncasey.com
penguin.com